Sapphire Seas

a story in the
RomantiSea Serenades
series

J.D. Harbor

Ebook ISBN: 979-8-9921213-3-9

Paperback ISBN: 979-8-9921213-1-5

Cover Design: J.D. Harbor

Editing and Proofreading: Mekhala Spencer, All The Proof Editing

Formatting: Nicole Kincaid, Naughty Nook PR

To DJ – Your enthusiasm and encouragement reminded me that stories aren't just meant to be written—they're meant to be shared. Thank you for igniting that spark.

One

Gleaming with sleek modernity, Brighton & Burke Advertising's office featured floor-to-ceiling windows that framed the cityscape, showcasing New York's architectural prowess in steel and glass. The room itself, with its minimalist design and pristine white walls, evoked creativity, but to Harper Brooks, it felt more like a sterile cage. The polished conference table stretched long between them, its reflective surface mirroring the carefully arranged faces of the clients seated across from her. Their smiles were polite, but their eyes seemed distant as if they were humoring her, waiting for their chance to talk.

Outside, New York pulsed with life. The mid-morning sun threw sharp angles of light between the towering skyscrapers, casting busy shadows that seemed to dance across the floor of her office. The city's symphony of honking taxis, steady footsteps, and occasional sirens reached Harper through the glass, reminding her of a dream she'd once treasured.

This city had been her fantasy. Years ago, when she was just a wide-eyed girl from Myrtle Beach, she had envisioned herself here, thriving amid the buzz of creativity, surrounded by thinkers, doers, and innovators. She saw herself burning the midnight oil, but not from stress, from excitement. She wanted to do campaigns that would be a big deal, set the pace, and make a difference. New York was her dream, the place she thought she'd finally make it big.

Now, it felt like a mirage that had dissolved the moment she reached out to touch it.

"Harper," the voice of Steven Knox, the client's CEO, broke into her thoughts, pulling her back to the present with a sudden snap. "We've been thinking about the campaign, and, well ..." He exchanged a glance with his marketing officer, who quickly nodded. "We'd really like to take a more, let's say, familiar approach."

Harper leaned forward, hiding the tension that was already tightening across her chest. Her professional smile, polished through years of practice, became her shield. "Of course, Steven. What do you have in mind?"

Knox swiped his tablet, scrolling through what Harper could only imagine was a portfolio of mediocrity. He paused, and with a swipe, a campaign popped up on the oversized screen in the middle of the room. It was bright, flashy, and disturbingly familiar.

Her heart sank.

"This," he said, with an enthusiasm that twisted in her stomach. "This is exactly what we're looking for. It's bold, but safe. We don't want to take unnecessary risks. You know, the public likes what it likes." He gave a light chuckle as if it were a joke they all shared.

Harper's eyes flicked to the screen. It was like a copy and paste job of every other campaign she'd seen, super slick but lacking any fresh ideas. Another campaign that felt like every other corporate ad trying to be hip, but in reality, offered nothing new. The creative fire in her flickered, then dimmed.

Her hands, folded neatly on the table, itched to swipe the screen clear and replace it with her own ideas. Bold, unconventional, disruptive ideas that she had stayed up late crafting, that she had poured her soul into. Campaigns designed to both engage the mind and move the heart. However, she simply nodded as Steven spoke glowingly about a competing company's successful campaign, which mirrored their own.

"I've seen this before," Harper said, her voice careful, controlled, though a quiet burn licked at her insides. "It's certainly effective, but wouldn't you rather stand out in the market, rather than blend in?" Her smile was inviting, suggesting understanding and a gentle push toward embracing difference. "We could take this concept and elevate it, add a twist unique to your brand."

Knox glanced at his marketing officer, and the woman beside him barely hid her sigh. "We're not looking to reinvent the wheel, Harper," Knox said, his tone affable but dismissive. "Let's go with something tried and true, you know, safe and recognizable. People prefer simplicity and clarity over excessive creativity. We're looking for results, not art."

The words struck her like a physical blow, knocking the wind from her lungs in the subtlest of ways. Not art. They never wanted art anymore. Harper's fingers curled slightly into the fabric of her pants under the table, the movement hidden but enough to release some of the tension building in her body. She took a slow, quiet breath, forcing herself to remain calm, to smooth out the edges of her frustration.

"Of course," she said, her voice steady, despite every fiber of her being recoiled at the thought. "We can make adjustments. I'll talk to the team about incorporating some of these elements, and we'll ensure it's exactly what you're looking for."

It felt like a betrayal. The artistic passion that had fueled her journey to New York felt betrayed and abandoned. And worse, it felt like a betrayal of herself. But this was the dance she had perfected. She could push the boundary just enough to offer something fresh, something daring, but when the clients came back with their "safe" requests, she had to bend. Every time she bent, she felt herself cracking just a little more, though.

"Great, great," Knox said, already moving on. "We need the revised drafts by the end of next week. Looking forward to seeing what your team can do."

The meeting wrapped up in a flurry of polite goodbyes and handshakes. Harper plastered on her most gracious smile, even though it felt like it might crack under the weight of her exhaustion. Once they left, she sank back into her chair and stared out the window, watching the city below churn with movement, energy, and life. The skyline that had once filled her with awe now felt oppressive, a towering reminder of dreams deferred.

The office felt too quiet, the ghost of the client's cologne lingering like an unwelcome presence. Her reflection in the window looked tired, the edges of her smile already slipping away, replaced by a deep-set weariness she hadn't noticed before.

Once upon a time, she had thought this life would make her feel alive. She had envisioned the thrill of building campaigns that made waves, that left a mark on the world. Instead, she was building cookie-cutter ads, nothing more than variations on someone else's work, dressed up just enough to look new. The ideas that used to fuel her fire were silenced, deemed "unrealistic" or "too bold," and neatly tucked away. The spark of creativity that fueled her journey, once blazing, now flickered, dimmed by the relentless pressure to conform.

Harper rose from her chair, crossing the office to the window. She pressed her fingers against the cool glass, her gaze fixed on the bustling streets below. Somewhere in the sea of yellow cabs and blurred figures rushing back and forth, she had lost herself. She had lost the spark that had brought her here in the first place, traded it for client appeasement and corporate satisfaction.

New York had once been her dream. Now, it felt like a gilded cage.

The city continued to buzz beneath her, indifferent to her struggle, its lights winking in the mid-morning sun.

Harper stood at the window a moment longer, the cool glass beneath her fingertips grounding her in the present, forcing her breath to slow. She could feel the tightness in her chest loosening slightly, though the knot of frustration still lingered just beneath her ribcage. Her eyes closed, a deep breath calming the turmoil within. She knew she had to keep it together. In this place, cool was king, emotions were weak, and everything you did mattered.

She took another breath, this one deeper than the last, feeling the city outside pulse beneath her, like some massive engine that never stopped. The familiar rhythm of New York had once excited her, fueled her ambition. Now it felt like background noise to the chaos from within.

"Get it together," she whispered to herself, her voice soft, barely audible over the faint hum of traffic below. The words weren't sharp but firm, like a hand on her shoulder guiding her back into focus. She needed to regain composure. There was no room for weakness, especially with her team relying on her.

She straightened, rolling her shoulders back as she stepped away from the window. Her hand drifted to the phone on her desk, her fingers hesitating for just a beat before she pressed the button to summon her assistant. Moments later, a quiet knock at the door preceded the entrance of Claire, her assistant, who slipped into the office with her usual grace.

Claire's calm presence was a welcome change from the chaotic office environment. Dressed in a sleek navy blazer and trousers, with her hair pulled back in a neat bun, she was the embodiment of calm efficiency. Her eyes met Harper's, and without a word, she knew something was off.

"Claire, could you gather the team for a quick meeting in the main conference room?" Harper asked, her voice steady now, the calm mask firmly back in place. She smoothed a hand over the front of her blouse, brushing away invisible creases, a gesture that gave her just a moment more to collect herself.

Claire nodded. "Right away. Anything specific I should tell them?"

"Just that I want to go over the client's feedback," Harper said, her smile professional but tight around the edges. "I'll explain the rest once everyone's there."

Claire gave a small nod, her eyes flicking over Harper as if assessing her state. Harper could see her assistant was ready to ask more, to offer help, but Claire, always insightful, knew it wasn't the right time to press for details. Without another word, she disappeared from the office, leaving Harper alone once again.

As the door clicked shut, Harper turned back toward her desk, bracing herself against its edge. Her reflection in the darkened screen of her laptop stared back at her, the faint outline of her own face barely visible but enough to remind her of the tension beneath the surface. She knew this dance well: the struggle to balance her creative passions with the relentless pressures of her corporate job. It wasn't just about one lost campaign or a single rejected idea; it was the constant erosion of everything that had once made her feel alive in this job.

Every compromise, client demanding imitation, and buried vision weighed heavily on her.

Her phone buzzed, breaking the silence. A message from Claire:

Claire

The team's ready in the conference room.

With a final exhale, Harper pushed off the desk, grabbed her tablet, and exited the office. As she walked down the hallway, the hum of chatter from the other rooms bled into the air. Some part of her envied the other teams, their smaller campaigns perhaps less glamorous, but free of the constant scrutiny of major clients. They could experiment, to innovate, while she had become a master at the art of the compromise.

She reached the glass doors of the main conference room and paused just for a beat before pushing them open. Her team, a tight-knit group of designers, copywriters, and strategists, their faces a blend of anticipation and, maybe, a touch of apprehension, surrounded the sleek table. They'd seen this look before; they knew what was coming.

"Hey, everyone," Harper said as she entered, her voice carrying a brightness she didn't feel. She walked to the head of the table, setting her tablet down with a soft thud. "Thanks for coming together so quickly."

There was a murmur of acknowledgment, but the room was heavy with anticipation. They had all been part of the brainstorm sessions for the Knox campaign, and had poured themselves into pitches that Harper had proudly led, believing, for a moment, that this time might be different. Maybe, just maybe, the client would finally want something that broke the mold and let them be truly creative.

But as Harper stood before them, she felt that tiny spark of hope flicker out.

"I just got out of the meeting with Steven Knox and his team," she began, her tone carefully measured. "The bad news is they're not interested in pursuing our original concept." With a moment of silence, she watched her team's faces transform from hopeful to defeated, then to barely concealed irritation.

"We pushed for something fresh, something unique," she continued, feeling the weight of their disappointment echo her own. "But they want us to, well ..." She hesitated, her throat tightening as the next words came out. "They want something that mirrors what another brand is doing."

There was a palpable silence in the room. The frustration and bitterness of the group were almost audible. Harper forced herself to keep her voice steady, even though the rejection felt personal, even though the creative fire in her was already sputtering again.

"They showed us a campaign that's ... safe," she added, struggling to keep the bitterness from creeping into her tone. "They want something tried and true, something that works." Her words felt bitter and hollow, but she forced a smile, a tight, controlled one because that's what a leader was supposed to do.

She could see the frustration ripple through the team. Jason, one of the copywriters, ran a hand through his hair, his lips pressed into a thin line. Sarah, the lead designer, folded her arms, her fingers tapping against her sleeve, her eyes narrowing slightly.

"So they want us to copy and paste someone else's work, essentially?" Sarah asked, her voice flat but edged with irritation.

Harper felt a pang of guilt. Sarah had poured herself into the design concepts, had stayed late for days, tweaking the visuals until they were exactly right. Jason, too, had delivered some of his best copy in months. They had all believed in the campaign.

"It's not ideal," Harper admitted, her hands resting on the back of the chair in front of her. The words "It's not right" hovered on the edge of her lips, itching to be spoken. It's not creative. It's not why we're here. But she smoothed over the edges of her frustration and added, "But it's what the client wants, and at the end of the day, our job is to give them something they'll approve. Something that works."

Another silence followed. She hated having to tell her team their work was useless. They were back to square one, doing another blah project because the client was too scared to do anything interesting.

"We'll pivot," Harper said, injecting a touch of optimism into her voice, though it felt forced. "We'll embrace their preferences but put our own spin on it, creating something polished that still feels uniquely us. It'll all work out.

But even as she said it, Harper could see the disappointment etched in the lines of their faces. It was a look she knew well, one she'd sported herself countless times in recent years.

As the meeting wrapped up, the team gathered their things, exchanging glances and murmured goodbyes as they filtered out of the room, their energy noticeably deflated. Harper stood at the head of the table, absently flipping through her notes on the tablet, her mind already racing with how they could salvage the campaign. The pressure was mounting, a familiar weight settling onto her shoulders.

Gradually, her team dwindled until only one person remained. Jason, her longtime copywriter, lingered at the door, his brow furrowed in thought. He hung back for a bit, unsure if he should talk, then breathed in and went back into the room.

"Hey, boss," he said, his voice quieter than usual, and Harper looked up from her tablet. Jason's unusual tone made her wary, as he was normally the one who could always find a silver lining in any situation. The look in his eyes had changed, becoming heavy and serious.

"Jason, what's up?" Harper asked, trying to keep her own voice light, though she could feel a knot forming in her stomach. The meeting, the client's rejection, and the deadline all piled up on her, and she felt an impending crisis.

A sigh escaped Jason's lips as he ran a hand through his unruly hair, moving closer to the table and tracing the edge of a chair with his fingers. He looked down at the polished surface momentarily, as if searching for the right words, before finally meeting her gaze.

"I don't know how much longer I can keep this up," he said, his voice steady but laced with exhaustion. "It's like ... every time we put our hearts into something, it gets shut down, or watered down, or turned into something that isn't even ours anymore." His eyes flicked toward the door, making sure the rest of the team was gone before he continued. "I think it might be time for me to look for something else."

The words hit Harper like a punch to the gut, but she kept her expression neutral, hiding the sudden surge of panic that flared in her chest. Jason had been with her for years, one of the few people she trusted implicitly, someone who understood the creative process as well as she did. She wasn't certain she could cope with losing him, not just as a talented copywriter but also as a trusted confidant.

"Jason ..." Harper started, her mind already scrambling for a response, something to reassure him, to convince him that things would get better, even though she wasn't sure she believed it herself. She let out a breath, leaning on the back of the chair. "I know it's frustrating. Believe me, I feel it, too. But we're in a rough patch right now. All campaigns come with their share of obstacles."

"Yeah, but it's not just a rough patch, is it?" Jason interrupted gently, shaking his head. "It's been like this for months, maybe even years. We keep getting told to aim for the stars, but then the clients yank us right back down to earth every single time. It feels like we're not creating anything anymore. Just ... filling orders."

Harper clenched her jaw, feeling the truth in his words hit hard. He wasn't wrong. The creation process didn't match the aspirations they had when they started out in the industry. What had once been an exciting challenge to break boundaries had become a monotonous routine of pleasing clients who didn't want innovation, only predictability. And it was draining.

Jason's eyes softened as he looked at her, reading the tension she was trying so hard to mask. "Look, I don't want to leave. I don't want to leave you, Harper. You've been a great boss, and you've always fought for us. But I'm getting burned out. And I know I'm not the only one."

A fresh wave of stress crashed over her, adding to the already heavy load she was carrying. The idea of losing Jason, or anyone else from her team, felt like another brick being placed on her chest, making it harder to breathe. The issue extended beyond replacing a skilled writer; it involved the departure of a rare individual who continued to champion their work in the face of seemingly insurmountable challenges.

"I get it," Harper said, her voice quieter. She could hear the exhaustion in her tone, the same exhaustion Jason was feeling. "I really do. And I wish I had a better answer for you right now. I wish I could tell you that the next client will be different, that we'll finally get to create something real again."

Jason's lips quirked up in a small, sad smile. "You don't have to have all the answers, Harper. I just … I don't want to feel like I'm giving up, but I don't know how much longer I can keep giving everything, just to have it shot down repeatedly."

She nodded, feeling a deep pang of understanding in his words. Overworked and depleted, she had been pushing herself beyond her limits for far too long, juggling deadlines, appeasing clients, and striving to inspire her team. She was wondering if she could keep it up, either. The pressure was unrelenting, and no matter how hard she worked, it seemed like it was never enough.

"I'll talk to the higher-ups," Harper said finally, forcing herself to sound hopeful even though her chest felt tight. "Maybe there's a way we can take on smaller, more creative projects between the bigger clients. Something to keep the spark alive."

Jason's smile was faint but grateful. "I appreciate that, Harper. I really do." He hesitated, then gave a small nod. "I'm not saying I'm gone tomorrow, but ... I just wanted to be honest with you."

"I'm glad you were," Harper said, managing a smile of her own, even if it felt fragile. "Let me see what I can do. We'll figure something out."

Jason gave her a quick, reassuring pat on the shoulder before heading out of the conference room, leaving Harper standing in the quiet space, her thoughts swirling with new layers of stress. She lingered, staring at the empty chairs, letting the weight of Jason's words settle.

How much longer could she keep this up?

The temptation to stay late tonight, to pour over the campaign until she figured out some way to make it work, tugged at her. She could already see the emails piling up, the revisions she'd have to make, the endless cycle of compromise that awaited her. If she just stayed a few extra hours, maybe she could come up with a new angle, something that would appease the client while still giving her team a sliver of creative freedom.

As she absently scanned her phone, a reminder pinged at the top of the screen, cutting through her work haze: Dinner with Dan: 7:30 pm.

Dan had always been her biggest cheerleader when it came to work. Early in their relationship, he'd stayed up late listening to her brainstorm ideas for campaigns, offering input when she asked, and pouring her another glass of wine when she didn't. "You're incredible," he'd told her once, brushing her hair back from her face as she scribbled in her notebook. "You're going to change the game, Harper Brooks."

But lately, his encouragement had felt ... muted. Tired. And she couldn't really blame him. Work wasn't fun anymore. She wasn't chasing dreams; she was putting out fires.

Harper stood suspended between two worlds: the relentless demands of her job and the steadfast love of a man who had spent years waiting—perhaps too patiently—for her to finally put him first.

However, the pull of the office was strong. The thought of not staying late tonight was already prompting questions in her mind. *What if I don't solve this? What if we lose this client?*

But a gentler, persistent voice asked: *How long before Dan stops waiting for me to choose him the way he's always chosen me?*

She pressed the power button, darkening the screen as she grabbed her bag and headed out of the conference room, determination settling over her like a mantle. Tonight, work will need to wait.

Two

The cab sped down the congested streets of Manhattan, weaving through the evening traffic with a kind of reckless ease that only New York cabbies had mastered. Harper sat in the back seat, staring out the window, her mind only half absorbing the passing scenery. Friday night energy pulsed through the city, with people rushing along the sidewalks, buildings glowing, and a sea of neon signs illuminating the distance. It was everything she had once loved about New York, everything she had once found electrifying. Now, it felt like a blur, a distraction from the constant undercurrent of stress pulling her in dozens of directions at once.

Her phone buzzed on the seat beside her. Instinctively, Harper glanced at the screen, her heart sinking when she saw the number.

Great. Just what I need right now, she thought as she picked it up, knowing she couldn't ignore this call. It was another client, and if the sinking feeling in her stomach was any indication, this would not be a call about a successful campaign.

"Harper Brooks," she answered, trying to inject her usual professionalism into her voice despite the gnawing sense of dread.

"Harper, hi, it's Matt from Crescent International." The tone on the other end was polite, but there was a tension in it, a stiffness that immediately set Harper on edge.

"Matt, hi! What can I do for you?" she asked, forcing brightness into her voice even as her mind raced, already trying to anticipate where this was going.

There was a pause, then a faint sigh on the other end of the line. "I'm really sorry to call you like this, Harper, but ... well, I wanted to let you know personally before anything official comes through tomorrow."

Harper's grip on the phone tightened. Here it comes.

"We've decided to go in a different direction with our marketing," Matt continued, his tone laced with the kind of practiced regret that made her want to scream. "It's nothing against you or your team. We've loved working with you, but the board has decided to bring everything in-house from now on. It's just a better fit for our new strategy."

Harper felt a rush of heat surge up her neck, a mixture of frustration and panic. Crescent International was one of their bigger clients, one of the few that still gave her some creative leeway. The loss was more than just financial for her agency; it was a personal setback. She had invested so much into their campaigns, worked long hours, skipped weekends, pushed her team to deliver something special. And now, just like that, it was over.

"I ... I see," Harper managed, though her voice sounded hollow in her own ears. "That makes me really sad to hear. I wish we could have discussed this before it came to this. We've really valued the partnership."

"I know, and trust me, this wasn't an easy call to make," Matt said, but his words felt as empty as the promises her clients always made before pulling the plug. "It's just ... we need something different, something more integrated with our new internal strategy. I didn't want you to hear this from anyone else, so we're sending an official letter to Sam tomorrow morning."

"Right." Harper's mouth was dry, but she forced herself to keep her tone steady, professional. "Thanks for letting me know directly, Matt. I appreciate it. If there's anything we can do to ease the transition, just let us know."

"Of course. You guys were great. It's nothing personal, Harper. You know how these things go."

"Yeah, I do," Harper replied, barely able to suppress the sarcasm that threatened to seep through. She ended the call with the usual pleasantries, though every muscle in her body felt tight, strung out like a wire about to snap.

She tossed the phone onto the seat next to her, staring blankly out the window, her pulse quickening with the anxiety she had been trying to keep at bay. Another client gone. Another rejection. And Sam ... Sam was going to have her head on a plate tomorrow when that letter came in. The weight of it all pressed down on her, the endless cycle of trying and failing to keep everything afloat.

As the cab pulled up to the restaurant, Harper glanced at her phone again, resisting the temptation to check her emails or make another work call. She could feel herself unraveling, her control slipping, but now wasn't the time to fall apart.

Dan was already standing outside the restaurant, arms crossed, his face pinched in a way that made her heart sink even further. In his crisp suit and freshly shined shoes, he looked like a model from a magazine. Harper, by comparison, felt like a crumpled mess in her coffee-stained blouse, her face a reflection of the sleepless night she'd had.

"Perfect," she muttered under her breath as she climbed out of the cab. "Dan's Prince Charming, and I'm Cinderella after a twelve-hour shift."

She was late. Again.

"Hey," she called as she approached, trying to plaster on a smile as if she wasn't coming apart at the seams. "Sorry, the traffic was crazy."

Dan gave her a long, knowing look, his eyes narrowing slightly. "Let me guess ... work?"

The words were flat, void of the warmth he usually greeted her with, and Harper flinched inwardly. The excuse had become predictable, even to her.

"Yeah," she admitted, running a hand through her hair, trying to suppress the flood of guilt. "There was an emergency with a client. They called me at the last minute. I couldn't just—"

"Of course not," Dan interrupted, his voice laced with a kind of weary resignation. "It's always work, Harper ... always."

She opened her mouth to respond, but he was already shaking his head, his lips pressed into a thin line. The tension between them was thick, almost tangible. Harper could feel it tightening around her chest, making it hard to breathe.

"Dan, I'm really sorry," she said, her voice softening as she reached out to him. "But I'm here now, and I promise, I'm going to be present for dinner tonight. No more work talk, no more distractions. Just you and me."

He raised an eyebrow, clearly skeptical. "You've said that before."

"I know, I know," she said quickly, raising her hands in mock surrender as she fumbled in her bag for her phone. "Look, I'm turning it off. See?" She held the phone up, showing him she'd put it on vibrate, then tossed it in her bag.

Dan's frown deepened as he glanced at her bag. He sighed, rubbing a hand over his face. "Harper, I'm trying to be patient here. I know your job is demanding, but it's getting harder and harder to feel like a priority. I get it, you're busy. But this isn't what I signed up for."

The words stung sharper than she'd expected. She felt the full weight of his frustration hit, mixing with the anxiety already twisting in her gut. This was supposed to be their special night, but everything went wrong. Now she was losing the client, her team, and maybe even Dan.

"I know," she said again, this time quieter, almost pleading. "But tonight's going to be different. I promise."

"I don't need you to be perfect, Harper," Dan continued, his tone low but insistent. "I just need you to be here. With me. Not your phone. Not your laptop. Just ... us."

"I know," she'd whispered, guilt pooling in her chest. But even as she said it, her phone buzzed in her purse, demanding her attention yet again, despite her feverish attempt to ignore it.

Dan studied her for a long moment, his expression softening just a touch, though the tension didn't fully leave his posture. "Okay," he said finally, though his tone lacked conviction. "Let's go inside."

They entered the restaurant, the warm glow of candlelight and the low hum of conversation surrounding them as a waiter guided them to their table. Harper could feel the weight of her phone, silent in her purse but still buzzing in her mind. She was physically present, yet an endless list of concerns had her mind elsewhere. That lost client, the doomed campaign, her to-do list ... she was stressing.

She tried to smile as Dan looked over the menu, but the nagging tension in her chest refused to ease. Even now, in this quiet, intimate space, work had its claws in her, pulling her away inch by inch.

She glanced down at her purse, the urge to check her phone gnawing at her, already chipping away at the promise she'd just made.

For the first time in what felt like months, Harper allowed herself to relax. The restaurant was super chill, with dim lights and hushed chatter. It felt like a total escape from her crazy office and demanding clients. Across the table, Dan was smiling, his frustration from earlier fading as they settled into the familiar rhythm of their relationship. They had ordered a bottle of wine and their usual dishes, and Harper relished the quiet, putting her phone away for nearly an hour, buried deep in her bag. She was doing her best to stick to her promise and just be present, like she said she would.

Dan beamed with excitement as he detailed the new project, which would expand his firm's reach into global markets. Harper listened, genuinely interested, letting herself sink into the moment. They even laughed, reminiscing about their early dates, when everything had felt easy and carefree.

"So, about next month," Dan said, his voice softening as he reached for his glass. "Are you excited about going back to Myrtle Beach? I know it's been a while since you've seen your family."

Harper smiled, a genuine one this time. "Yeah, I am. Helen's been texting me non-stop about how much Channing has grown since I last saw him. I feel like I'm missing everything. And the beach ... God, I miss it. The air here just doesn't compare."

Dan nodded, his expression lightening. "I'm looking forward to it, too. A few days of sun, some downtime ... away from all this." He longed for sunshine and relaxation, a break from the city's relentless pace: the work, the noise, and the endless responsibilities.

She reached across the table and touched his hand, feeling a swell of gratitude that he was still trying, that they could still have moments like this. It made her believe, for a brief second, that maybe things could work out. She believed she could manage both her demanding career and the life she wanted with Dan.

They were just deciding where to eat on the drive down when their food arrived. Dan got salmon, and she got risotto. The smell of rosemary and lemon filled the air, and for once, Harper felt a flicker of contentment.

But as the waiter set the plates down, she felt a series of subtle vibrations against her foot, like a faint tremor in the floor beneath her. The familiar, unwelcome buzz of her phone jolted her out of the calm she had been trying to maintain.

She stiffened. The phone, tucked in her bag and leaning against her foot, buzzed incessantly. Her pulse quickened, dread settling into her stomach like a stone. Harper knew, without even needing to check, that Sam had called several times. The news from Crescent International about the lost client had surely reached her boss's ears.

Her hand hesitated for a moment, hovering above her bag. She could feel Dan's eyes, could sense the shift between them. Dan longed for a night free from her work, a night where she would devote herself to him. But the phone buzzed again, and the pull was too strong; the fear of letting things unravel even further was too consuming.

She couldn't afford to ignore this.

"I'm just going to ..." Harper started, her hand reaching for the phone, but the moment her fingers brushed against it, Dan stood abruptly. His chair scraped back against the floor with a sharp screech, causing a few heads from nearby tables to turn.

"Dan ..." Harper began, but he was already storming toward the door.

"I need some air," he muttered, his voice low and tight. "Do whatever you need to, Harper. Clearly, this dinner doesn't matter." He pushed the door open, and before she could say another word, he disappeared into the cool night, the door swinging shut behind him with a soft thud.

Harper felt a cold rush of panic as she fumbled with her phone. The screen lit up, revealing the missed calls from Sam and a barrage of texts. Without thinking, she quickly fired off a message: I already know. I'll handle it tomorrow. Her fingers hovered over the screen for a moment longer, and then she locked the phone and shoved it back into her bag.

"Dan, wait ... I'm sorry," she called, her voice breaking as she hurried toward him, her heels clicking against the slick sidewalk. "I ... I wasn't ... it wasn't supposed to happen like this."

Dan turned slowly to face her, his eyes heavy with exhaustion, but there was also a simmering disappointment beneath the weariness that made Harper's stomach churn.

"It's never supposed to happen like this, Harper," he said, his voice steady but edged with pain. "But it always does. And every time, I tell myself it'll get better. That you'll figure it out. That you'll come back to me." He paused, his shoulders sagging. "But you don't. And I ... I can't keep holding on to something that's slipping away."

Her heart stuttered, the panic rising. "What do you mean?" She stepped closer, her voice cracking at the edges. "It was just one call ... I ... I told Sam I'd handle it tomorrow. I swear, Dan, I ... I'm here now. Okay? I'm here."

Dan's eyes softened for a moment, but the weight of his words hung between them, heavy and irreversible. He shook his head, the rain catching in his hair, making it curl slightly at the ends.

"It's never just one call. It's always work! Even when you're physically here, Harper, you're not really here. I feel like I'm constantly fighting for scraps of your attention. I've tried to be patient, I've tried to support you, but I ... I ..." Dan hesitated, his Adam's apple shifting as he swallowed hard, nerves tightening his expression.

But then, the words came out like a dagger, "I'm done trying."

She opened her mouth to respond, but all that came out was a strangled gasp, her throat tightening with an icy dread that sunk like a stone into her chest.

"Dan, wait ... I ... I didn't mean for this to happen." Her voice cracked, the words tumbling out. "It's just ... I don't know how to stop. I'm trying, I really am, but ... please don't do this."

"No, Harp, I can't keep doing this," he said, his voice softer now but no less final. "I can't keep feeling like I'm second place to your job. I love you, Harper. I love ... the way you used to light up when you talked about your ideas. The way you made me believe we could take on the world together." He hesitated, his voice breaking slightly. "But now? It feels like the person I loved has disappeared. And I don't see how we get back to that."

Her mind churned, desperate for a solution, but all she could hear was his finality: *I'm done trying.*

"Are you ... are you saying ..." Her throat tightened, the rest of her sentence barely a whisper. She could already feel the tears pricking at the corners of her eyes, but she refused to let them fall.

Not here. Not now.

"Yes, I'm saying we are done." Dan's face softened, but the resolve in his eyes didn't waver. "I'm calling off the engagement, Harper. I don't want to keep pretending that things will get better when we both know they won't."

Harper stood rooted to the slick pavement, watching Dan disappear into the rain. His words echoed in her head: *I can't keep doing this ... I'm done trying.*

Harper traced the edge of her engagement ring, the diamond flickering beneath the streetlamp's glow. A year ago, it had felt like a promise—one she had let slip through the cracks of her ambition. Now, it rested heavy against her skin, a reminder of the man she had taken for granted. She twisted it absently, the band's cold bite grounding her as a painful knot formed deep in her gut.

The city churned on, indifferent to her unraveling. Taxis splashed through puddles. People hurried by, umbrellas bobbing, their laughter and voices blurring into meaningless noise. Harper felt like she was sinking, the weight of everything—her job, her failure, her heartbreak—pressing down on her.

Her phone buzzed, the glow of the screen piercing through the rain. Sam. Of course. Because if there was one thing she could count on, it was work demanding her attention when everything else was falling apart.

She snatched the phone out of her bag and stared at it, her thumb hovering over the screen. But instead of answering, she hit *decline* and shoved it back into her bag. She couldn't deal with Sam or Crescent International or anything else tonight. Not after this.

Harper looked up, blinking against the rain. She didn't want to go back to the apartment—not to *their* apartment. The thought of sitting alone on the couch Dan wouldn't come back to was unbearable. She needed somewhere else, anywhere else, but the weight of the city suddenly felt suffocating.

Her mind drifted to Cierra. Her friend had always been her emergency escape hatch, the one person who didn't judge her when things fell apart. *You always have a place with me,* Cierra had told her once, and Harper knew she meant it.

Her hands trembled as she pulled out her phone again, scrolling through her contacts. She hesitated for only a moment before hitting *call*.

"Harper?" Cierra's voice came through, warm and familiar.

"Hey," Harper said, her voice cracking. "Is your couch still available?"

"Always. What's wrong?" Cierra's voice was laced with concern. "Do you need me to come get you?"

Harper's throat tightened. "No. I'm getting a cab now. I just ... I just need to crash somewhere tonight."

"You've got it," Cierra said without hesitation. "I'll leave the door unlocked. And I've got wine and leftover pizza."

Harper let out a choked laugh, a small release of the tension clawing at her. "You're the best."

"See you soon," Cierra said lightly.

Harper hung up and wiped at her rain-streaked face. Her breath was shaky as she flagged down a cab, exhaustion settling deep into her bones. Dan and the apartment could wait. The fallout with Sam could wait. For now, she just needed a safe harbor.

Three

Harper lay awake on the pull-out sofa bed, staring up at the ceiling, her body sinking deep into the worn mattress. The dim light filtering through the small windows barely touched the far corners in the room, casting it in a perpetual twilight. A cold, gray light spilled across the floor, but it was weak, suffocated by the brick wall that loomed just outside the window, cutting off any direct sunlight. It was like living at the bottom of a well, with the narrowest slit of sky peeking in, reminding her that daylight was out there somewhere, just out of reach.

Cierra's apartment was functional but cramped, a sharp contrast to the light-filled, airy loft Harper shared with Dan. Their old place had been all glass and open spaces. That apartment glowed in the mornings with warm, golden light, spilling into every corner, making it feel like the day ahead was always full of possibilities.

The boxes she'd managed to haul to Cierra's apartment over the weekend still sat in the corner, untouched. She couldn't bring herself to unpack them—not when she still had to go back to the loft to finish sorting through what was left.

Harper was no longer in her own world, instead, she was in a place of shadows and confined spaces. Cierra's artistic touch adorned the dark gray walls, her indie film posters and sketchpads scattered across mismatched furniture. The space was cozy, though cluttered, its closeness pressing in on Harper like the weight of her own thoughts.

Harper shifted on the creaky pull-out sofa, glaring at the ceiling as she adjusted the lumpy pillow beneath her head. The bed wasn't the problem. It was everything else—the persistent ache of failure, loss, and displacement. Her heart still throbbed with the memory of Dan's words, the rain soaking through her clothes as he walked away, leaving her standing alone on the slick Manhattan sidewalk.

"Still awake, Harp?" Cierra's voice drifted from the doorway, soft but alert.

Harper turned her head, catching sight of her best friend leaning casually against the frame in her usual pajama uniform—loose sweatpants, an oversized band tee, and a messy bun holding her curls in place. Everything about Cierra radiated ease, the kind of comfort Harper hadn't felt in months.

"Yeah," Harper muttered, rubbing a hand over her face. "Couldn't sleep much."

"Couldn't sleep or didn't try?" Cierra asked, stepping into the room with a steaming mug in hand. She held it out to Harper, the rich aroma of fresh coffee cutting through the stale air.

Harper sat up, her movements sluggish, and took the mug like it was a lifeline. She breathed in deeply before taking a tentative sip.

"Coffee. The first miracle of the day," she said with a weak smile. "It's the only thing keeping me upright at this point."

Cierra raised an eyebrow, perching herself on the arm of the sofa. "You say that like you've already had a pot. This is cup one, right?"

Harper managed a faint smirk. "Cup one. I'm not vibrating, yet."

Cierra snorted. "Good, because this apartment can only handle one caffeinated meltdown at a time."

Harper took another sip, letting the heat seep through her like a slow wake-up call. "Trust me, you don't want me functioning without coffee. The alternative is zombie mode, and this bed is giving 'undead' vibes. Pretty sure it was designed to destroy spines."

"Hey," Cierra shot back with mock indignation, gesturing around her apartment. "My place might not be five-star luxury, but at least you get coffee delivery. Room service doesn't come with judgment."

"Room service," Harper murmured with a faint chuckle, holding the mug aloft like a toast. "Five stars for the coffee, two stars for the mattress."

"You could always sleep in my bed," Cierra offered casually, dropping onto the edge of the pull-out sofa.

Harper's rigid demeanor melted just slightly, a ghost of a smile breaking through the storm clouds of her thoughts. "How would your girlfriend feel about you sneaking another woman into bed while she's out of town?"

Cierra laughed, unfazed. "Toni wouldn't mind. She's commented on your sexy ass before, actually."

Harper blinked, then laughed, genuine and warm, despite herself. "Wow. High praise from your hot girlfriend. Maybe it's time I switch teams. I mean, if I'm gonna rebound, you're a pretty great option."

"Please," Cierra said with an exaggerated eye roll. "You wouldn't last a week on this team, Harp. Too much emotional baggage. We've got a strict carry-on policy."

Harper laughed again, the sound soft and tentative but real. "Fair point. Still, it's nice to know I'd be in demand."

Cierra grinned, nudging her shoulder. "You're a catch, Harp. Don't let Dan walking away make you forget that."

Harper's smile wavered, but she forced herself to hold onto the lightness of the moment. "Yeah, well, apparently, I wasn't enough of a catch for him."

Cierra rolled her eyes. "Please. Dan wasn't catching anything. He was coasting. And let's be real—was he really the great love of your life, or was he just the safe option? The guy who checked all the right boxes but never really made your heart race?"

Harper opened her mouth to protest, but no words came. She closed it again, gripping her mug a little tighter.

Harper's amusement dimmed, the familiar ache stirring again, but a trace of humor remained, keeping her steady. She took another sip of coffee, letting its heat spread through her like a quiet comfort.

"You need a break," Cierra said gently, her tone shifting. "You've been going non-stop since the breakup, burying yourself in work like it's going to magically fix everything."

Harper shrugged, gripping the mug tighter. "It's better than sitting around feeling sorry for myself. There's too much to do."

"There's always too much to do," Cierra countered. "But at some point, you have to put yourself first. You're human, Harp, not a robot. You used to know how to take a break. You used to have balance."

Harper stared into her mug, her jaw tightening. She didn't want to have this conversation, not now. Not when she felt like she might shatter under the weight of it.

Sensing her resistance, Cierra leaned back, giving her space. "Just ... think about it, okay? What do *you* want? Not for your clients, not for Sam—what do *you* need right now?"

Harper didn't answer, the question too heavy, too raw to process. Instead, she forced a faint smile and took another sip. "What I need is for this mattress to stop attacking me."

Cierra laughed, standing and ruffling Harper's hair as she walked toward the kitchen. "Keep cracking jokes, Harp. Maybe one day, you'll even mean them."

The sound of dishes clinking and a kettle boiling drifted from the kitchen as Harper stared down at the blanket pooled around her legs. Her smile faded, the weight creeping back in. But for a moment—just a moment—she felt lighter, like maybe, just maybe, she could figure out how to get through this. As she made her way toward the bathroom, she passed the small window again, her eyes drawn to the brick wall blocking most of the light. The metaphor hit her like a sudden gust of wind. Like a sliver of sunlight unable to fully penetrate the gloom, she felt barely there, out of reach. She had been running on autopilot for months now—long before the breakup made it impossible to ignore. Driven by pursuing the next deadline, the next office victory, she deluded herself into thinking it would be enough to fill the expanding hole within.

But now, with Dan gone and work feeling like a sinking ship, she felt the darkness closing in. She stepped into the bathroom, flipped on the light switch and stared at her reflection in the small mirror above the sink. Her reflection looked back at her with weary eyes, shadowed by dark circles, her pale skin stretched tight over her gaunt face, and her hair limply hanging down.

With a sigh, she turned on the shower, letting the steam fill the room. She stripped off her clothes and stepped under the spray, the water hot and comforting against her skin. The rushing water enveloped her, its steady rhythm a calming counterpoint to the chaos of her thoughts.

Her fingers dragged through her hair, slick with water, as if scrubbing hard enough might somehow lift the weight pressing down on her. She needed to focus. Losing Crescent International had shaken her more than she cared to admit. They had been with her for years, one of the few clients she could count on to appreciate her vision, and now they were gone, taking a sizable chunk of revenue with them.

The thought twisted in her mind like a dull knife. If she didn't land this new client today, the agency would feel the blow, and she knew Sam was watching. He had said nothing outright, but she could sense the pressure in his clipped emails, and in the way his tone had shifted during their last call. *We can't afford another loss, Harper.*

The steaming water poured over her face, the heat a temporary relief, like washing away a layer of failure. The lost client. The uncertainty pressing in. The breakup—

Her jaw clenched. Not now.

She reached for the shampoo, forcing herself to think through the pitch. She had rehearsed it a hundred times, fine-tuned every slide, every transition. If she nailed this, if she secured the client, it would mean stability for the agency. It would mean proving—to Sam, to the team, to herself—that she was still at the top of her game.

But beneath the rush of water, another thought curled at the edges of her mind, uninvited.

Dan.

His voice, his expression when he had walked away from her outside the restaurant. The exhaustion in his eyes—or was it relief? A hollow feeling spread through her chest, an ache she refused to name.

Stop!

She exhaled sharply, pressing her forehead against the cool tile. This isn't about him.

The water continued to pour over her, the steady rhythm helping to drown out everything else. Work. She had to focus on work.

I have to nail this pitch. The thought repeated itself over and over, a relentless mantra that kept her heart racing. *I can't lose another client. I can't let the team down.*

Still, as she reached for the faucet, her hands unsteady, a stray thought whispered through her mind, unbidden.

Was Dan really the love of my life, or was he just ... safe?

A sharp inhale caught in her throat, but she shoved the thought away, locking it beneath a fortress of strategy and well-rehearsed lines. She twisted the faucet, cutting off the stream, and the only sound left was the slow patter of droplets hitting the tile.

She reached for the towel and wrapped it tightly around herself, stepping out into the humid air that clung to her. A blurry haze of fog distorted her reflection in the mirror. She wiped it clean with her palm, the condensation smearing under her touch and obscuring the woman looking back at her.

She barely recognized herself. Her eyes, usually sharp and focused, were dull, rimmed with dark circles that makeup could only partially hide. Her hair hung in wet, limp strands around her face, and the deep frown lines between her brows seemed etched there permanently. She tried to smile at her reflection, tried to summon some flicker of the confident woman she had once been, but the smile faltered, falling apart before it even began.

Who are you? she thought bitterly.

Since that night with Dan, her life had felt off-kilter, spinning in a direction she couldn't control. She had thrown herself back into work, hoping the frenzy of deadlines would fill the void. But it wasn't working. Nothing was.

She sighed, reaching for her makeup bag, her fingers trembling slightly as she unzipped it. Each stroke of concealer, every careful brush of foundation, felt like another layer of armor. Concealer to erase the dark circles that betrayed sleepless nights. Foundation to smooth over the unevenness that hinted at stress. She dabbed on blush, blending until her cheeks held the faintest hint of life, a pale imitation of the confidence she used to carry. She moved with clinical precision, her actions almost robotic, as if perfect execution could mask the truth that she was losing control.

Her fingers stilled on the lipstick.

She had laughed when Cierra had asked her—half-joking, half-serious—if Dan had been her great love or just the safe choice. Brushed it off, pretended it wasn't a question worth asking.

But now, staring into the mirror, the words lingered.

Dan had been safe. Steady. Dependable. But had he ever made her heart race? Had she ever burned for him the way she had always imagined love should feel? Or had she simply convinced herself that love was supposed to be practical?

A lump rose in her throat. Had she spent all these years mistaking comfort for passion?

She studied her reflection, searching for an answer in her own eyes. Even beneath the concealer and blush, they looked ... lost.

With a sharp sigh, she tossed the lipstick back into the bag.

"Well, that's encouraging," she muttered.

Harper turned away from the mirror, her reflection still haunting her, and braced herself for the day ahead.

Four

Harper smoothed her blazer with deliberate precision, her hands trailing over fabric that needed no adjustment. The polished glass of the conference table reflected the dim glow of the projection screen, every detail meticulously arranged. And yet, her thoughts remained restless.

"You've got this, Harper," Claire, her assistant, said from across the room. She methodically straightened the last of the binders, each one packed with polished sales materials crafted to make an impact. "It's a great pitch. They're going to love it."

Harper nodded, trying to summon a smile, but it felt tight and forced. "Thanks, Claire. Let's hope you're right." She noticed the time on the wall clock, a quiet reminder of the critical meeting about to begin.

In truth, Harper had been over the pitch a dozen times, tweaking it obsessively until it was as perfect as she could make it. Persuasion was the goal, achieved through every graph, every slide, and every word.

Even after thinking about it a bunch, she still worried, *What if it's not good enough? What if they don't bite?*

With Crescent International gone and her relationship with Dan crumbling in the background, this pitch had taken on extra pressure. She wasn't just seeking a client; she needed to regain a sense of control. This account could be her lifeline, a way to save everything.

Claire finished arranging the folders, then walked over to Harper, her face softening with concern. "Harper," she said, her voice hushed, "It's been tough, but you're incredible at what you do. No one works harder than you, and no one knows these clients better. You've got this."

Harper's resolve softened, her shoulders dropping just slightly as she took in Claire's words. Harper appreciated the sentiment, but she felt far from amazing. She was exhausted, her emotions barely contained. She felt overwhelmed by the loss of Dan, Sam's pressure, and the constant deadlines. While she wished to believe Claire, a deep-seated doubt held her captive, refusing to loosen its grasp.

"Thanks, Claire," Harper said, her voice quieter now, tinged with exhaustion. "I just ... I need this one to go well." Her fingers drummed lightly against the table as she took a breath, trying to center herself. "If it doesn't, I'm not sure what ..."

The door to the boardroom swung open before she could finish the thought, and in walked Sam Waters, the CEO of the agency. His presence immediately filled the room with a subtle tension. Harper felt the pressure radiating off him, despite his unreadable expression and sharp suit. The prospective clients followed him in with their sharp suits and polite smiles, but she could feel their critical gaze evaluating her worth.

"Harper," Sam said, his voice clipped but polite as he nodded in her direction. "This is Mr. Porter and Ms. Avery from Sterling Brands. They're looking forward to hearing what you've prepared for them."

"Mr. Porter, Ms. Avery," Harper greeted, her voice smooth and professional as she extended her hand. "It's a pleasure to meet you. Thank you for taking the time to come in today."

Mr. Porter, a towering figure with salt-and-pepper hair and a firm grip, flashed a smile, but Harper caught the distant chill in his eyes. He disregarded the charm, prioritizing the numbers. Ms. Avery, his younger counterpart with sleek dark hair and sharp, calculating eyes, barely spared a nod before shifting focus to the projection screen.

"We're eager to see what you've put together," Ms. Avery said, her tone professional but guarded.

Harper gestured to the folders on the table, keeping her voice composed even as her pulse pounded. "We've prepared materials for you to follow along. I think you'll find we've designed a strategy that not only aligns with your brand but elevates it in ways that will truly set you apart in the market."

Claire gave Harper a tiny nod from across the room just to let her know she was there for her. Harper took a deep breath, steadying herself as she prepared to begin the presentation.

This was it. Everything was riding on this pitch.

Harper took her place at the front of the room, the remote for the presentation in hand, and began. "Sterling Brands has an incredible reputation in the market," her voice remained steady and clear. "But with shifting consumer trends, there's a tremendous opportunity here to pivot in a way that not only strengthens your presence but transforms it."

As Harper moved through the presentation, the rhythm of her words and the fluidity of the pitch pulled her out of the fog that clouded her mind for days. Suddenly, she felt on fire. Everything just made sense, and she knew what to do. The polished slides flashed behind her, outlining the data, the vision, the strategy she had crafted so painstakingly to impress Sterling Brands. Her voice was steady, her tone persuasive as all her other worries faded into the background.

She glanced at Mr. Porter, whose head was nodding slightly as she spoke, and Ms. Avery, who seemed to follow along with keen interest. Even Sam, seated at the far end of the table, appeared satisfied, his posture relaxed as he leaned back in his chair. The pressure that had weighed so heavily on Harper's shoulders loosened, if only for a moment. *Maybe this will work*, she thought, feeling a flicker of hope.

"Now," Harper continued, gesturing to the next slide, "with this strategy, we'll be able to engage your core audience while expanding your reach into new, untapped markets. This pivot ..."

"Hold on a second," Mr. Porter interjected, raising a hand as his brow furrowed slightly. "Sounds good, but what about our rivals? Specifically, from Lansing & Co."

The name Lansing & Co. hit Harper like an icy wave, and she froze for just a fraction of a second, her grip tightening around the remote in her hand. She forced a smile, though it felt strained at the edges. "Lansing & Co.?" she repeated, buying herself a moment to gather her thoughts. Of course, it had to be them.

"Yes," Mr. Porter said, leaning forward. "Their latest campaign has been making waves in the market, we're curious if your team has considered how you'd, let's say, take a fresh spin on their approach. We'd like to see something that works as well as theirs, but with a unique twist. Something ... safer but impactful, like what they're doing."

Harper's heart thudded, a familiar feeling of frustration rising in her throat. Safer? It was always the same. Clients, echoing Knox from last week, desired a product replicating the current market trend. There was no room for originality, no appetite for risk. Just a demand to "play it safe" while "standing out." The contradiction grated on her nerves like nails on a chalkboard.

Harper fought to maintain composure as the words pressed against her throat. "Well, Lansing & Co. has certainly made an impression with their latest campaign," Harper said, carefully choosing her words. "We've customized this for Sterling Brands. We want to ensure your voice is distinct in the market, not a reflection of what your competitors are doing. Innovation ..."

"Of course," Mr. Porter said, cutting in again, "but we also can't ignore the success of Lansing's approach. Their numbers are impressive. I'm sure your team could give it your own spin. We're not asking for a copy, just something that feels ... aligned with what's already working."

Harper's smile tightened, and she felt a burning heat rise to her cheeks. *Aligned with what's already working*. Once again, the identical demand surfaced, choking her creativity in the same way Knox had pushed her to the brink.

Harper tried to steady her voice, but Sam's sharp glance from across the table told her he could sense the shift in her tone. "Mr. Porter, I understand the desire to replicate success," Harper said, her voice firm but with a noticeable edge. "Lansing's campaign works for them, but what about Sterling's story?"

She could feel the familiar frustration rising, the same hollow ache that had lingered since Knox. Why couldn't they see that originality set brands apart? Is following the safe path truly leadership, or simply fear in disguise?

"Harper," Sam's voice cut through the air like a blade, calm but firm. He stood from his chair, offering a measured smile to Mr. Porter and Ms. Avery before returning his attention to Harper. "I think this is a good point to pause and let me take over for the rest of the meeting."

Harper blinked, her frustration still simmering. She met Sam's attention, and the look in his eyes, though not hostile, was an obvious message: Retreat before you lose your composure.

"Why don't you head back to your office for now?" Sam continued smoothly. "I'll handle the remaining discussions with Mr. Porter and Ms. Avery."

For a moment, Harper wanted to argue, to defend her stance, but she swallowed the words. She knew Sam could tell she was on the verge of losing her composure, and the last thing she needed was to unravel in front of the clients. Nodding stiffly, Harper set the remote down on the table, her fingers brushing it lightly as she stepped back.

"Of course," she said, her voice clipped but controlled. "Thank you again for your time."

Harper kept her face carefully blank as she stepped out of the boardroom, her heels clicking against the polished floor in a steady, practiced rhythm. With each step, the adrenaline from the pitch drained out of her, replaced by a creeping sense of humiliation that spread like a stain. She could still feel Sam's calm, authoritative voice cutting her off, his smile directed at the clients as he took over and eased them away from her "unreasonable" ideas.

Heat flooded her face, her cheeks turning red with the shame of a reprimanded child. Someone who just couldn't stop.

Is that what Sam thinks of me? The question pulsed in her mind, jagged and insistent. Too much? Too ambitious? She'd always believed that her drive, her refusal to settle for bland, derivative work, was part of what made her good at this job. But in that quiet exchange, Sam's detached stare made her feel exposed, as if her passion were something reckless, something to rein in.

Her hands shook slightly as she pushed open the door to her office, the glass walls offering her little refuge from the prying eyes of her coworkers. She could feel the stares following her, their expressions carefully blank but curious. She forced herself to keep her head high, her steps measured, but inside, the pressure was mounting, her thoughts circling faster and faster.

Safe but impactful. The phrase echoed in her mind, mocking her. It was the same corporate buzzword nonsense she'd heard a hundred times, a subtle insult disguised as a compliment. She was good enough to execute, but not trusted enough to lead, to truly innovate. The unspoken frustration, resentment, and feeling of being trapped within a suffocating role made her feel like she was choking on her own words.

Harper closed the door to her office and pressed her back against it, breathing hard, as if the air itself had turned against her. The pristine walls, the polished surfaces, all felt like they were closing in, offering no comfort, no release. Her chest tightened, and she tried to swallow down the lump in her throat, tried to force herself to calm down.

But the more she tried to hold it in, the more the pressure built, like a ticking clock, counting down to a detonation she couldn't stop.

She could still see Mr. Porter's face, the way he'd looked at her with polite dismissal. Sam's look, too, was one of sympathy, but it also carried a touch of patronizing, sending the message: *Let the adults deal with this, Harper.*

Her vision blurred as tears pricked at her eyes. She tried to focus on breathing, on staying composed, on not letting it all spill out, but it was no use. The relentless burden of proving herself overwhelmed her, the pressure to create safe and forgettable content, and the loneliness of feeling misunderstood.

Her legs gave out, and she slid down the door, landing hard on the floor as the first sob tore free, raw and desperate. She clamped a hand over her mouth as if she could silence herself, but the tears came faster, her body shaking with the force of her grief and anger and exhaustion.

Alone in her glass-walled office, she let it all out. The disappointment, the fear that she wasn't enough, that she was losing herself in a world that didn't value her voice. For so long, she'd been holding everything together, pretending she was fine, pretending the sacrifices were worth it. But now, there was nothing left to hold.

As Harper sat on the floor, her tears slowing to shaky breaths, one thought cut through the haze: She couldn't keep doing this. She didn't know what the answer was yet, but for the first time, she admitted to herself that something had to give.

The office had fallen silent as people turned to watch her breakdown, but she was too absorbed in her own emotions to notice. The glass partition that separated her office from the rest of the workspace offered no real privacy, and in that moment of vulnerability, Harper was fully visible to her coworkers.

The scene unfolded as if in slow motion; a car crash playing out in front of everyone's eyes. Frozen, the crowd witnessed their leader's collapse. A few exchanged awkward glances, unsure whether to look away or offer help. A couple of them just stared like they'd seen a ghost. Harper Brooks, known for her composure, was visibly unraveling in front of them.

And then, through her blurry vision, Harper glimpsed movement outside her office. Tears blurred her vision, and she gasped, catching her breath, as she realized who was watching.

Sam. And the clients.

Her heart dropped to her stomach.

From her spot on the floor, Harper could just make out Sam escorting Mr. Porter and Ms. Avery out of the boardroom. Through the glass walls of her office, she watched their polite, professional conversation play out, the faint hum of their voices muffled by the distance. Sam's calm demeanor never wavered as he gestured toward the exit, his movements smooth and practiced, the perfect picture of control.

But then his eyes flicked toward her office.

He stopped mid-sentence, his focus snapping to her through the glass. Harper's breath caught in her throat as she realized what he was seeing: her crumpled on the floor, blotchy and tear-streaked, her chest still heaving from the force of her sobs.

She didn't have to hear the words to know what was happening. Mr. Porter and Ms. Avery noticed Sam's pause and followed his line of sight. The way their eyes landed on her, heavy with unspoken accusation, made Harper's stomach twist. Their faces were a kaleidoscope of confusion, discomfort, and shock, a silent language that spoke of a judgment she couldn't decipher. She could feel it even from across the room, their judgment was like a spotlight burning through the glass.

Panic rose in her, hot and suffocating. She scrambled to her feet, wiping furiously at her face as if she could erase the evidence of her breakdown. Her hands shook as she tried to pull herself together, but it was pointless. It was too late.

They had seen everything.

Her entire office had seen everything.

Through the blur of humiliation, Harper could see Sam turn back to the clients, his lips moving in a steady stream of words she couldn't hear but could only imagine. Was he smoothing it over? Reassuring them that this wasn't what it looked like? That she wasn't what she looked like?

The clients gave polite nods, their awkwardness palpable even at a distance. Harper caught the faintest glimpse of Mr. Porter's tight smile and Ms. Avery's brief glance away, as if to avoid acknowledging what they'd just seen. Her humiliation deepened, spreading like fire across her skin.

Sam ushered them toward the exit, his expression carefully neutral, his body language composed. Harper pressed her back against the wall of her office, trying to stay out of sight, though she knew it was useless. Everyone had seen her come undone.

As the office door clicked shut behind the clients, Sam turned back toward her. He hovered in the boardroom doorway, his attention drifting once more toward her office. His face was a mask, but a glimmer of pity and disappointment shone in his eyes.

Harper's pulse hammered in her ears, a frantic rhythm of disbelief. She averted her eyes, as if refusing to meet their stares could somehow erase what had just happened. Shame curled in her stomach, panic seeping through the cracks of her composure. The realization hit her with brutal clarity: she had just fallen apart right in front of the clients. The very people she had been so desperate to impress had just witnessed her at her lowest, and there was no undoing it.

The meeting wasn't the disaster. I was the disaster.

Her body faltered, legs on the verge of failing, yet she willed herself to stand tall, pressing down on the desk to keep steady. Meeting her own reflection, she felt it—a cold, irreversible certainty settling in her gut. There was no going back.

And yet, she couldn't bring herself to move. She stood there, frozen in the aftermath of her own breakdown, knowing the fallout was only just beginning.

Harper turned away, retreating deeper into her office, her body trembling with the aftershocks. She stood by the window, her back to the glass wall, lifting her arms and pressing her palms to her face as if she could somehow erase the last five minutes from existence.

But the damage was already done.

The dam finally broke, her unraveling laid bare before the entire office. Now, she stood in the aftermath—isolated, stripped of pretense, and struggling to find solid ground beneath her feet.

Well ... shit!

Five

Outside Cierra's apartment, the sky was a dreary, suffocating gray, with thick clouds hanging low and heavy over the city. The overcast weather had lasted for days, and the meager light filtering through the apartment's tiny windows created a washed-out glow that made the room feel even more dismal. Harper's laptop was the only light in the room, making her face look cold and blue. She sat slumped on the pull-out sofa, unmoving, her eyes fixed on the wall, though she wasn't really seeing it.

She hadn't left the apartment since the blow-up at work. Three days. Three days of doing nothing but sitting on the sofa in the same crumpled sweatpants, the same oversized T-shirt, and ignoring the outside world. She ran her fingers through her tangled hair, the grease from days of neglect making her scalp itch. But she didn't care.

Why bother?

The door clicked open, and Cierra walked in. The thud of her gym bag against her shoulder echoing in the quiet apartment, followed by the rustling of the grocery bags in her other hand. As she stepped inside, her eyes landed on Harper, tracing the exhaustion etched into her slumped form.

"Harper, seriously?" Cierra's voice cut through the silence as she dropped her gym bag on the kitchen counter. "You've been in the same spot for three days. Are you planning on ever moving again?"

Harper shifted, rolling her eyes as she pulled the blanket tighter around her shoulders, sinking deeper into the sofa. "I'm fine," she muttered, her voice flat, sulky. "I just ... don't feel like doing anything right now."

Cierra gave her a pointed look and started unpacking the groceries, placing cans and boxes in the cupboards. "You haven't even opened the blinds. It's depressing in here. You need some fresh air, sunlight ... anything. You've been sitting in the dark, staring at the wall like you're in a cave."

Harper snorted softly, barely glancing up. "There's no sunlight to let in. Have you seen outside? It's gross. It's not like I'm missing anything."

Cierra paused and looked at her, hands on her hips. "That's not the point. You can't keep doing this. You can't just sit here and expect things to get better."

Harper slouched lower, crossing her arms over her chest. "I just need a few more days. I'll be fine." There was a distinct teenage weariness in her tone, a mix of annoyance and a reluctance to engage in a full-blown argument.

Cierra sighed, her patience wearing thin as she leaned against the counter. "No, Harper. No more days of this. You've got an entire month of forced time off to figure things out—use it. Sam basically handed you a sabbatical, and you're wasting it sitting here like a lump. By Monday, I want you out of this apartment."

Harper's head snapped up, alarmed. "What? Are you seriously kicking me out? Where am I supposed to go?"

"I'm not kicking you out," Cierra replied, her tone firm but not unkind. "But you need to get away. You've been sulking in here for days, and it's not helping you. You need to get out of your head. Go somewhere, anywhere. A beach, the mountains ... I don't care. You need to clear your mind."

Cierra tilted her head slightly as if the answer was obvious. "You already had plans to visit Myrtle Beach next month with Dan, right? Why not just go early? Spend some time with your family. It's the perfect escape."

Harper froze, her stomach twisting. The mention of Myrtle Beach stung more than she expected. This wasn't just any ordinary trip, this trip was special for them. A week of family barbecues, lazy beach afternoons, and her mom's relentless key lime pie offerings. A lump formed in her throat as she recalled her mom's contagious enthusiasm when she'd shared the news about bringing Dan along.

"No," Harper said quickly, her voice tight. "That's not happening."

Cierra frowned. "Why not? You love the beach, and your mom's been begging you to visit. Just call her, say you're coming early. She'd be thrilled."

Harper let out a bitter laugh, a sharp edge cutting through the sound. "Yeah, thrilled to interrogate me about why I showed up alone. 'What happened with Dan?' 'Are you sure things can't still work out?'" She pulled the blanket higher over her lap, her jaw tightening.

"I can't deal with that right now. Not after ..." Her voice trailed off, but Cierra didn't push.

She could already picture her mom's worried eyes softening as she placed a hand on Harper's arm. "You two were so good together. Are you sure things can't still work out?" The questions themselves were manageable, but the heavy burden of her mother's expectations hung over her like a dark cloud. The way it would wrap around her like a too-tight hug, making her chest ache.

Harper shook her head, her voice hardening as she continued. "Look ... their version of 'help' is convincing me to fix something that's already broken. They'll never understand. I'd spend the entire trip explaining why it's really over while my mom gives me those big, pitying eyes." Her jaw tightened. "It's not exactly my idea of a relaxing getaway."

Cierra studied her for a moment, then sighed. "Okay. No, Myrtle Beach. But you still need to get out of here. Somewhere you don't have to answer questions or explain yourself. Anywhere but this apartment."

Harper groaned and flopped back against the cushions. "What's the point?" she grumbled, folding her arms and staring at the ceiling. "It's not like going somewhere's gonna fix anything. I'll still be dealing with the same crap when I get back."

Cierra, now dressed in her running leggings and sports bra, walked back into the living room, wiping her hands on a towel. "Harper, I'm not saying a trip is going to solve all your problems. But you'll lose your mind if you keep doing this." She gestured toward the blanket and the disarrayed state of the living room. "Just get away for a while. A change of scenery. You used to love traveling."

Harper grumbled something unintelligible, then pulled the blanket up over her face in exaggerated defiance. "Yeah, but I don't feel like it."

Cierra crossed her arms and leaned against the doorway, staring Harper down. "Well, you need to start feeling like it. I'm not asking anymore. You've got until Monday to figure out where you're going because you're not spending another week moping in my apartment."

Harper peeked out from under the blanket, her brows knitting together in a pout. "What am I supposed to do? Go on some random trip by myself? That sounds ... boring."

Cierra raised an eyebrow. "You used to love going on cruises. Why don't you look into that? Just get on a boat, soak up some sun, and not think about anything for a week."

Harper sighed, dragging the blanket tighter around herself. "A cruise? I don't know. I haven't done anything like that in years. Feels pointless."

Cierra walked over to grab her gym bag, rolling her eyes as she slung it over her shoulder. "Well, get yourself in the mood because this whole brooding-in-the-dark thing isn't a good look for you, Harper. You need to snap out of it. Like, yesterday."

Harper didn't respond, just stared moodily at the wall, her arms still crossed.

Cierra paused at the door, her hand on the knob. "You want anything from the bodega when I get back?"

After a long, exaggerated pause, Harper muttered, "A donut ...?"

Cierra laughed, shaking her head. "You can have a donut after you take a shower. Deal?"

Harper shot her a half-hearted glare, but a tiny smile tugged at the corner of her lips. "Fine. Deal."

With that, Cierra left for her run, leaving Harper in the same dim apartment, the faint sound of her footsteps fading away.

Alone again, Harper sighed, staring blankly at the ceiling before grabbing her phone off the coffee table. She opened up a travel app and began half-heartedly scrolling through vacation options, her thumb lazily swiping past beach resorts and hotels.

Her finger hovered over the search bar, and with a reluctant groan, she typed Caribbean cruises.

The screen filled with pictures of sparkling blue waters and sun-drenched decks, the open sea stretching out as far as the eye could see. Though she squinted at the vibrant images, Harper's frown eased as a reluctant spark of interest ignited inside her.

Maybe Cierra was right.

Maybe she needed to get away.

Harper sat back against the sofa, her thumb lazily scrolling through endless cruise listings. Pictures of white-sandy beaches, impossibly blue waters, and massive, gleaming ships filled the screen, but none of them stirred any excitement in her. She had once fantasized about escaping to a tropical paradise, sailing away on a ship and leaving her duties behind. But now, all she could think about was the fact that she'd be alone. *Just me ... paying double for a cabin designed for two.* Rolling her eyes, she imagined herself alone, awkwardly seated at tables for two, surrounded by couples and families on their vacations, was almost unbearable.

Great. Just me and my cocktail for six days straight.

Another overpriced cruise flashed across her screen, and irritation prickled at the edges of her patience. After a few more minutes of aimless browsing, she typed "cruises for single people" into the search bar, not really expecting much. But then something caught her eye.

A site called Mingle at Sea popped up with a tagline that read: **Where solo journeys turn into shared memories.**

Harper paused, intrigued, and tapped on the link. The homepage opened with vibrant photos of groups of people laughing over cocktails, exploring tropical destinations, dancing on deck under a sky full of stars. There was a warmth to the pictures, something inviting.

At Mingle at Sea, we believe that travel is better when it's shared.

Harper's eyes skimmed the text, taking in the pitch. **As the premier single sailors' travel agency, we bring together adventurous solo travelers from all walks of life to explore the world's most breathtaking destinations.**

The more she read, the more she leaned forward, drawn in by the promise of connection. The idea of not being alone. Of meeting new people, other solo travelers like herself who were just trying to escape for a while. Whether you're seeking new friendships, looking to connect with like-minded individuals, or simply ready to leave behind the routine for some fun on the open ocean, our cruises offer the perfect opportunity to dive into exciting experiences. Harper's eyes lingered on those words, her pulse quickening.

She scrolled further down and found more details about how the agency worked. Instead of forcing the double occupancy rate, Mingle at Sea works with travelers to assign a roommate to share the cabin cost, easing the financial burden for solo adventurers.

A wave of relief settled over her. Finally, a trip that didn't make solo travel feel like a punishment. They weren't just trying to get people together; they were making the whole thing perfect for people going solo. She read on, her curiosity piqued: **With our carefully curated itineraries and a laid-back, inclusive vibe, you'll never feel out of place or alone on your adventure. There's always someone new to meet, a conversation waiting to happen, or a laugh to be shared.**

Harper felt a flicker of excitement rise for the first time in days. She clicked on the "Upcoming Cruises" tab, scanning the options. Next week, a luxurious and sleek vessel called the Elysian Serenade was departing for a six-night sailing that looked straight out of a dream. The itinerary promised a journey through the Caribbean, with stops at stunning coastal cities, white-sandy beaches, and opportunities for sunset cocktails, snorkeling excursions, and dance parties under the stars.

This might actually be perfect, Harper thought, her heart picking up pace as she read further. No awkward solo dinners. No paying double for a cabin. Six days to explore new landscapes, meet new people, and have some fun. This might be exactly what she needed to escape her life for a while.

Your next adventure is just a wave away, the website promised.

Harper bit her lip, hesitating. *Could I really do this?* She thought about what Cierra had said, about getting away, about snapping out of her funk and doing something for herself. The thought of hanging out here, moping in Cierra's apartment, was just too depressing. She could stay stuck, or she could shake things up, something completely outside her comfort zone.

Her finger hovered over the "Book Now" button, her heart pounding as a million doubts flickered through her mind. What if it was a mistake? What if it made her feel even lonelier? The thought of the cold, gray walls of Cierra's apartment urged her thumb forward, even as she hesitated. The suffocating weight of the past three days.

With a deep breath, Harper clicked.

A flicker of doubt gripped her, but surprisingly dissolved as the reality of her decision sank in. The release felt almost … light. For the first time in days, she'd done something just for herself. Six nights on the Elysian Serenade. Six nights to escape the city, the questions, the heartbreak. It wasn't about solving anything. It was about breathing again.

Information about dates, prices, and rooming options scrolled across the screen, and Harper booked a shared cabin, trusting the agency to pair her with someone else traveling alone. She submitted the forms, entered her payment, and watched as the confirmation solidified her decision.

She was going.

Harper stared at the confirmation email, her heart still racing with the thrill of what she'd just done.

Six nights on the Elysian Serenade, leaving behind work, heartbreak, and the suffocating city. It wasn't about fixing things. It wasn't about anyone else. For the first time in far too long, Harper had done something just for her.

She glanced out the window at the gray sky, still thick with clouds that seemed to choke the light from the day. The same dreary view she'd been staring at for days. But now, it didn't feel so suffocating. She no longer felt trapped. It seemed like there was a way out, a break, on the horizon.

Despite the gloomy weather outside, Harper felt a change within her, like the sun finally emerging from behind storm clouds. Your next adventure is just a wave away, the site had promised, and for the first time in a long time, it felt true.

With a deep breath, Harper closed her laptop and stood up, stretching her stiff limbs as she glanced at herself in the mirror. She still looked disheveled, still felt a bit lost, but there was a flicker of something else now, too. A glimmer of hope. And just like that, the clouds that had hung over her life didn't seem so permanent anymore.

The sun was coming. This time, she was sailing straight toward it.

Six

The crisp scent of saltwater mixed with the hum of anticipation as Harper stepped onto the gangway, the soft click of luggage wheels echoing beneath her. The Elysian Serenade rose before her, its gleaming white hull catching the light, reflecting sea and sky as one. She stilled, breath hitching as she let the moment settle—this was real.

This was nothing like the tired, crowded ships she remembered from past family vacations. Every inch of the Elysian Serenade was dripping with refinement, resembling a grand, floating castle urging her toward something extraordinary she had long yearned for. The ship seemed to shimmer, its curves smooth and flawless, each deck glistening in the sunlight like a promise of the perfect escape. The glee of fellow passengers created a subtle hum of activity, adding to the air of anticipation that made her heart race just a little faster.

As she walked up the gangway and crossed onto the ship, Harper felt a wave of awe wash over her. It wasn't just the breathtaking scale; it was the feeling of venturing into uncharted territory, a feeling that had been absent from her life for months. Something unburdened by her past, her stress, or her mistakes. The moment her feet touched the deck, the city's clamor, the urgency of deadlines, and the weight of Dan's expectations all dissolved, replaced by the refreshing scent of salt air and the calming sway of the ship.

It felt strange, almost wrong, to leave those burdens behind so easily. They'd clung to her, a part of her identity. Who was she without them?

She entered the ship's grand atrium, and immediately Harper's breath hitched. Golden light poured through the glass skylights, casting a soft, warm glow over the room, illuminating the soaring ceilings that reached up like the heart of a cathedral, a testament to its masterful design. The marble floors gleamed beneath her feet, and a spiral staircase with intricate gold balustrades wound up to the higher decks, inviting passengers to explore the ship's treasures.

The space was alive with possibility.

This vacation was unlike any she'd had before. The grandeur was undeniable, but there was something more. There was romance in the air, an elegance that seemed to surpass even her wildest expectations. Velvet couches in deep blush tones filled the lounge areas, while oversized windows framed the endless blue of the ocean outside.

A feeling of hope, something she hadn't felt in weeks, blossomed in Harper's chest as she sighed softly. It was like the Elysian Serenade was telling her that this, this floating sanctuary, would be the place where everything changed. Where she could breathe again, where she could be herself. She ran her hand along the smooth banister as she walked deeper into the atrium, admiring the shimmer of the chandeliers overhead.

This place is beautiful, Harper thought, her lips curving into a faint smile. *Better than I ever imagined.*

So absorbed in wonder, Harper barely noticed the older woman standing beside the grand piano, silently observing the stream of boarding passengers. Harper remained oblivious to the woman's scrutiny until their eyes locked.

"First time on the Elysian Serenade?" the woman asked, her voice smooth and warm, like a sunbeam cutting through the bustle of the ship. The woman's sun-kissed skin, silver hair, and effortless grace made her seem as natural to the ship as its opulent furnishings, captivating Harper immediately. Her teal dress flowed like the sea, and her ocean-blue eyes twinkled with amusement and wisdom.

"Yeah," Harper replied, a little breathless. "This ... this is ... I've never quite seen just anything quite like this." Her eyes drifted back to the grandeur of the atrium, unable to fully hide her awe.

The woman smiled knowingly, her lips curving as if she'd heard the same reaction a thousand times but never tired of it. "It's something, isn't it?" She stepped closer, her eyes soft but sharp, as though she saw more than just the surface of things. "Are you part of the singles group?"

Harper blinked, startled by the question. She hadn't even mentioned it, but then again, it wasn't hard to guess. She was clearly here alone, with no partner or group trailing behind her. "I am, actually," she said, nodding. "Are you ...?"

The woman's smile widened, her eyes glinting with a playful spark. "Maude Nereida," she said, extending her hand. "I'm with Mingle at Sea. You might've gotten a few emails from me before the cruise."

Harper's eyes lit up with recognition as she shook Maude's hand. "Oh, of course! It's nice to put a face to the name. Your emails were really helpful. I've never done something like this before ... a singles cruise, I mean."

Maude's smile deepened, her presence radiating a calm, welcoming energy. "Well, you're in the right place. Trust me, you're going to have more fun than you expect." She tilted her head, studying Harper, her voice dropping to a softer, more knowing tone. "This is a chance to leave everything behind for a little while. To inhale, to investigate, and perhaps even to discover something fresh, be it a companion or something ... more. And the best part? You're not doing it alone."

Harper felt a strange sense of relief wash over her at Maude's words as if the woman had somehow read her mind, and seen the tension she'd been carrying. Maude possessed a quality of resilience, an unwavering strength that suggested she'd weathered countless storms.

"You're not just talking about the cruise, are you?" Harper asked, smiling a little despite herself.

Maude's eyes sparkled with a hint of mystery. "The tide always knows where it's going, even if we don't," she said softly. "All you have to do is follow the flow."

Harper felt something tighten, a mix of emotions she couldn't fully untangle. Relief? Fear? Maybe both. She'd been fighting the tide for so long, clawing against the currents of work, of Dan, of everything—and what had it gotten her? Nothing but exhaustion. The idea of letting go, of following the flow felt foreign, even a little frightening. But also ... freeing. She couldn't remember the last time she had let herself drift.

She laughed softly, almost to herself. "I think I'll try that," she said, tasting the words like something unfamiliar yet promising. A quiet thrill flickered to life, tentative but real.

Maude gave her a wink. "Good. We've got some great events lined up for you and the others ... starting with a cocktail mixer tonight in the Topaz Lounge. You'll meet your fellow travelers soon enough."

When Maude turned to greet another passenger, Harper experienced a sense of excitement greater than she'd felt in a long time. Not just for the cruise, but for what might come next. The ship's grandeur, Maude's warm welcome, and the promise of new possibilities all combined to feel like a new beginning.

Harper stood still in the grand atrium, the ship's quiet hum and the murmur of voices fading into the background. She breathed in deeply, a rich aroma dancing around her senses with a heady mix of floral perfume and briny sea breeze. *This is it*, she thought as something within her shifted, stretching toward the light. The burden she had carried for so long didn't vanish, but in its place, a quiet sense of hope began to bloom.

With one last glance around, Harper headed toward the glass-enclosed elevators, the centerpiece of the atrium. As she stepped inside, she couldn't help but marvel at the panoramic view the glass walls provided. As the elevator glided upward, the atrium spread out before her like a magnificent tapestry, the soft, filtered light from above illuminating the ornate railings, the cool, smooth marble, and the plush, inviting seating. The grand staircase spiraled beneath her, passengers like tiny figures moving up and down, exploring the ship's splendor.

Harper's breath caught in her throat as she rose higher. The immense atrium, with its massive windows, revealed a breathtaking vista of the ocean. The endless horizon, meeting the sky in a blurry line, hinted at a vast unknown beyond the ship and the journey, a realm of possibilities. She smiled to herself as the elevator dinged softly and the doors slid open.

As Harper stepped off the elevator, her excitement grew with each stride as she hurried toward her cabin. She navigated the plush, carpeted hallway until she reached her door, her heart giving a small flutter as she slid the key card through the slot. The door unlatched, and she stepped inside. She was home for the next six nights.

The cabin was brighter and more spacious than she had imagined, creating a welcoming atmosphere. The walls were a soft cream, accented with warm wood tones and nautical-themed décor.

A stunning panorama of the bustling Miami port and downtown skyline stretched out before her from the large balcony window, the noise and movement a sharp reminder of New York's relentless rhythm. But beyond the port, the ocean waited—quiet, boundless, and limitless. It was a clean break, a line drawn in the water between the life she was leaving behind and whatever came next. Soon, the city would disappear entirely, swallowed by the horizon, and all that would remain was the open sea.

With a deep sigh, Harper dropped her bags onto the floor and kicked off her shoes. She crossed the room in a few steps and collapsed onto the bed, her body sinking into the soft mattress. For the first time in weeks, she felt the tension leave her body, her muscles slowly unwinding. She lay there, staring up at the ceiling, letting the cool air and the soft hum of the ship lull her into a state of relaxation. Stepping onto the Elysian Serenade, she seemed to release all her burdens as if the weight of the world had vanished.

She didn't know how long she lay there, drifting in the quiet, when suddenly, the sound of the door unlocking snapped her back to the present. She sat up quickly, smoothing her hair as the door swung open, revealing her new cabin mate.

A young woman with a beaming smile and sun-kissed skin stepped into the room, her presence immediately filling the space with an infectious energy. She wore a brightly patterned sundress, the vibrant colors bursting with life against the backdrop of her blonde hair pulled back in a high ponytail, a perfect ensemble for the tropical getaway they were about to embark on. A small duffel bag completed her look, draped over her shoulder and a pair of large sunglasses perched atop her head.

"Hey, roomie!" she said brightly, her eyes lighting up when she saw Harper. "You must be Harper, right? I'm Paige Turner. Yes, that's my real name."

Harper blinked, taken aback by Paige's warm, easygoing demeanor. But she quickly smiled, feeling some of her nerves ease. "Yeah, that's me. Nice to meet you, Paige."

Paige flopped down on her own bed, kicking off her sandals with a casual toss and stretching out, much like Harper had before. "I've been on my fair share of cruises, but this one really blows the others out of the water. It's like stepping into a dream. I mean, this is fancy, right?"

Harper nodded, relaxing a little more. "It really is. I've been on some family cruises, but nothing like this. It feels ... special."

Paige grinned, her eyes twinkling. "Oh, it's special alright. Trust me. But you've seen nothing yet! The rest of the ship is absolutely breathtaking. I'm already planning how to hit every bar by the end of the week." She laughed, the sound full of light and mischief as if life was one big adventure, and she was ready to dive right in.

Harper smiled again, feeling the warmth of Paige's energy lift her mood. It was hard not to get caught up in it, to feel like maybe this was the start of something good. Something fun. "That sounds like a solid plan," she said, leaning back against her pillows.

Paige sat up suddenly, pointing toward the balcony. "And look at that view! How can you be in a bad mood when that's your view?" She flashed Harper another bright smile. "We are not gonna waste a second of this trip, okay?"

Paige plopped onto her bed, stretching out with an exaggerated sigh. "I say we spend the entire week pretending real life doesn't exist. This ship? This view? Nothing else is as important." She flashed Harper a grin, her energy practically radiating from her like sunlight.

Harper nodded, feeling a surprising surge of excitement bubble up inside her. Maybe Paige was right. Maybe this was her opportunity to ultimately ditch it all and start fresh.

"Deal," Harper agreed, smiling for what felt like the first time in forever. "Let's make the most of it."

Paige grinned, leaping off the bed. "Good! Now, I'm going to unpack and then scope out the best spots for sunset cocktails. You in?"

Harper hesitated, thinking about the past few weeks, the stress, the disappointment, the exhaustion. As her eyes shifted from Paige's serene expression to the sun-drenched balcony, a subtle shift in her emotions became undeniable.

"Absolutely," she said, standing up. "Let's do it."

Paige pumped her fist in the air, clearly pleased. "Yes! That's the spirit!" She turned toward her bags, and Harper couldn't help but laugh quietly to herself. Maybe this cruise was her chance to escape the stress and figure out who she really is.

For the first time in a long time, Harper felt a flicker of excitement, a sense of readiness for whatever the future could hold.

Seven

The steady rhythm of the ship's engines vibrated softly beneath Harper's feet as she stood alone on the promenade deck, leaning against the railing. Behind her, the glittering Miami skyline slowly shrank into the distance, its lights winking out one by one, swallowed by the horizon. The sky above was a watercolor of lavender and deep orange, the last streaks of sunset fading into the encroaching night.

Harper stayed rooted to the spot, watching until the city was nothing more than a faint glow on the edge of the vast, open sea. She exhaled slowly, the cool salt air rushing in to fill the quiet spaces within her. As the last trace of land vanished, it felt like the past loosening its grip—fading into the waves, just like everything she was leaving behind.

The bustling city life of New York, with its fast pace, soaring buildings, and constant pressures, seemed a distant memory. It was fading away, just as the Miami skyline disappeared as the ship ventured out into the vast ocean. Out here, surrounded by nothing but endless water and the soft hiss of waves, Harper felt small but not insignificant.

It was as though the sea itself was inviting her to let go of the old, to lose herself in the vastness and find something new, something she hadn't even realized she was searching for.

She let her fingers drift over the railing's smooth metal, the sensation keeping her tethered as she hovered between the life she knew and the unknown ahead.

With one last glance at the fading lights, Harper turned and headed inside toward the Topaz Lounge, where the hum of conversation and the promise of connection awaited her.

The room radiated a golden warmth, its deep rose velvet seating lending it an unexpected elegance. Elegant windows framed the vast ocean, where the first stars had reflected on the water's surface. She could almost see why people got lost in this type of atmosphere; there was something so undeniably romantic about it.

Her heels clicked softly against the varnished floor as she moved deeper into the room, her eyes theatrically scanning for someone in the crowd. Small clusters of people formed, some laughing and sharing drinks, others awkwardly introducing themselves. The entire space was relaxed, intimate, and easy like everybody was here for a brief escape and a little adventure.

As much as she wanted to relax, there was a part of her still stiff, almost like an impersonation. Unconsciously, she played with the hem of her black dress, questioning if it was too formal for the relaxed atmosphere. The dress itself was simple yet elegant, curving at all the right points of her figure. With her dark hair cascading in soft waves upon her shoulders, she knew she looked good. But that knowledge was a double-edged sword. Her armor was her stunning appearance, a carefully crafted facade to ward off criticism. But here, surrounded by strangers who didn't know her, the cracks in that armor felt glaringly obvious.

And yet, it never quite felt like enough. Beneath the polished exterior, there was always the fear that one crack in the façade would be all it took to unravel her. Despite her surroundings, she couldn't shake feeling like an outsider, as if she couldn't embrace the present without anticipating what was to come or worrying about making the wrong impression.

Just then, a familiar voice reached her from behind, as she was about to make a bee-line for a corner where she could hide and drink.

She turned to see Paige bounding toward her in a riot of color from her sundress, hair pulled up high into a bouncy ponytail that threatened to bob off her head with each step. It was almost impossible not to smile around her energy.

"Hey, Harper! Come meet these guys!" Paige said, seizing Harper's hand before she could get a word of protest out. "They're great, Brody and Aidan. You'll like them, I promise."

Harper passively followed Paige through the throngs of passengers in the lounge, eventually reaching a spot close to the bar. Two men stood side by side, one with a martini glass in hand, the other enjoying a beer.

"This is Brody," Paige said, presenting the taller of the two, already flashing his broad smile as he gave Harper a playful wink. "And this is Aidan," she followed, gesturing toward the other man.

When Harper noticed him, something shifted—like the first stroke of color on a blank canvas, subtle yet intentional. He wasn't flashy, not like Brody. His red hair, streaked with silver, was neither neatly combed nor unruly, resting somewhere in between. The lines on his face, the faint blemishes, the unshaven stubble along his jaw—all of it told a story she couldn't yet read. He was well-dressed but indifferent to fashion, as if he had learned long ago that presence mattered more than polish. And somehow, that made him more compelling than someone who tried too hard to be seen.

"This is my roommate, Harper," Paige said. "She's basically the classiest person here, so I figured you two should meet."

"Nice to meet you," Harper acknowledged, her smile polite and composed.

Aidan replied, "Uh, nice to meet you too," sounding a little self-conscious.

Meanwhile, Brody was all charm. "Harper, huh? Love the name. So, what brings you on this cruise?"

Harper turned to Paige, who was grinning proudly beside her, quite pleased with herself for having dragged Harper into the mix. Her shoulders relaxed just a fraction as she leaned in, a soft chuckle escaping her lips. "Let's just say I needed a change of scenery."

Brody raised his martini in a toast. "I can definitely relate to that. You've certainly come to the right place. This is where all the action takes place."

Harper couldn't help but laugh at his exuberance, though it was the quiet form beside him that drew all of her attention. He wasn't pushing hard to overpower the conversation like Brody had; he watched, listened, and waited for the right moment to say anything. There was something about that patience that was intriguing.

Before they could continue further, the room dimmed slightly, and a light chime reverberated off the lounge walls. All the chatter around the area dissipated as a woman emerged onto a small, uplifted stage-like area near the middle of the room. Harper knew right then and there who she was: Maude Nereida, the Mingle at Sea hostess. Harper had met her earlier that day when she went through the atrium alone, and Maude welcomed her in with an enlightened smile.

Now, Maude seemed to effortlessly fill the room with her commanding presence. Subtle grace marked her movements, and her sun-kissed skin and streaked hair gave her the appearance of one born of the sea itself. It all signaled quiet authority.

"Good evening, everyone," Maude started with a voice as smooth and rich. "Welcome aboard the Elysian Serenade—and more importantly, welcome to the start of what I hope will be a week full of adventure, laughter, and maybe even a little romance." A playful wink and a teasing tone drew gentle chuckles from the crowd. "I'm Maude, your host for this journey, here with Mingle at Sea, and I'll be guiding you through all the fun events we've got lined up. So get comfortable, get to know each other, and let's make this a week to remember."

The room erupted in gentle applause. Maude acknowledged them with a brief wave before exiting, and the conversation picked up where it left off. The atmosphere buzzed with a newfound vibrancy sparked by Maude's words that resonated with everyone.

Besides her, Paige was already deep in conversation with Brody, their banter lively and full of energy. Again and again, Harper's attention drifted to Aidan, standing removed from the crowd. His thoughtful look at the gathering was neither cold nor aloof.

The whole standing thing felt a little weird, so Harper looked toward the bar. "Fancy getting another drink?" Aidan asked, sensing her unease.

Her eyes locked with his, and she nodded in agreement. "Yeah, why not?"

They made for the bar, weaving through knots of people and catching snatches of laughter and clinking glasses as they went. A woman in a sequined dress gestured wildly, sending the contents of her cocktail splashing over her companion's arm. Someone burst into a high-pitched laugh near the piano, the sound blending with the gentle strains of jazz from the band. The room was alive with motion, with connection, and Harper felt the faintest tug of a longing stir as she reached the bar.

"Another red ale for me," he said to the bartender, turning to Harper. "And for you?"

"Dry martini," Harper said smoothly, leaning against the bar. It was her go-to drink: simple, classic, and strong. Aidan's eyes lingered on her, not in a way that felt intrusive, but as though he were sketching an outline in his mind, collecting details beyond the words she'd spoken.

They remained in the quiet, the rhythmic chime of glasses and the dusky lull of jazz folding around them like a slow-moving tide. Harper wasn't sure what to say, but the silence between them didn't feel awkward. It felt … steady. They both enjoyed the peaceful silence, neither of them wanting to break it.

"So," Aidan finally said, turning his drink slowly in his hands, "what brings you on this cruise?"

Harper exhaled softly, her lips curving into a small smile that didn't quite reach her eyes. "I needed to step away from work for a while. Clear my head, you know? Take a break."

Aidan nodded, his attention drifting before settling back on her. "Yeah, same. Life at home started to feel like a grind. Figured maybe some time away would help me figure out a few things."

Harper's head tipped slightly as she studied him, sensing a quiet gravity in the space between them—an echo of the burdens she knew too well. "Seems like we're all here for the same reason ..." she said, her voice soft. "Escape."

He glanced at her, a faint smile tugging at his lips, one that didn't quite erase the weariness in his eyes. "Or to find something."

The words landed heavier than she expected, her chest tightening as they struck closer to home than she cared to admit. She lifted her martini and took a slow sip, letting the pause stretch. "And have you figured out what you're looking for yet?" she asked, her tone quiet, almost hesitant.

Aidan let out a low chuckle, rough around the edges, but not unkind. "Not yet," he said, the corner of his mouth lifting in a wry smile. "But I've got six days. Guess I'll find out."

The tension that had been tightly bound within Harper loosened like a tiny crack in a shell that had been protecting her. This moment, this sense of ease, was precisely why she had come. Not necessarily to meet someone, but to step outside the life slowly closing in on her.

"I've never really done anything like this," she admitted, her gaze wandering briefly over the room. "I'm usually more ... structured. This is kind of out of my element."

Aidan nodded, his expression softening. "Same here. I'm not exactly the 'singles' cruise' type. Or the 'mixer' type, really. But here we are."

Harper smiled, and this time, it was genuine. "Here we are."

The silence that followed wasn't heavy. If anything, it felt light, as if they were two people sharing the same unspoken understanding with no need to elaborate. She relaxed into it, letting the moment breathe.

Before either of them could say more, a familiar voice drifted over to them, warm and melodic.

"Hello there. I hope you two are settling in."

Harper turned to see Maude standing beside them, her ocean-blue eyes sparkling with a knowing calm. She gave them both a warm smile, her presence somehow both grounding and mysterious.

"Hi, I'm Maude," she said, offering her hand to Aidan first, then Harper. "I'm the host for the singles group, in case you didn't catch my little speech earlier."

Harper smiled politely, shaking Maude's hand. "We're getting there. It's been ... a bit of an adjustment."

"Oh, absolutely," Maude replied with a playful glint in her eye. "The sea has a rhythm, a way of drawing things out of us. Things we don't always expect. That's why we're here. Solo travelers find themselves in good company. Just remember to let the tide take you where it wants. You might be surprised where you end up."

Harper chuckled, but Maude's words stuck with her, resonating in a way she hadn't expected. Maybe there was something to be said about letting go, about allowing herself to be carried by whatever this journey had in store for her.

As Maude drifted away, disappearing back into the crowd, Harper felt a strange sense of anticipation settle over her. The evening wasn't over, and yet, she wasn't afraid of what might come next.

She took another sip of her martini, her eyes drifting back to Aidan. "Do you think she knows something we don't?" Harper asked with a playful smirk.

Aidan smiled, a faint but genuine one. "She definitely gives off that vibe. Maybe we should stick close to her if we want to figure it out."

"Maybe," Harper mused, feeling lighter than she had in weeks. Then she raised her glass slightly, her smile softening. "Here's to letting the tide take us where it wants."

Aidan clinked his glass against hers. "To the tide."

As if out of nowhere, a tiny but significant feeling came over Harper. Maybe it was just the gentle rocking of the ship as it cut through the darkening waters, the rhythmic motion of the ocean beneath her feet. Or maybe, just maybe, it was something more. Something deeper. Something she hadn't even realized she needed until this very moment.

She took another sip of her drink, letting the warmth of the martini settle as she glanced at Aidan, who seemed equally lost in his thoughts. Tonight, she wasn't thinking about work, or Dan, or the endless pressures waiting for her back home. On a ship that felt like a sanctuary, surrounded by the endless possibilities of the open sea, she found herself here, in this moment.

Eight

The afternoon of the next day, the Elysian Serenade brimmed with life as passengers scurried from one activity to another, salty breeze picking up soft peals of laughter and the hum of distant conversations across its decks. Harper found her way to Hestia's Hearth, along with Paige, whose bright energy contrasted sharply with the rather subdued mood hanging over her. Her private class in pasta-making on board was just the right setting where she could set aside—for a couple of hours or so—the cares she had brought with her from New York. The state-of-the-art kitchen gleamed under the bright lights, its sleek countertops and commercial-grade appliances straight out of a cooking show set. Large floor-to-ceiling windows wrapped around the suite, framing a view of open sea and reminding one of the great, interrupting vastness beyond the ship's polished walls.

"Come on, Harper! Let's get our hands dirty," Paige beamed, tying on her apron with a melodramatic flourish.

Harper smiled at Paige's enthusiasm, though it didn't quite reach her eyes. "You do know I have never made fresh pasta before, right?"

"That's the fun part!" Paige said, her eyes scanning the room before settling on a figure who could only be Brody. Harper caught the playful grin spreading across Paige's face, and before she could question her friend's intentions, Paige was already weaving through the crowd in his direction.

"Brody! You look like you need a partner!" Paige called out, abandoning Harper in a heartbeat.

Sighing, Harper cinched her apron a little tighter. Of course, she should have seen that one coming. She wasn't surprised when Paige promptly abandoned her to partner up with Brody, who gave her a wave from across the room, clearly enjoying Paige's bubbly energy. As the group paired up, Harper scanned the room, inhaling fresh herbs and olive oil.

"Looks like we've both been left in the dust," a familiar voice said from behind her.

She turned, coming face-to-face with Aidan himself, a slight smirk playing at his lips. The breeze from the open windows tousled his light red hair, catching the sunlight just right and making him seem almost illuminated. There was just something refreshingly unpolished about him, though he carried himself with a quiet confidence. His apron, haphazardly tied around his waist, suggested a seasoned kitchen veteran rather than a tourist pretending to be a chef for the day.

She laughed low in her throat, raising an eyebrow. "Abandoned again, huh?"

Aidan dramatically sighed. "It's starting to be a motif, this whole vacation. It's gonna be a fight to keep those two separated."

"Well," Harper said, giving a weak smile, "looks like we'll make do."

The head chef, exuberant with a deep Italian accent, clapped his hands to gain everyone's attention and boomed out the steps they'd take to make fresh pasta from scratch. Harper's hands worked through flour and eggs, and that was all she focused on. The plain tactile process of combining ingredients, then kneading and rolling out the dough, was a minor balm against the non-stop static that had interfered with her, it seemed, since the sabbatical she'd started.

"So," Aidan said after a few minutes, his tone casual but laced with curiosity, "how's life?"

The question landed unexpectedly, like the first cool breeze of autumn catching her off guard. Harper's hands stilled for a fraction of a second, her fingers dusted white with flour. A smile stretched across her face, but it was brittle as if constructed of glass, fragile and liable to break if handled too roughly.

"You really want to know?" she said, trying for a lightness in her voice, though the tension beneath it was unmistakable.

Aidan let out a low chuckle from the back of his throat; his eyes snagged on hers with a glint in their depths that seemed fully apprised of how far from telling it like it was she had strayed. "That good, huh?"

Harper uttered a small, bitter laugh; she was surprised at herself. "Yeah," she said softly, her hands resuming the work with the dough. "Something like that."

They stood in silence for a moment, the rhythmic kneading of the pasta dough filling the quiet between them. It was strange how easy it was to speak with Aidan, how there wasn't that pressing need to fill every gap with words. She noticed, with a flicker of curiosity, how confidently he moved his hands through the task, suggesting an experience beyond the beginner level of the cooking class.

"You've done this before," she said, her eyes narrowing a fraction as if curiosity got the better of her.

The smirk twisted on his face, but there was something self-deprecating about it. "You could say I've had some practice."

Harper lifted an eyebrow, intrigued. "Professional pasta maker on the side?"

He shrugged. "Not quite. I run a restaurant back home. It's essentially a family business. We don't do much pasta, but ... I've spent more time in kitchens than I care to admit."

Again, at that, Harper's hands slowed. "A restaurant?"

Aidan nodded, his tone casual, but there was a tinge of weariness in his voice. "Yeah. Irish place in Charlotte. It's been in the family for years. My dad built it from scratch. I've been running it with my brother for ... longer than I thought I would."

"And do you like it?"

The silence spoke volumes from Aidan. He looked out the window, his jaw tightening ever so slightly as if weighing his response. "I love cooking," he said finally, his voice quieter, "but the restaurant ... it's complicated. Family business comes with family expectations, you know?"

Harper nodded as a spark of comprehension leaped between them. She lacked experience in running a restaurant, but she was acutely aware of the pressures she had placed on herself. "I get it," she whispered, resuming her own work. "I've spent the last several years chasing a career that I thought would bring happiness." She paused as she reflected. "And now? Well, I'm not so sure anymore."

Again, his green eyes settled on her, his face softening. "Advertising, right?"

"Yeah," Harper sighed, "creative manager at an agency in New York. Big city, big job, big burnout."

Aidan smiled empathically. "That's a lot of baggage to carry."

Harper looked down at the dough she'd been working, pondering his words. He understood her subtext quickly. It was as if he was reading her backstory written on her forehead. "Yeah. I thought if I worked hard enough, if I pushed myself, I could get to this place where ... I don't know, everything would make sense. But now I'm here ..."

"It's hard, isn't it? Realizing that what you thought you wanted isn't what you need."

She shook her head. "Yeah, something like that. I wanted to be the best ... make a name for myself," she hesitated, "but now, all I feel is tired. Like I'm trying to hold on, but it doesn't even matter anymore."

Aidan's hands stilled, and for a minute, he said nothing. Then, softly, he said, "You're not alone in that."

Harper turned to him, and those eyes reflected right back at her mirrored frustrations. They didn't know everything about each other, but they understood each other. They were both in the same boat.

"You ever think about walking?" Harper asked, her tone low, almost tentative.

Aidan chuckled, a small smile tugging at the corner of his lips. "Every damn day."

They laughed softly, a warm camaraderie settling over them. Despite not having all the answers sorted out yet, those moments of togetherness meant more than words could express.

In that instant, Harper felt a connection with him. It wasn't romantic, not yet anyway, but a warm feeling of shared understanding and trust blossomed between them, forged in the crucible of their demanding work. Despite showing a hint of openness, she still kept her distance, unwilling to fully divulge her personal life. She wasn't ready for that. Not yet.

For now, just sharing a part of this moment in the cooking class-room, with its flour and olive oil scents, would suffice.

"Looks like you're pretty good at this," he said, looking down at her dough. "Maybe we should open a pasta restaurant together."

Harper laughed, loosening up for the first time all week. "One problem. I hate cooking."

Aidan nodded and smiled. "That could be an issue."

Harper wiped her flour-covered hands on her apron and smiled playfully. "Maybe someday I'll have to come and sample your cooking. You know, to see if you live up to all the hype."

Aidan arched an eyebrow and smiled. "You're welcome anytime, and I promise, it'll be the best dish just for you."

"Better be," she teased lightly, feeling strange the sense of warmth despite herself.

As her hands worked the dough, pressing and shaping, Harper felt something loosen inside her—like a knot slowly unraveling. Perhaps this was what she needed, time to sift through the pieces of her life, to shape something new.

For now, she let herself be consumed by something simpler: the dusting of flour on her skin, the boundless ocean meeting the sky, and the quiet company of someone who saw her, even without words.

As Harper and Aidan continued working through the steps of making their fresh pasta, the rhythmic kneading and rolling of dough offered a strange sort of calm. Yet Harper's mind wandered, drawn by the infectious energy from the station across the room where Paige and Brody were working. Their laughter cut through the soft hum of conversation in the kitchen, rising like an exuberant melody above the quieter rhythms around them.

Harper's attention lingered on them. Their connection was immediate and undeniable, both captivated by each other. Paige tossed a playful handful of flour in Brody's direction, her laugh bright and unrestrained as he ducked in mock surrender. Moments later, Brody retaliated by smearing a dollop of sauce on her apron, earning a delighted squeal from Paige. They looked so carefree, so alive, like nothing else in the world mattered except the ridiculous game they were playing.

Harper couldn't remember the last time she'd let herself laugh like that, unburdened and untethered by expectations. The scene was magnetic, a sharp contrast to her own approach to life. While Paige and Brody leaned into the lightness of the moment, Harper found herself caught between a smile and a sigh. Harper was happy for Paige, thrilled to see her so relaxed and carefree. But watching them together also stirred something in her that she couldn't quite name.

"They're certainly hitting it off," she said finally, her voice carrying a touch of wry humor as she glanced back at Aidan.

Aidan's eyes followed hers, and he couldn't help but grin. "Looks like a fun fling in the making, doesn't it?"

Harper nodded, but her smile faded slightly. "Yeah, it does. Good for them, I guess. It's nice to see them so carefree."

She glanced back at Paige and Brody, who were now feeding each other spoonfuls of sauce with dramatic, exaggerated gestures, their laughter bubbling up like champagne. Brody leaned in with another spoonful; his actions met with a flush of happiness on Paige's face and sparkling joy in her eyes. Sauce smudged her cheek, and instead of recoiling or fretting, she simply laughed harder, swiping at it with her flour-covered hand.

It was enviable, really. That kind of ease. Being fully absorbed in the present, free from anxieties about what's coming next. Harper's focus shifted to her hands, working the dough in smooth, measured strokes. The motion was steady, methodical, keeping her tethered to something solid. When had she last let herself exist like this, untangled from worry? The answer felt just out of reach.

"You don't sound too convinced," Aidan said, his tone cutting gently through her thoughts.

Harper shrugged, keeping her hands busy with the pasta dough. "It's just ... I don't know. I used to think things like that were supposed to be simple. Fun. But they never turn out that way, do they?"

Aidan rolled out a piece of dough, his movements calm and methodical, as if the conversation didn't surprise him. "Not often, no. Things get ... complicated."

"That's an understatement," Harper said with a short laugh, shaking her head. "Watching them, I can't help but think it's just a vacation thing. Something light and fleeting. You know, something light that won't follow them home. But then I think about all the times I thought I was going to have something simple and ... well, it never worked out that way."

Aidan glanced at her, his expression thoughtful but not intrusive. "Yeah, I know what you mean. Simple's good in theory, but real life tends to mess it up."

Harper's head tilted just enough to suggest intrigue, a smirk curling at the edges of her mouth as she slid him a knowing glance. "Speaking from experience?"

Aidan let out a quiet sigh, leaning slightly against the counter as they continued working. "You could say that. Had a relationship back home that started simple enough. We were both busy, so we didn't expect much. But the thing about busy lives is, eventually, someone starts wanting more, and when you can't give it …"

"Things fall apart," Harper finished for him, her voice quieter now.

Aidan nodded. "Yeah."

Harper bit her lip, focusing on the dough. She wasn't ready to dive into her own relationship mess, not just yet, but something about Aidan's straightforward nature made it easier to talk. Like he wouldn't judge because he'd been there, too.

"What about you?" Aidan asked after a moment, his tone gentle but curious. "Any … complications?"

Harper gave a small, humorless laugh. "Complications is putting it mildly."

Aidan let the conversation drift, his hands deftly rolling out the pasta dough, but Harper could feel his attention quietly on her, waiting. There was a gentleness to him, an unspoken permission to speak or stay silent. That kind of patience was rare, and it made her feel less guarded than she had been with others.

After a beat, Harper broke the silence. "I was engaged once," she said carefully, the words feeling heavier than she expected as they left her lips. She focused on the dough, smoothing it with more intent than necessary, as if trying to knead the weight of the past away. "We were together for a while."

Aidan didn't press her. He simply nodded, letting the words settle between them. "Engaged, huh? That's ... a big step."

"Yeah," Harper said, the word heavier than it should have been, trailing off into silence. Something unfinished lurked beneath it, but she left it there, unspoken. She didn't explain that the breakup was only weeks old, that the wounds still felt raw, or that a part of her wasn't sure how to move forward. She wasn't ready to unpack it all—not here, not now, not with someone she was only beginning to know.

"So, what happened?" Aidan asked, but not with the edge of someone prying. His tone was soft, cautious, giving her an out if she didn't want to go further.

Harper's hands pressed into the dough, the tension in her grip betraying what her voice tried to conceal. "Life happened. Work happened. I thought I could juggle everything. I thought ... if I just worked hard enough, I could make it all fit. But in the end, I lost him." She gave a soft shrug, trying to mask the deeper hurt beneath the simple statement. "It's funny how you think you're doing the right thing, but when you look back ... you wonder if you missed the point entirely."

Aidan's expression shifted, his eyes gentler now, as if he recognized something familiar in her words that didn't require an immediate response. "I get that," he said finally. "Trying to hold on to everything and ending up with nothing."

Harper studied him for a beat, as if surprised by how well he understood. "Yeah, exactly. It feels like that."

He nodded, folding his dough carefully. "It's hard to know when to let go. Or even what to let go of. I guess it's something we're all still figuring out."

A genuine smile danced across her lips, different from the rehearsed expression she so often used as an emotional shield. "It's like that saying, 'You can have it all, just not all at once.' I'm still trying to learn that part."

Aidan nodded. "Same here. My dad always says life's about balance, but the more I try to find it, the more unbalanced everything feels."

They fell back into a comfortable silence, both of them working through the motions of the cooking class but now sharing something beyond just the ingredients. Harper's focus shifted back to Paige and Brody, who were now theatrically taste-testing their sauces, spooning bites to each other like giddy contestants in a game show. Brody's cheek sported a flour streak and tomato sauce splattered on Paige's apron; yet they were oblivious.

Harper smiled, but there was a flicker of something else—doubt, maybe—as she watched them. "They seem to be having fun." A beat passed before she spoke again, quieter this time. "Makes me wonder if it's just a vacation thing, you know? Something that won't follow them home."

Aidan nodded, following her gaze to the playful duo. "Maybe. But sometimes ... that's enough. It doesn't have to be anything more."

Harper tilted her head, pondering that. "You think?"

He shrugged, wiping his hands on a dish towel. "Yeah. I think not everything has to be serious to matter. Sometimes, a little fun, a little lightness, is all you need. And if it ends when the cruise ends, well ... maybe that's okay, too."

Harper considered his words. Maybe he was right. Maybe not everything was meant to be permanent. Some connections arrived when you needed them most, leaving behind something valuable before slipping away.

She turned back to Aidan. "I guess we'll see. Either way, they're making the most of it."

"Looks like it," Aidan agreed, his green eyes catching hers with a glint of humor. "Maybe we should take notes."

Harper laughed, feeling a little lighter than she had in days. "Maybe."

As they finished rolling out the pasta, Harper felt the tension that had been gripping her begin to ease. Aidan's presence was comforting. He didn't offer solutions or clichés, he just understood. Maybe that's all she needed right now. Someone who got it.

She peered out at the waves; her focus was drawn to the horizon where the ocean stretched endlessly into the distance. At last, the burden of New York, Dan, and her past felt lighter, as if the sea was washing it away.

"Thanks for this," Harper said quietly, her voice softer than she intended. "For listening. And for not ... pushing."

Aidan smiled, a smile that felt like an unspoken promise. "Anytime. We've got each other's backs this week, right?"

Harper raised an eyebrow, catching his teasing tone. "If Paige and Brody keep this up, I think we'll both need all the support we can get."

They looked back at their friends, laughing hysterically as Brody pretended to drop a spoonful of sauce into Paige's hair. Harper rolled her eyes, but a genuine smile surfaced, and she didn't suppress it.

"Looks like it's going to be an interesting week," Aidan said.

Harper's eyes found his, the silence between them shifting, lighter somehow—less burdened. She turned back to the window, the endless ocean stretching out before them.

"Interesting, for sure," she murmured, her smile lingering.

They returned to their cooking, their quiet connection deepening as the class continued. Harper didn't feel the pull of everything she'd left behind in New York. She surrendered to the moment, embracing the ship's presence and the enigmatic man beside her.

And perhaps, in the rhythm of the waves and the quiet of this journey, this week could become something more than just an escape.

Nine

The Bubbly Bar sparkled like a glittering dream as Harper and Paige sank into plush seats, each holding a bubbly cocktail. Soft jazz played in the background, the smooth notes weaving through the gentle hum of conversation. Elegance defined the bar; marble counters shimmered under the light of crystal chandeliers, scattering tiny rainbows. Around them, couples and small groups lounged in comfortable clusters, sipping cocktails and laughing in that easy, carefree way Harper hadn't felt in what seemed like forever.

Harper took a slow sip of the lounge's signature cocktail, the Scarlet Surrender, its bright citrus vodka and house-made strawberry syrup coating her tongue in a perfect balance of sweet and tart. A gentle fizz from the splash of Prosecco lifted the flavors, light and effervescent, like a sunlit breeze on a summer afternoon. It was indulgent yet refreshing, like a strawberry lemonade with a sophisticated, seductive twist.

Her eyes swept over the sleek décor, trying to soak in the atmosphere. It was peaceful here, even romantic. Yet, despite the quiet elegance, her thoughts kept pulling her back to New York—her office, her clients, the ever-looming deadlines trailing her like shadows she couldn't quite shake.

Paige, on the other hand, looked completely at ease. She leaned back in her chair, her champagne glass dangling casually from her fingers, her bright eyes sparkling like she had already discovered the secret to life. "Okay," she said, grinning as she raised her glass toward Harper. "What do you think so far? Pretty sweet deal, right?"

Harper gave a small smile, swirling the deep red liquid in her glass. "Yeah, it's nice. Definitely not the thing I do every day." She glanced around the opulent bar, taking in the sparkling chandeliers reflected in the polished marble counters, the air thick with expensive perfume and old money. "It's just ... I can't seem to stop thinking about everything I left behind. The office. Projects. Deadlines."

Paige's grin morphed into a smirk as she nudged Harper with her elbow. "Seriously? You've been on vacation for, like, what, two days? You're already breaking the cardinal rule of cruising: no thinking about work."

Harper let out a heavy sigh, sinking deeper into the plush seat. "Easier said than done. My job's intense. Advertising in New York isn't exactly a nine-to-five kind of gig. There's always something blowing up, something urgent to fix. Sometimes I feel like I'm just ... running on autopilot."

Paige tilted her head, watching Harper curiously. "But you've made it, right? You're working at some big-deal ad agency in New York City. That's, like, the dream, isn't it?"

Harper laughed softly, but there was no humor in it. "It used to be. I mean, I worked my ass off to get there. The big city, the high-powered job, all the 'Madison Avenue' glitz and glam. I moved to New York, thinking it would be everything I wanted. But now ..." Her words trailed off as she stared into her drink, watching the bubbles rise and pop.

Paige leaned forward, her playful demeanor softening. "But now what?" she asked gently.

Harper hesitated, searching for the right words. "Now, it just feels like ... I don't know, like I'm stuck. I don't feel creative anymore. I dedicate half my time to firefighting and the other half to diluting ideas to increase their safety. It's not ... fulfilling."

Paige's brow furrowed as she took that in. "But you're successful, right?" she said, like she was trying to piece it together. "I mean, you've got this amazing job in New York. Isn't that what everyone wants? You're living the life people fantasize about."

Harper smiled faintly, but it didn't reach her eyes. "Sure, on paper. But what about you? You seem so ... content. You're always traveling and working a job you actually like. I wish I had your freedom!"

Paige blinked, surprised. Her lips quirked into a half-smile as she shook her head. "Me? You think I've got it all figured out?"

Harper shrugged, her tone light but tinged with something heavier. "You've got that spark, Paige. I used to have it. But now ... now it just feels like the more successful I get, the more trapped I feel."

Paige leaned back in her chair, swirling her champagne thoughtfully. For a moment, she said nothing, which was rare for her. When she spoke, her voice was quieter than usual. "But you worked so hard to get where you are, Harp. That's not nothing."

"I know," Harper said, exhaling slowly. She studied her drink, mesmerized by the bubbles dancing to the surface. "But sometimes I wonder if I'm climbing a ladder I don't even want to be on anymore. Like, every step I take, I'm just getting farther away from the things I actually love. Some days ... I barely even recognize myself."

Paige tilted her head, her lips twitching like she was about to say something cheeky, but stopped herself at the last second. Instead, she let out a long whistle, shaking her head. "Okay, that's deep. Like, seriously deep, Harp. Are we still talking about jobs, or did we just wander into the meaning-of-life zone?"

Harper rolled her eyes, but a small smile tugged at the corner of her mouth. "Come on, I'm being serious."

"I know, I know," Paige said, holding her hands in mock surrender. "I'm just saying ... it sounds like you're at an existential career crossroads. And honestly? Yeah, that tracks. You've got the fancy, skyscraper-office life, but if it's not feeding your soul ..." she trailed off, swirling her champagne. "Maybe you're right. Maybe it's time to look for something else."

Her attention drifted briefly before snapping back, her energy returning like a spark reignited. "But listen—I'm jealous of you! You've got roots, this real, grown-up career. Me? I'm winging it, bouncing from one thing to the next. It's fun, sure, but sometimes I think ... what if I wake up one day and realize I've built nothing? Nothing that really matters."

Harper blinked, startled by the rare flash of vulnerability from Paige. "Really? I mean, I always figured you were living your best life, going wherever the wind takes you."

"Yeah, well ..." Paige shrugged, a sheepish grin tugging at her lips. "The wind's great and all, but you can only drift for so long before you wonder where the hell you're actually going. And don't get me started on watching all my friends settle down, buying houses, having careers and babies, and whatever. Sometimes I'm like, 'Hey, Paige, when are you gonna get it together?' And then other times I'm like, 'Fuck it! Let's go skydiving in Bali.'" She laughed, the sound bright but not without a trace of uncertainty.

Harper's brow furrowed, processing Paige's admission. "So ... you're saying you kind of want what I have, and I kind of want what you have?"

Paige smirked, leaning forward and clinking her glass against Harper's. "Classic grass-is-greener situation, huh? Let's just trade lives for a week and call it even."

Harper chuckled, shaking her head. "If only it were that easy."

Paige leaned back in her chair, watching Harper thoughtfully for a beat. Then her eyes suddenly widened, the playfulness rushing back into her voice like a wave crashing to shore. "Oh, wait! Speaking of soul-searching ... look who's coming!" She shot up in her seat, waving so enthusiastically it was a wonder she didn't spill her champagne. "Maude! Over here!"

Harper turned to see Maude gliding past the lounge, her deep blue eyes sparkling with an almost magnetic energy. Her long, wavy hair, tied back with a bright scarf, flowed like it was alive. Harper felt the same pull as before, a quiet wisdom emanating from Maude that commanded attention, a feeling both powerful and serene.

Maude's smile widened as she approached, a graceful confidence in every step. "Well, if it isn't my two favorite travelers," she said with a soft laugh, her voice as soothing as the sea itself. "How's the champagne treating you?"

"Perfectly bubbly, as always," Paige replied with a grin, motioning to the seat beside her. "Sit down! We need some of your signature sage advice."

Maude raised an eyebrow, amused, as she lowered herself gracefully into the chair. "Uh-oh. Sounds serious. What's the dilemma?"

Before Harper could answer, Maude waved down the attendant with a flick of her fingers, effortlessly commanding attention. "Hey Chrisanto, good to see you again. Could you grab me a glass of my usual please, and another round for these two." she said with a knowing smile. "This one's on me."

Paige didn't miss a beat, waving her champagne glass for emphasis. "Okay, so Harper here ..." She threw an arm around Harper's shoulders, pulling her in like a proud older sister. "Big-shot ad exec in New York ... skyscrapers, power heels, the whole thing. But ... get this plot twist ..." Paige hesitated for dramatic effect, then plunged ahead with gusto. "She's burned out! Like, the creative spark? Pfft. Gone. She's successful, sure, but totally stuck. You feel me?"

"Paige," Harper muttered with a sigh, shooting her a look, though her voice lacked heat. Still, she jabbed her elbow lightly into Paige's side, earning a mock yelp. "Thanks for the delicate delivery."

"What?" Paige said with an unapologetic grin, rubbing her side as if Harper had wounded her. "I'm just telling it like it is!" She turned back to Maude, eyes wide, her words spilling like a waterfall. "So here's the big mystery: how does someone who's worked her butt off to climb the ladder end up feeling, like, totally lost? Isn't New York supposed to be the dream?"

Harper winced slightly at the bluntness but couldn't suppress her smile. Paige had a way of delivering the truth like a punchline, and somehow, it made everything feel a little lighter. Still, her attention drifted back to Maude, her curiosity sharpening. Maude's quiet confidence and graceful movements drew Harper in, making her eager to hear what Maude had to say.

Maude cradled her glass, swirling the Prosecco Rosé thoughtfully. She spoke with gentle tranquility, a peaceful aura surrounding her. "It's not really about having the dream job or living in the perfect city," Maude said, her words measured. Her eyes met Harper's, steady and knowing like she already understood the weight Harper carried. "It's gotta be your dream, not someone else's. Society dictates its version of happiness, and we chase it blindly, often neglecting to reassess whether those societal standards of happiness still apply in our own lives."

Harper blinked, her breath catching slightly as the words sank in. *Your dream, not someone else's.* She thought about how long she'd clung to the idea of New York, how much of herself she'd poured into reaching a goal that no longer felt like hers. Was she climbing someone else's ladder? Had she been chasing an idea of success that didn't belong to her anymore?

Maude's voice was quiet, almost tender, yet each word landed with quiet force. "You might have outgrown it," she continued, her tone full of understanding. "And that doesn't mean you've failed. It just means your heart is pulling you in a new direction. You don't have to stick with the same dream forever, Harper. Life changes, and so do we."

Harper stared at her glass, her mind turning over Maude's words. She had never considered that outgrowing things wasn't a failure; it was simply part of life's process. The idea was both comforting and unsettling, like standing at the edge of a cliff and realizing you weren't afraid to jump.

Paige leaned forward, breaking the reflective silence. "So, what's the solution? Ditch New York? Trade skyscrapers for palm trees?"

Maude laughed softly, her eyes twinkling with amusement. "Not necessarily. Sometimes, it's not about running away but finding space to hear yourself again. Space to figure out what you truly want, without all the noise."

Harper nodded slowly, the words settling into her like pieces of a puzzle she didn't even know she'd been trying to solve. She glanced at Maude, who seemed to carry an aura of quiet certainty, like someone who had lived through enough to know when to speak and when to let silence do the talking.

Maude swayed with the ship, graceful as could be. Harper felt Maude's role extended beyond the cruise hostess, but its exact nature eluded her.

"You don't need to have all the answers right now," Maude said, her voice steady but laced with something more profound that felt like an undercurrent of truth. "Sometimes the answers find you when you're not even looking."

Harper tilted her head, intrigued. There was something cryptic in Maude's words, which seemed to carry layers of meaning that Harper wasn't sure she was ready to unpack. Maude smiled knowingly, her deep blue eyes reflecting the ocean beyond the windows. "Trust the tide, my dear," she added, her tone low, almost a whisper. "It has a way of bringing you exactly where you need to be."

With that, Maude turned and glided away, her scarf trailing behind her like the wake of a boat. Harper and Paige sat silently, watching her disappear into the crowd. The faint scent of sea mist seemed to linger in her absence.

"She's unreal," Paige said, breaking the quiet.

Harper didn't respond immediately, her mind still swirling with Maude's words. *The tide. Outgrowing dreams. Answers finding you.* There was something about the way Maude spoke, the way she seemed to know things, that sent a shiver down Harper's spine.

Paige leaned back in her chair, shaking her head in wonder. "I don't know what she meant by all that 'trust the tide' stuff, but it makes me want to just … let life happen, you know?"

Harper nodded absently, her fingers tracing the rim of her glass. Whatever it was, it invigorated her spirit and ushered in a bold new perspective.

"She's something else," Harper murmured, her voice barely above a whisper, as if speaking too loudly might break the spell Maude had left in her wake.

"Totally," Paige agreed, her eyes still lingering on Maude's retreating figure. "She's like the oracle of the high seas or something."

Harper bit her lip as her curiosity lingered. Who was Maude, really? Her thoughtful way of speaking was captivating, revealing layers that Harper was excited to uncover. Her warm, melodic voice suggested a rich understanding waiting to be explored. It was more than just guidance; it opened a window to deeper insights, inviting Harper to reflect on the meaningful possibilities.

Harper sipped her cocktail, her thoughts swirling. Maybe Maude was right. The answers she desired might have been beyond her control. Perhaps they'd come to her, like the tide, when she wasn't trying so hard to find them. But what if Maude wasn't just speaking in metaphors? What if she really did know where the tide would lead her?

The thought triggered an icy shiver that traced a path down Harper's spine, a disconcerting yet oddly soothing sensation. Something undeniable about Maude's presence, an inexplicable gravity, made Harper feel like their paths had crossed for a reason. It was as though Maude had shown up not just to guide the group but to guide her precisely.

Who is she? Harper wondered, the question echoing quietly in her mind.

Maybe she'd figure it out before the journey was over. Or maybe, just like Maude had said, she'd have to let the tide bring her the answers when it was ready. For now, though, Harper felt lighter than she had in weeks. And that, she decided, was enough.

Ten

The Elysian Serenade floated like a gleaming pearl off the coast of a private Bahamian island. Harper watched tender boats ferry passengers toward the white sand and turquoise water from their cabin window. It was a postcard-perfect escape; where palms swayed gently, and the ocean shimmered in the sun.

Inside the cabin, Harper was pulling on her worn denim shorts over her bikini bottoms when she glanced at Paige. She smirked, unable to resist a lighthearted jab. "Leaving very little to the imagination, huh?"

Paige twirled in front of the mirror, her sheer cover-up swirling dramatically around her neon pink bikini like a spotlight following her every move. "Well, when in paradise ..." she said with a mischievous wink. "And don't forget, Harp, we're in a singles group with, like, a hundred eligible bachelors on this ship. If you're not dressing to impress, what's even the point?" She struck a mock runway pose, one hand on her hip and the other tossing her ponytail over her shoulder. "Gotta keep the competition on their toes!"

"Trust me," Harper said, adjusting the brim of her straw hat, "you'll have no problem there."

They laughed, the teasing lightening Harper's mood as she finished getting ready. It had been a long time since she'd dressed for pure relaxation. Compared to the constricting designer outfits she wore for work, the cut-off shorts and simple cropped swim top felt like armor she could actually breathe in.

As they left their cabin, the sound of children's laughter drifted from the pool area where they were to meet the boys before heading ashore, filling Harper with unexpected excitement for the day—a world away from her gloomy mood of just a few days prior. The promise of the gentle ocean breeze and warm sand between her toes suggested this island might be precisely what she needed—a temporary escape.

When they reached the pool deck, the scent of sunscreen and the salt-laced breeze wrapped around them like summer itself. The sun burned bright overhead, casting shimmering reflections across the water. Brody spotted them first, waving with a grin, his arms already weighed down by beach towels and gear.

"Ready to hit the beach?!" Paige practically squealed, bouncing on her toes like an overexcited kid on Christmas morning. Her eyes locked onto Brody with a playful spark, and she fluffed her ponytail for extra effect. "Hope you're ready for some sunshine and a whole lot of me!" she teased, shooting him a flirty grin that could've melted the deck underfoot.

Brody smirked. "As long as there's a hammock with my name on it, I'm good to go."

Harper noticed Aidan standing by the railing, his posture unguarded. The sunlight caught the red in his hair, brightening the silver streaks near his temples. He looked far more at ease now, relaxed in his worn tee and swimming trunks, as if he had finally settled into the rhythm of the trip.

They exited the ship and stepped onto one of the tender boats that would take them to the island. As they neared, the island sprang into full view, its pristine white sands shimmering under the sun, starkly contrasting the vibrant turquoise water stretching endlessly beyond. It felt untouched, like something out of a dream.

The island was pristine and secluded, reserved exclusively for cruise passengers. Palm trees swayed lazily over rows of colorful cabanas, their shadows dancing across the sand. Harper found a rare sense of peace as the sun warmed her skin and the salty air filled her lungs.

Once they reached the beach, they quickly found a few chairs beneath large, coral-colored umbrellas. Harper kicked off her sandals, the sun-warmed sand spilling over her toes like tiny grains of light. The breeze carried the sound of laughter and the distant crash of waves, blending into a harmonious soundtrack of island life.

They lounged beneath the umbrellas, the occasional wind ruffling the wide brims of Harper and Paige's straw hats. Paige launched into an animated story about a California road trip, her hands flying as she spoke. Brody countered with exaggerated tales, insisting his adventures were "way more dangerous." Harper let their banter wash over her, amused by the easy rhythm of their energy. Next to her, Aidan sat quietly, sipping from a bottle of water, his smile steady.

"You know," Brody said, lounging back with a grin, "we could stay here. Open a tiki bar. I'm mixing drinks, Aidan's doing food, Harper's bringing the cool factor, and Paige is in charge of entertainment."

Paige gasped dramatically, tossing a bit of sand at him. "Excuse me? Entertainment? Please, I'd be running the whole thing. You'd all be working for me."

Brody laughed, brushing off the sand. "Sure, boss lady. But let's not forget—I'm the face of the bar. People come for the charm, stay for the cocktails."

"More like the mascot," Paige shot back, smirking. "A flamingo, maybe."

"Flamingos are classy!" Brody said, puffing out his chest. "Perfect fit."

Harper tilted her hat back, eyeing him. "Still not seeing how 'refined charm' fits into this tiki bar."

"It doesn't," Aidan said, grinning. "But I'm more worried about me. Am I stuck flipping burgers while you all lounge around?"

"No way," Paige said, waving him off. "You're the broody chef everyone swoons over."

Aidan chuckled, shaking his head. "Flip-flops and an apron? Very mysterious."

"Own it," Paige teased. "Flip-flops, apron, and a smolder."

Harper laughed as Aidan sighed. "Fine, but I'm charging extra for the smolder," he deadpanned.

Brody grinned. "Worth every penny."

They were mid-conversation when a guy with shaggy, sun-bleached hair and a faded band tee strolled up, a volleyball tucked under his arm like it was part of him.

"Hey, I know you guys," he said, flashing a lazy grin. His eyes bounced between Harper and Paige before landing on Brody and Aidan. "You're in the Mingles group, right?"

Aidan nodded, recognizing him. As the group's unofficial cruise cheerleader, Steve enthusiastically promoted activities.

"That's us," Brody said, leaning forward with a grin. "What's up?"

Steve spun the ball in his palm. "Beach volleyball. We've got a solid group but need a couple more players. You in?"

Brody lit up. "Volleyball? Hell yeah. Harper, you're in, right?"

Harper hesitated, casting a sideways glance at Aidan, as if waiting for a cue. When none came, she shrugged, pushing up from her chair with an easy grin. "Sure. It's been a while, but why not?"

Aidan leaned back, smirking. "Think I'll sit this one out."

Paige waved her hand dramatically. "Same. Someone's gotta hold down the fort."

Steve nodded. "Alright, let's do this. Brody, Harper ... give 'em a show!"

As Harper placed her hat in Aidan's hands, their fingers met—light, fleeting, but enough to send a spark up her spine. "Wish me luck."

His smile was soft, warm—steady in a way that felt like an anchor. "You don't need it," he said, his voice steady. "You've got this."

Harper nodded, feeling his words settle somewhere deeper than expected. She turned toward the volleyball court before she could overthink it.

Brody slapped Aidan's shoulder. "I got this, dude."

Aidan called back as they jogged away. "That's what I'm worried about."

The moment Harper and Brody stepped onto the volleyball court, a flicker of energy rose inside her, light and unexpected. The sand, hot and silken, shifted beneath her toes, and the air hummed with bursts of laughter and playful banter. Brody was already in his element, cracking jokes and stretching like he was about to play in some made-up beach league finals.

"Alright, let's show 'em how it's done!" Brody shouted, tossing the ball to Steve with an exaggerated windup.

The game kicked off, full of quick volleys, missteps, and bursts of laughter. Harper wasn't exactly a pro, but she held her own, even as Brody hammed it up, diving theatrically for shots and narrating his "game highlights" mid-play. His energy was infectious, and Harper couldn't help but laugh at his antics. It felt good to just let go for a while.

Harper wiped the sweat from her brow during a break and glanced back at the umbrellas. Paige was laughing, gesturing wildly as Aidan leaned in, his expression steady and unhurried. They looked easy together, their energy an effortless contrast. Harper's chest tightened, a flicker of something she didn't quite understand. She shook it off, letting the ocean breeze tug at her hair.

"So," Brody said, "What's going on with you and Aidan?"

Harper blinked, surprised. "What do you mean?"

Brody grinned, folding his arms. "Oh, come on. You two have been having these quiet moments. Don't tell me nothing is going on."

Harper followed his gaze back to Aidan, who now had his head tilted slightly as Paige teased him, her laughter loud and uninhibited. Harper shrugged, kicking the sand lightly with her toe. "There's nothing to tell. Aidan's ..." she hesitated, searching for the right word, "he's solid. Easy to talk to. We've got some common ground, but it's not like that."

Brody raised an eyebrow, unconvinced. "Uh-huh. Quiet and brooding ... that's romantic gold. You sure there's no spark?"

Harper laughed, rolling her eyes. "Quiet and brooding? Is that your professional analysis?"

"Absolutely," Brody replied with mock seriousness. "Trust me, I know a thing or two about chemistry."

"Please," Harper said, smirking. "You'd probably flirt with a volley-ball if it winked at you."

"Only if it bought me dinner first," Brody shot back with a grin, nudging her shoulder.

Harper shook her head, laughing, but she couldn't help noticing how Brody's usual bravado dimmed slightly when she shifted the conversation. "What about you and Paige? Seems like you two are getting pretty cozy."

Brody hesitated briefly, his grin faltering before he puffed out his chest. "What can I say? She's fun, gorgeous, and into me. It's a win-win."

"Hmm," Harper said, narrowing her eyes playfully. "That hesitation sounded like a red flag."

"No hesitation," Brody insisted, his tone too casual. "It's just ... fast, that's all."

"Fast, huh?" Harper teased, her smirk widening. "Maybe she'll have you wrapped around her finger by the end of the week."

Feigning dramatic offense, Brody let a teasing grin tug at his lips before flexing his fingers in a suggestive rhythm. "If anything, I'll have her wrapped around my fingers ... if you know what I mean."

"Gross!" Harper groaned, rolling her eyes as she swatted at him. "I don't need to hear all that."

Brody smirked, leaning back like he'd won some imaginary contest. "Just keeping it real, Harp. You know me. I'm classy all the way.

Harper shook her head, laughing despite herself. "Classy isn't the word I'd use."

Before Brody could fire off another one-liner, Steve called them back to the game. Harper jogged toward the court, her feet sinking into the warm sand, letting the teasing slip away with the breeze. She glanced again toward the umbrellas, where Paige was leaning close to Aidan, her laughter bright and uninhibited. Aidan looked at ease, nodding with an almost imperceptible smile, his steady energy contrasting Paige's wildfire spark.

Paige and Brody were a storm of passion, all heat and reckless energy. With Aidan, things felt softer, more like a story unfolding in whispers rather than flames. Harper wasn't sure if that contrast meant anything, but in this moment, surrounded by glistening ocean, she decided she didn't need to figure it out.

Eleven

Dinner had been fun. Surprisingly so. Harper laughed more in one evening than in days, thanks mainly to the lively energy of Brody and Paige across from her. He was cracking jokes left and right, but Paige kept pace, quick-witted with infectious laughter. The banter had been so easy between the four of them; it seemed the meal was over before it had even gotten underway. Harper had even forgotten, for a while, about everything waiting for her back home in New York. But as the night wore on, Harper could tell that Brody was growing restless, his eyes darting around the room like he was already working out his next move.

"Okay, we're off to the comedy club," Brody declared, pushing his chair back and preparing for a good time. He threw Aidan a teasing look. "Are you guys coming, or do you have fancier plans for tonight?" He clearly found his own joke funny, showed by the wiggle of his eyebrows.

A silent understanding passed between Harper and Aidan as they exchanged a look. While the comedy club's lively atmosphere and expected laughter beckoned, she found herself drawn to the prospect of a peaceful evening, away from the press of people and the din of loud conversation. "I think we'll pass," she murmured, soothing and resolute.

Aidan shrugged, a casual smile spreading across his face. "Comedy's not really my thing tonight."

"Suit yourselves," Paige teased, tugging on Brody's arm. "Have fun, you two!" she called playfully over her shoulder as she winked at them, dragging Brody toward the exit and leaving Harper and Aidan at the table.

After they left, the ship's hum resounded in the space; the indistinct murmur of other diners and the intermittent clinking of glasses created a soft backdrop. Harper enjoyed the quiet that settled between her and Aidan, comfortable without being awkward. It was a pleasant change of pace from the earlier frenetic energy.

"So now?" he asked, leaning back in his chair and regarding her with a silent interest.

Harper was quiet as she paused collecting her thoughts. There was something she had been meaning to do since they boarded the ship, something that tugged at the back of her mind. "Actually," she said, almost bashfully, "I've wanted to check out the art gallery on board. Care to join me?"

Aidan blinked, taken aback, before smiling and nodding. "Sure," he said, gesturing for her to lead the way. "Lead the way."

Harper felt an inner change coming on as they neared the ship's art gallery. Hopefully, surrounding herself with art's beauty and peace would reignite her artistic soul.

The modern, sleek gallery gleamed: its floor reflected soft light from overhead, and its wall space was alive with popping bright colors of abstract pieces against the white walls. As they stepped inside, Harper could feel her pace grow sluggish, her eyes scanning the paintings immediately for all the details. That space revitalized her, erasing the memories of work stress and her split with Dan.

She walked toward a giant canvas splashed with fiery reds and deep, brooding purples. The strokes were wild, almost chaotic, yet there was a rhythm to them, a kind of unspoken intensity that seemed to reverberate deep inside Harper. "Look at the way the brushstrokes flow," she whispered. "It's so intense ... like you can feel the emotion in every movement."

Aidan stepped beside her, his gaze following hers to the painting. He squinted at the abstract shapes, his brow furrowed slightly. "What is it supposed to be?" he asked, puzzled.

Harper returned his smile, a twinkle of amusement in her eyes. "It's not about what it's supposed to be," she explained softly. It's how it makes you feel. Observe how the colors collide, a riot of pigment that somehow resolves into a unified whole. You can feel a wordless conversation with the artist through their artwork. You feel it here." She placed a hand lightly over her heart. "Not here." She tapped her temple with a playful smirk.

Aidan shook his head. "I don't know if I'm wired that way."

"Perhaps not," Harper teased, looking up at him. "But I think you're capable of embracing new things, and with my help, you can unlock your full potential."

As they wandered through the gallery, Harper settled effortlessly into her element. She guided him from one piece to the next, animatedly discussing techniques, compositions, and the emotions she believed the artists had poured into their work. It wasn't just the vibrant colors and sweeping brushstrokes that captivated her, but the untold stories woven into each canvas. For a change, she didn't feel the pressure to be anything other than who she was—a woman who found herself in the language of art.

"You're really into this stuff, aren't you?" Aidan asked as they stopped before one with sharp lines contrasting black and white.

"I am, yes," Harper said, her voice softening. "Art's always been my escape. When the farcical din becomes too loud, too unbearable … I come back to this." She passed a hand over the painting in front of them. "It reminds me that there's more to life than deadlines and schedules. There's beauty in chaos, too."

Aidan nodded slowly, his face contemplative as he took in her words. "I get that," he said after a moment. "It's like cooking for me. When I'm in the kitchen, everything just … makes sense. But it hasn't felt that way lately."

Harper turned to him, a glint of understanding in her eyes. "Why not?"

Aidan shrugged. "Too many expectations. It used to be about the food, about the process. Now, it just feels like work. I don't know … it's hard to explain."

"I get that," Harper said, thoughtful. "Maybe you just need to find the passion again."

"Maybe," he said, though his voice held doubt. Yet something in his eyes told her he was searching, too. He was looking for the missing spark, the part of himself he'd neglected amidst life's chaos.

As they continued through the gallery, the conversation became easy and free-flowing. Harper spoke openly about art, her frustrations at work, and even her struggles. Subsequently, Aidan discussed his career, explaining the strain of managing his family's restaurant and losing his initial enthusiasm.

Harper felt an unexpected sense of peace when they finished touring the gallery. Something was different. She wasn't sure if it was the art or the conversation. In any case, she felt lighter, more connected to herself than she had in a long time.

"Thanks for bringing me here," Aidan said, breaking the comfortable silence. "I never thought I'd say this, but ... I actually enjoyed it."

Harper smiled, "You're welcome. Glad you came."

They stood there, lingering with the quiet of the gallery wrapping around them like a cocoon. Harper felt a flicker of something she hadn't felt in a while: hope. Maybe, just maybe, things could be different. Perhaps she could find a way back to herself. And maybe, she thought as she glanced at Aidan, she didn't have to do it alone.

With the gallery tour complete, Harper and Aidan wandered into the boisterous bar called El Corazón. Stepping inside, Harper was instantly enveloped by the sultry rhythm of Latin music, the beat pulsated like a heartbeat she could feel in her bones. Spices lingered in the air, clinging to the sweat-slicked bodies on the dance floor swaying in wild, effortless harmony. The bar was a riotous blur of deep red, vibrant tropical greens, and golds, accented with wall-sized murals depicting palm trees and sun-drenched beaches. Not being alive was basically impossible here, amidst all this hum of energy and the rhythmic beats of the conga drums.

Harper smiled to herself. "It's always a holiday here at this house."

Aidan took it in, glancing around at the festive décor and twinkling lights above the bar. "Well, this is a change of pace," he said with a grin, letting the upbeat rhythm wash over him.

"El Corazón is one of my favorite places on the ship," Harper said warmly, striding toward the bar. "It's got good vibes and even better mojitos."

Aidan's fingers tapped idly against the bar as he studied the choices. "Guess I'll have to mix it up then." Harper had noticed his preference for beer throughout the trip, but tonight, something had changed. Maybe it was the lingering energy from the gallery, or maybe it was her. Either way, she caught the subtle shift in him—the quiet desire for something bolder, something that fit the moment.

They slid up to the counter, and Aidan signaled to the bartender. "Two mojitos," he ordered, flashing Harper a quick grin. "Seems like the right choice."

Harper watched him, a little impressed by his willingness to change things up. "Good call," she said, the playful glint in her eyes sparkling. "A mojito's hard to beat."

Tall glasses brimming with crushed ice, lime wedges, and mint sprigs arrived, the vibrant green of the mint contrasting beautifully with the clear ice. With its clean scent, a refreshing wave of cool lime and mint cut through the pulsing music's heat and the thick, humid air around them.

Aidan took a drink, his eyebrows rising in appreciation. "Not bad," he admitted, smiling at her over the rim of his glass.

Harper sipped her mojito, letting the crisp lime and mint cool her tongue as she took in the lively energy of the bar. The atmosphere was different tonight—lighter, easier. They sat in comfortable silence allowing hum of surrounding conversation to fill the space between them. When she glanced at Aidan, she caught him watching her over his drink, his expression thoughtful, as if still lost in the echoes of the gallery.

"You know," Aidan began, his voice cutting through her thoughts, "I never thought I'd be the guy to get into art. But watching you in that gallery ... I don't know. You've got a real passion for it. You made me see things I wouldn't have noticed otherwise."

Harper's face softened into a smile as a warm flush crept up the back of her neck. She wasn't used to receiving compliments like this, and this one felt different. "I guess I can get a little carried away when I talk about art," she admitted, shy yet proud. "It's just always been my escape. My way of making sense of things."

"Well, you're a good teacher," Aidan said, unwilling to break eye contact. "You've got that sort of passion people don't see daily. It's infectious."

Harper felt a jolt at his words, a brief, intense connection that transcended their previous lighthearted exchange. "Thanks," she said. "That means a lot."

The music changed to a loud salsa rhythm just before the moment could stretch too long. The bass reverberated through the floor, and Harper's body responded before her mind caught up. Her hips moved instinctively, drawn into the rhythm, and when she turned to Aidan, her smile came effortlessly, playful and unguarded.

She arched a teasing brow.. "You know how to salsa?"

Aidan blinked, surprised. A sheepish grin tugged at his lips. "Not exactly. But I've got two feet. I can try to follow your lead."

Harper laughed, bright and infectious. "Come on, then," she said, grabbing his hand. Before he could protest, she pulled him off the barstool and onto the small dance floor, where couples swayed to the rhythm. Maracas and trumpets filled the vibrant room, their music weaving into the steady conga beat; every note pulsing with life.

The music found them instantly. His hand, hesitant yet warm, settled lightly on her lower back, a comforting weight against her. Harper felt the press of his fingers, the heat of his touch sparking something electric. She looked up, surprised by his quiet shift. Gone was the playful banter. In its place was something unspoken, something that made her pulse quicken.

His usual simple grin had softened, replaced by something more vibrant. The colored lights danced across his face, highlighting the red in his hair. His eyes remained locked on her, steady, searching, as if he saw past the version of herself she showed the world and into something deeper.

Her heart skipped. The laughter and hum of the room blurred into a soft hum. The rhythm of the music pulled them closer, steady yet intoxicating. Around them, the world faded, leaving only them moving together in perfect time.

He spun her, the motion smooth and seamless, as if they had done this a hundred times before. As she twirled, his nearness engulfed her—his breath a whisper against her skin, his scent weaving into the moment like a thread of something unspoken. The music surged, stretching the silence taut between them.

"Not bad for a guy who doesn't salsa," she murmured, her voice quieter now.

"Maybe I'm a quick study," he replied, his tone light.

The sway of the music carried them deeper into the evening, but Harper was lost in something else entirely—the pull of him, the way his hand pressed warm and steady at her back, the quiet brush of his fingertips that left her pulse unsteady. His presence surrounded her, all warmth and quiet strength, his nearness a force she wasn't sure she wanted to resist.

His eyes drifted briefly to her lips, and her heart stuttered. The moment stretched, delicate and full, their lips poised on the edge of something inevitable. When his eyes lifted to hers again, she saw it—that flicker of restraint, a hesitation that echoed her own.

Then, the music shifted, the spell breaking like a retreating wave. Aidan sighed, stepping back, his fingers slipping away—but not before the ghostly warmth sent a shiver down her spine.

"You're a natural," he said, his voice steady.

Harper struggled to catch her breath. "You're not so bad yourself."

For a moment, they stood there, the charged silence between them saying more than either was ready to admit. Then, Aidan extended his hand with an almost playful tilt of his head. "Drink?"

Harper nodded, her heart still racing. "Yeah. I think I need one."

They left the floor, but the space between them remained charged, the tension a quiet undercurrent neither of them acknowledged but both could feel. The music continued to swirl behind them, the rhythm still thrumming in her veins. Harper felt an irresistible pull toward him, a thrill mixed with a terrifying uncertainty that sent shivers down her spine. But for now, the night stretched before them, the question left hanging, like the final note of a song that refused to fade.

Twelve

Harper returned to the cabin, carrying her heels in one hand to give her feet a break. The night breeze carried the soft scent of the sea, mingling with the traces of Aidan's cologne, still faintly clinging to her senses. The dancing, drinks, and hot connection they'd shared still buzzing.

She couldn't shake the feeling that something had almost happened in the bar, that just one more moment in Aidan's arms might have tipped the night into uncharted territory. Secretly, she was happy he hadn't tried to kiss her; everything felt so early and delicate. But another part of her, the part that was still caught in the salsa's rhythm, wished he had. There had been moments when their eyes locked, and she thought he would lean in. She could still feel the warmth of his hand on her waist, the way his attention never faltered as they moved together, the silent pull that had thrummed between them.

Harper sighed softly, tucking a stray lock of hair behind her ear as she reached her cabin door. She grasped the handle and gently twisted it, but it didn't budge. She scowled and tried again, putting more muscle into it. Still nothing.

Then she heard it. Muffled yet unmistakable, soft, pained moans, heavy gasps, and the rhythmic groaning of the bed frame beyond the door vibrated through the floor, each sound thick with unspoken meaning. Harper's face flushed as the realization hit her like a wave. Paige and Brody.

"Of course," she muttered under her breath, letting go of the handle with a huff. Despite her efforts, her mind conjured Paige and Brody, passionately infatuated, just beyond the doorway. Good for them, she supposed. They certainly didn't waste any time. She stood there biting her lip and debating whether to knock, interrupt, or just turn away. But with how things sounded, Paige and Brody weren't nearly finished with their ... evening.

Harper rolled her eyes, a mix of amusement and slight frustration bubbling inside her. "Guess I'm not getting into my pajamas tonight," she muttered. Her thoughts drifted back to Aidan, and suddenly, the solution became obvious.

Turning on her heel, she walked with purpose down the hall, back toward Aidan's cabin. Excitement and nerves caused her heart to race as she neared his door. This wasn't exactly how she pictured the night ending, but there was no way she was going to spend the night listening to Paige and Brody going at it like teenagers.

Harper knocked softly, praying Aidan wasn't already asleep. After a few moments, the door swung open to reveal Aidan standing in a plain T-shirt and sweatpants, his hair slightly tousled. He blinked in surprise when he saw her, but quickly smiled.

"Hey," he said. "What's up?"

Harper shifted slightly, feeling suddenly awkward now that she was actually here. "Uh, Paige and Brody ..." she started, gesturing vaguely back toward her cabin. "They're, um, a little busy. And by 'a little,' I mean ... really busy. I can't get into my room. Do you think I can crash here tonight?"

Aidan's eyebrows shot up in amusement as he stepped aside and gestured for her to come in. "Sure, you can stay here. Sounds like Brody won't be needing his bed tonight."

She stepped inside, feeling relieved as the door clicked shut behind her. Aidan's cabin was nearly identical to hers, though his side of the room was surprisingly tidy. Apart from a few clothes and an empty beer bottle on the nightstand, Brody's bed was untouched. Harper glanced around, feeling the tension from earlier still thrumming beneath her skin.

"Thanks," she said, turning to face him. "I, uh, didn't exactly plan on ending up here, but ... desperate times, you know?"

Aidan's nod was just a fraction too quick, his body language betraying a moment of uncertainty. "No worries," he said, his voice as steady as ever, but Harper caught the hesitation—small, but there—before he added, "Make yourself at home."

She was still in her jeans and tank top, which were not exactly bedtime attire. Harper bit her lip. "Actually, do you think I could borrow a shirt or something to sleep in? My pajamas are ... well ... you know."

Aidan nodded, already moving toward the small closet. "Yeah, of course. Here." He pulled out a soft, well-worn T-shirt and handed it to her. "This should do."

Harper took it with a grateful smile. "Thanks." She glanced toward the small bathroom. "I'll just, um, change real quick."

Aidan gave a casual nod, and Harper slipped into the bathroom, closing the door behind her. She leaned against it briefly, exhaling as she looked at herself in the mirror. The evening's events left her cheeks flushed and her hair tousled, but more than that, she radiated a confidence she hadn't felt in years. Excitement. The thrill of the unexpected.

After changing into his shirt, Harper gathered her thoughts. Uncertainty draped over the night like a heavy veil, but one truth lingered—the spare bed beside Aidan's seemed unbearably empty, a stark contrast to the electric charge that had crackled between them all evening.

Harper stepped back into the room, the oversized T-shirt brushing her thighs as she moved. She felt Aidan's eyes focus on her, a quiet, steady weight that made her skin hum with awareness, like a low thrumming of energy. Every step toward him only deepened the tension, the slow sway of fabric offering fleeting glimpses of black lace beneath.

When she finally locked eyes with him, the look he gave her sent heat surging beneath her skin. There was no mistaking it—he'd noticed her. And despite his best effort, he couldn't quite keep himself from looking again. His usual confidence had faltered, his posture subtly rigid, his gaze lingering just a moment too long before he tore it away, almost reluctantly.

"Looks better on you," he said, his voice low and teasing, though the softness in his tone hinted at something deeper.

"Does it now?" Harper plucked at the hem, feigning nonchalance, though her heart thudded in her chest. "I guess it's not every day your wardrobe gets stolen."

"Not every day someone makes it look that good," he replied smoothly, his smirk widening as his eyes briefly, but pointedly, dropped to her figure. The charged silence that followed said more than either of them was willing to admit.

Feeling the heat rise to her face, Harper crossed to the other bed, folding her legs beneath her in a casual but intentional way. She leaned back on her hands, letting the shirt ride up just slightly, testing the waters. Aidan's jaw shifted almost imperceptibly, his restraint clear, but the tension crackling.

"Comfortable?" he asked, his voice light but edged with something that made her pulse skip.

"Getting there," she quipped, tilting her head with a sly smile. "But you seem ... distracted."

His low laugh rumbled in the quiet. "Oh, I'm paying attention," he said, his voice smooth, his eyes never leaving hers. "Believe me."

"Hey," she said, her voice hesitant but playful, "you mind if we ... I don't know, maybe cuddle? Just for a little while. No funny business. It's just ... been a long day."

Harper saw the flicker of surprise in Aidan's eyes, the way his head tilted slightly, as if testing whether she was serious. When she didn't take it back, his smile stretched, slow and easy. "Cuddle, huh?" He echoed, but didn't hesitate as he scooted over, patting the space beside him. "Sure, I think I can handle that. Boundaries included."

Harper grinned, her heart fluttering as she climbed into his bed. She lay down next to him, feeling the heat of his body as he wrapped an arm around her, pulling her close but keeping it light. She'd only asked for comfort and closeness in the dim light, but the way her head lay on his chest and his steady breathing made her feel safe.

Harper nestled deeper into Aidan's arms, feeling the steady rhythm of his breathing as she settled against him. He felt warm and comforting, but there was this weird tension between them, a silence until Harper finally broke.

"Bet you didn't expect to get me into bed tonight," she quipped with a sly grin, looking up at him through her lashes.

He pulled her in just slightly, his voice rich with the same warmth that lingered in his touch. "Yeah, not exactly how I saw the night going, but I'm not complaining."

A quiet, almost forgotten lightness spread through Harper as she smiled. They lay together in quiet companionship, the ship's steady hum a soft reminder of the world beyond the cabin. Time felt slower here, the warmth of the sheets and the gentle rocking of the vessel cocooning them in a world all their own.

After a few minutes, Aidan spoke again, his voice low, almost thoughtful. "So ... Paige and Brody. Do you think that's gonna flame out after the cruise? Or do you actually stand a chance?"

Harper tilted her head, eyes drifting toward the door as she pictured Paige and Brody, lost in their own orbit. "Hard to say. They're definitely having fun now, but it's all pretty fast. Could be just a cruise fling, you know?"

Aidan nodded. "Yeah, it feels like that. But who knows? Stranger things have happened."

They lapsed into a more serious conversation, their energy shifting as they settled into something more profound. "Long distance is hard," Aidan added quietly, his tone more reflective. "Even if they tried to make it work, once the cruise is over, they're in completely different places. It's tough to keep something going when you're not in the same world."

Harper shifted slightly, thinking about what he said. Her mind wandered back to her relationship with Dan. Despite sharing the same city and apartment, they sometimes felt worlds apart. She lay silent at first, but the weight of that truth pressed down on her. Sometimes, you didn't need an ocean between you to feel worlds apart.

"It doesn't even have to be long distance," Harper finally murmured, her voice soft, almost contemplative. "You could be sitting right next to someone and feel like you're miles away. Like you're not even speaking the same language anymore."

She didn't feel the need to elaborate, sensing that Aidan understood the undertone of her words. It was a familiar ache, one she had been carrying with her for weeks. That simple reflection brought back a flood of memories of the distance, the drift. Harper had been living with its weight for so long now, not fully processing the emotions, just existing within the hollow it had left behind.

But there was something different about this moment. Something about being here, lying next to Aidan, made it feel safer to let her guard down, even just a little. It might have been his gentle touch or the quiet empathy in his eyes; he instinctively understood her emotions. He wasn't pushing her to explain or revisit the painful memories she'd been avoiding. And that silence, that space to just be, was a gift she hadn't realized she needed.

Harper felt a small but significant inner shift as his hand caressed her back. After Dan left, she'd built up walls so high, layers of protection around her heart. She was determined not to experience that vulnerability again. Fear of the inevitable heartbreak and slow disintegration of trust kept her from fully committing. But those walls didn't feel as necessary lying here, wrapped in Aidan's quiet reassurance.

Her heart, still tender from the breakup, softened against his touch. The walls she'd built didn't seem so impenetrable anymore. Maybe they didn't need to be. Harper wasn't ready to fully admit anything to herself, not yet. But the small cracks forming in her defenses, the way she was feeling something again, something more than the numbing grief she'd wrapped herself in since Dan.

It wasn't just Aidan's physical presence; it was how he made her feel, demanding nothing in return. He didn't pry, but simply held her close, giving her space to feel whatever she needed. Only then did she understand her need for unconditional acceptance and effortless intimacy.

In Aidan's arms, the familiar ache in her chest didn't feel as sharp. There was still pain there, but it wasn't overwhelming. It didn't consume her. It felt manageable, even possible, that she could relinquish some of the burden. Maybe she could trust again, even if it was just for tonight. Maybe she could let someone in, just a little.

And, surprisingly, that idea didn't scare her.

Breaking the silence, Harper whispered, "This is nice."

Aidan tilted his head slightly, looking down at her. "What's that?"

"This," she said softly, barely above a murmur. "Just ... being here. Being in the moment. It's nice to have someone to really connect with on this cruise. Even if it's just for now. Even if it's just a fleeting wave."

Aidan's expression softened, his eyes meeting hers in the dim light. "Yeah," he agreed quietly. "It is nice. Ya know, sometimes a connection is enough, even if it doesn't last."

Harper's heart raced, caught between the safety of the moment and the pull of something more. She felt a deep connection with Aidan, a warmth that went beyond the physical comfort of their embrace. She wondered if this was more than just a passing thing. What if she took a chance here and now?

She took a deep breath, gathering the courage to take fate into her own hands. "Aidan," she whispered, with a tinge of vulnerability.

"Yeah?" he quietly responded, intrigued but clearly growing sleepy.

"Would you like to kiss me?" she asked.

His eyes flickered with mild surprise, and then a warmth bloomed, deepening into something akin to affection. He said nothing, but the look in his eyes was enough. Gently, he tilted her chin up, his fingers brushing softly against her skin as he leaned down. A quiet pull, a breathless hesitation, a heartbeat stretching impossibly long. And then, finally, his lips found hers.

Their lips met in a slow, savoring caress, the kind of kiss meant to be memorized. But restraint didn't last long. Aidan's hand slid to the nape of her neck, his fingertips pressing into her skin, pulling her deeper into him. Harper's heart hammered as the kiss grew urgent, a collision of longing and need. Heat crackled between them, their bodies molding together as if drawn by gravity, as if this had been inevitable from the start.

When they finally broke apart, Harper's breath came uneven, her lips tingling, her heart hammering against her ribs. A quiet stillness settled between them—not awkward, but thick with meaning. The taste of the kiss still lingered, warm and intoxicating, as their hands remained tangled, fingertips tracing silent messages neither of them dared to speak aloud. His hands still held her lightly, fingertips pressing gently against her, as if committing the moment to memory.

With a soft sigh, Harper melted into Aidan's arms, the steady rise and fall of his chest beneath her cheek lulling her into quiet contentment. His arm curled around her, not to hold her in place, but to keep her close—secure, wanted. She wasn't just with him; she was here, fully present ... she felt like she had nowhere else to be.

As her eyes fluttered closed, she smiled softly, feeling the world's weight lift from her shoulders. Whatever tomorrow brought, she would not worry about it now.

Right now, she had everything she needed.

"Goodnight," she whispered, her voice barely audible.

Aidan's hand gave her back a gentle squeeze as he murmured, "Goodnight, Harper."

And with that, they drifted to sleep, wrapped in each other's arms, sharing a quiet, unspoken comfort that only the night could hold.

The signs of a long night were evident on Harper as she walked back into the cabin: her jeans wrinkled, her tank top hung loosely, and her hair looked like it had been through a wild night. She felt less like a fresh breeze and more like a reminder that she hadn't showered yet. Morning light streamed through the small circular window, casting soft rays across the mess of clothes and shoes strewn about the room.

But nothing, no matter how much she expected, could have prepared her for what was before her.

Paige sprawled across her bed like a shipwreck survivor who'd surrendered to chaos. Her mermaid-inspired pajamas were a complete disaster: the tank top was only half-on, with one arm successfully through its proper armhole while the other flopped out like it had given up entirely. Her bright teal shorts? Halfway up one leg, seemingly abandoned in their mission to reach the other. And her tan-line-accented butt cheeks greeted the world without shame.

Harper stopped dead in her tracks, one brow arching so high it threatened to escape into her hairline. "Well, this is ... a look," she teased, tossing her shoes into the corner. "Please tell me this is some sort of avant-garde fashion statement and not the aftermath of Brody sweeping you off your feet."

Paige let out a muffled groan, her head buried in a tangle of pillows. "Ugh. Morning, Sunshine. Didn't realize the decency police were on duty this early." Her voice, though muffled, was laced with sarcasm.

"I'm not the decency police," Harper quipped, leaning casually against the wall, "but I am the friend who's about two seconds away from tossing a blanket over your exposed butt cheeks. Cover up, woman."

Paige cracked one eye open and made a lazy attempt to tug her shorts the rest of the way up. They barely budged. With a dramatic groan, she flopped back onto the bed, spreading out like a starfish in defeat. "What's the point? Brody's already seen all the best parts," she said, her smirk lazy and dripping unapologetic sass. "Besides, Harp, it's not like you've never seen a butt before. Let's be honest, mine's a work of art. Like, frame it, put it in a museum, charge admission."

"Appreciate the sales pitch," Harper snorted, grabbing the nearest pillow and hurling it at her. "But I think I'll pass on admiring your 'masterpiece,' thanks. Now pull yourself together before someone mistakes you for performance art titled Tragic Mermaid in Disarray."

Paige batted the pillow away with the grace of a sleepy cat, yawning theatrically. "Relax. It's just a butt. We all have one, Harp. Mine is just above average." She finally pushed herself up on one elbow, her tank top still stubbornly a one-arm wonder. With another exaggerated yawn, she made a half-hearted effort to tug her shorts into place. "Better?" she asked, giving Harper a lopsided, sleepy grin.

"Marginally," Harper replied, crossing her arms as she perched on the edge of her bed. Her lips twitched with amusement. "Do I even want to know what went on in here last night? Because honestly, it sounded like gym class gone rogue."

Paige snorted, her face lighting up despite her sleepy state. "Oh, Harper. Where do I even start?" She flopped onto her back again, her legs kicking lazily in the air like a kid recounting their favorite birthday party. "Brody? Total sleeper hit. I was expecting cocky and passable, but he's ... MUAH! Chef's kiss. Phenomenal. Like a gift to women everywhere."

Harper raised a skeptical eyebrow. "Phenomenal, huh? What, does he juggle or something?"

Paige grinned, her eyes sparkling with mischief as she leaned in conspiratorially. "Not juggling, exactly. More like ... multi-tasking. The man pays attention, Harper. A-level effort across the board."

Harper tilted her head, intrigued despite herself. "Attention, huh? I'm almost afraid to ask, but ... what kind of 'attention' are we talking about here?"

Paige propped herself up on her elbows, her eyes practically gleaming with mischief. "Oh, Harper. Everything. The way he looked at me like I was the only woman in the world. Sweet, right? But then ..." She leaned in closer, lowering her voice as if about to reveal a world-altering secret. "The man has skills. Like, let me tell you, the way he finessed his tongue around my pearl—"

"NOPE! Nope, nope, nope—" Harper nearly launched off the bed, waving her hands frantically as though trying to physically swat the words out of the air. "Too much information! Way too much! I was here for the sweet, romantic highlights—not a play-by-play of Brody's oral resumé."

Paige dissolved into laughter, throwing herself back against the pillows, delighting in Harper's dramatic reaction. "Oh, come on," she teased, wiping away a tear. "I was just setting the scene. You know, painting a vivid picture."

"Stop!" Harper groaned, grabbing another pillow and launching it at her.

Paige caught the pillow mid-air, grinning as she pressed a hand to her chest. "Oh, I love a challenge. Shall I compare his tongue to a summer's breeze? A tempest of pleasure upon uncharted shores?"

Harper let out a full-body shudder, snatching up another pillow. "No. Absolutely not. You are forbidden from pirate metaphors, Shakespearean sonnets, and—God help me—nautical-themed erotica. Ever again."

Paige giggled, rolling onto her side. "Fine, fine. I'll stick to the warm, hard facts ... much like his hard—"

"Paige!" Harper fired off another pillow, laughing despite herself.

"Cock." Paige's laughter rang through the room, absolutely delighted with herself, while Harper groaned and flopped back onto the bed, mentally scrubbing her brain.

"Fine, fine," Paige relented, grinning from ear to ear. "Come on, you must be a little envious, right?"

Harper rolled her eyes, though the smile tugging at her lips betrayed her. "Jealous of the tan lines I just endured? Hardly."

"Oh, please," Paige smirked, finally tugging her tank top into place as she swung her legs over the side of the bed, her mermaid-inspired shorts still slightly askew. "You were the one sneaking back in this morning looking way too satisfied for someone who didn't get any. So, spill. Where'd you end up? And don't say the shuffleboard deck."

Harper headed for the bathroom, unzipping her jeans as she called over her shoulder, "Let's just say your ... enthusiastic bedroom performance last night left me homeless. I ended up crashing with Aidan."

Paige's eyes widened with giddy delight as she grabbed a brush off the nightstand, running it through her tangled hair. "I knew it! So, you get some?"

"It wasn't like that," Harper shot back, her voice echoing from the bathroom as she peeled off her tank top.

"Yeah, right!" Paige chuckled, tossing the brush aside. "Come on, what happened? Did he 'fill you up at the gas pump'?"

"Ugh, Paige Turner!" Harper emerged from the bathroom in her bra and panties, her tank top and jeans crumpled in one hand. "Alright, fine. We shared a bed, okay? But if you're imagining anything remotely juicy, let me stop you right there." She tossed her clothes into a corner with a frustrated huff and rummaged through her suitcase for something clean to wear.

Paige's lips quirked, her eyes sweeping over Harper's pink lace bra with obvious appreciation. "First, that bra is adorable. Really makes your boobs pop."

Harper paused, glancing down at herself. "Thanks ... I think?"

"I mean it," Paige said, grinning. "If I had a cleavage like that, I'd weaponize it."

"Well, maybe that's what I did wrong," Harper muttered, yanking a fresh T-shirt from her bag and shaking it out with unnecessary force. "Because apparently, even weaponized cleavage wasn't enough to get Aidan to make a move."

Paige's eyebrows shot up. "Wait, what? You mean ... nothing happened?"

"Oh, something happened," Harper said bitterly, pulling the shirt over her head. "We kissed. It was nice. Sweet, even. But after that? Nothing. No petting, no hands 'accidentally' wandering, and definitely no sex." She stormed back into the bathroom, muttering as she grabbed her toothbrush.

Paige's jaw dropped. She followed Harper to the bathroom door, leaning casually against the frame. "Hold on. Back up. You're telling me you spent the night in his bed, kissed him, and then cuddled?"

Harper stuck the toothbrush in her mouth, mumbling around the bristles. "Yup. Kissed. Cuddled. Slept."

Paige blinked, then burst into laughter, clutching her sides. "Harper, that is the saddest thing I've ever heard. What were you wearing? A chastity belt?"

"No pants, Paige. His shirt, my underwear. I practically gift-wrapped myself. I even asked for a kiss! What was I supposed to do, write him a personalized invite? 'Dear Aidan, please proceed with ravishing me at your earliest convenience'?"

Paige dissolved into laughter. "Oh, sweetie. You said 'no funny business,' didn't you?"

Harper groaned. "I thought that was code for 'Yes, funny business. Proceed immediately.'"

Paige dissolved into another round of laughter, leaning against the frame for support. "Wait, wait. Let me get this straight. You asked him to cuddle, then told him, 'No funny business'? And now you're mad he didn't make a move?" She tossed her head back, laughing so hard she nearly toppled over.

Harper flushed, crossing her arms defensively. "I was being playful! It was supposed to be flirty. "

"Flirty?!" Paige snorted.

"Yeah, don't guys like the whole hard to get shtick?"

"Boys, maybe. But honey, men aren't that complicated. You might as well have handed him a signed contract that said, 'Do Not Touch.'"

Harper groaned, pressing the heels of her hands to her temples. "God, maybe I am out of practice. Dan wasn't exactly a master class in seduction. I didn't need to try because he was just there half the time."

The mere mention of Dan stirred something inside her—a small, sharp tug, fleeting but undeniable. *Had that been part of it?* She'd told Aidan not to make a move, but deep down, had she really wanted him to? Or had she been protecting herself, keeping a safe distance because, for all her talk, she wasn't ready to let someone else in just yet?

Paige flopped onto the bed beside her, bumping their shoulders together. "Well, Aidan isn't Dan," she said pointedly. "Which, by the way, is a good thing. So what if he didn't pounce on you last night? Maybe he's just not the type to rush into things."

Harper sighed. "Maybe I've just forgotten how to ... you know, be flirty. It's been so long since I've felt like this, and I thought I was sending all the right signals. But maybe I'm just awkward now."

Paige gave her a knowing look. "You're overthinking it. The guy let you stay in his bed, kissed you, and cuddled you all night. He's clearly attracted to you; he's just taking his time. Honestly, it sounds kind of ... sweet."

"Sweet isn't what I was going for," Harper muttered, "at least not last night."

"Well, next time, ditch the 'no funny business' line and try something more direct," Paige teased, leaning back on her hands. "Like, 'Hey, Aidan, take off your shirt and let me sit on your face.'"

Harper burst into laughter, the tension finally breaking. "Oh my gawd, you're impossible."

"And you love me for it," Paige said, flashing her most self-satisfied grin. "Harp, let's be honest, every epic romance needs a comical supporting character."

Thirteen

The days aboard the Elysian Serenade blurred together in a pleasant haze of sun, sea, and laughter. Day by day, the cruise's carefree vibe lessened Harper's burden. After that night with Aidan, when she had sought comfort in his cabin and they'd fallen asleep wrapped up in each other, Harper had felt even more at ease around him. There was something sweetly natural about how they now gravitated toward each other. Since then, they'd exchanged a few tender, slow, relaxed kisses that felt natural, neither trying to rush into anything. It was a kind of simplicity Harper hadn't realized she'd been craving until now.

Paige and Brody, on the other hand, had been all fire and passion from the start. Their fling had yet to cool down, and though they hadn't spent any more nights together, they hadn't refrained from sneaking off for a quick, heated moment whenever they could. Each time, without fail, Paige would return looking thoroughly pleased with herself, flashing Harper a wicked grin before winking as if to say, *Yep, still winning.*

On the day they reached Grand Cayman, their final stop before a sea day on their way back to Miami, the group had spent the morning exploring the port, sipping fruity cocktails under swaying palm trees, and wandering in and out of the local shops filled with bright fabrics and colorful souvenirs. It was the sun-drenched afternoon that felt timeless, as if they could have spent forever on this little island, basking in the warmth of it all.

Around lunchtime, though, Paige, leaning casually into Brody's side, claimed to have a "small headache," giving Harper a knowing look that was anything but subtle. "We're just going to head back to the ship early," Paige said, barely containing her grin. "Maybe rest up a little. You two okay here?"

"Sure," Harper said, not bothering to challenge Paige's excuse. By now, she knew better than to question the inevitable. She shot Aidan a small smile as the other two wandered off, hand-in-hand, clearly in no rush to "rest."

With Paige and Brody gone down the busy street toward the ship, Harper and Aidan were alone, the tropical air heavy with the aroma of salt and sunscreen. The mood between them was easy. Aidan gestured toward a small beachside bar, its thatched roof offering shade from the midday sun. "How about another round of cocktails before we head back?"

Harper nodded, following him to the bar, where they found a couple of high-top seats under a large palm umbrella. The ocean glittered in the background, its waves rolling gently onto the soft white sand. There was a subtle magic at the moment, a postcard-perfect scene that could almost make you forget about the real world waiting on the other side of this trip.

After the server delivered their icy mojitos, garnished with fresh mint, Aidan gazed intently at Harper, his quiet intensity causing her heart to flutter. "So," he began, his voice casual but laced with something deeper, "I was thinking ..."

She raised an eyebrow, sipping her drink. "Oh? About what?"

Aidan glanced toward the ocean, as if gathering his thoughts, before his eyes found hers again. "Would you like to have dinner with me tonight? Like ... a date?"

Harper blinked, taken by surprise. "A date date?" she asked.

Aidan grinned, a boyish charm lighting up his face. "Yeah. It's formal night, so I thought ... it might be nice. We could check out that Greek restaurant. I've heard good things."

"That sounds ... really nice," she admitted, her heart fluttering. "I'd love to."

"Great," Aidan said, his smile widening. "I'll pick you up around seven? We can take our time and enjoy it."

Harper nodded with a giddy energy. "It's a date, then."

The afternoon sunlight stretched lazily over the beach, glittering against the turquoise waves of Grand Cayman as they finished their cocktails. A warm breeze carried the scent of salt and frangipani, mixing with the steady rhythm of the ocean. Harper felt the familiar spark of anticipation— soon, she'd be dining under an endless sky, the sea stretching beyond sight, and Aidan across from her, making the night feel like more than just another evening.

After lingering over their drinks in the beachside bar, Harper and Aidan returned to the tender port, where small boats waited to shuttle passengers back to the Elysian Serenade. Neither of them had to say anything. Harper could feel the rhythm of the day shifting, moving from the carefree laughter of the morning to something quieter, more intimate.

Only a few other passengers trickled onto the tender, sun-drenched and content from their time ashore. Harper settled into a seat near the back, Aidan sliding in beside her. As the boat pulled away from the dock and started toward the looming ship, she leaned into him, her body fitting perfectly against his side. Despite their newness to each other, their movements felt familiar and effortless, as if rehearsed.

Without hesitation, Aidan slipped his arm around her shoulders, drawing her close. The boat rocked gently beneath them, the low hum of the engine blending with the rhythmic lap of water against the hull. A warm breeze carried the scent of salt and sunscreen, wrapping around them like an embrace. Harper closed her eyes, sinking into the feeling of being held. She couldn't remember the last time she'd felt this weightless, as if, for once, she didn't have to carry everything alone.

As they neared the ship, Harper opened her eyes and spotted Maude sitting a few rows ahead. The older woman must have boarded unnoticed, her quiet presence blending into the background. However, when Maude glanced at Harper, a warm, knowing look in her eyes hinted she perceived more than just two people sitting quietly on a boat.

Maude's smile was spattered with something playful, yet Harper felt the warmth of unspoken approval in it. A quiet understanding passed between them, unacknowledged but felt, as if Maude had already seen the shift in Harper's heart before she had recognized it herself. Her words from earlier floated back—*The tide always knows where it's going.* And right now, with Aidan by her side, Harper felt as though the tide had led her exactly where she belonged.

Unaware of the exchange, Aidan pressed a soft kiss to the crown of her head, his lips lingering just long enough. The warmth melted through Harper, and she leaned further into him, letting out a quiet, contented sigh as the tender boat neared the gleaming hull of the Elysian Serenade.

When the boat bumped gently against the ship and the passengers rose, Harper and Aidan pulled apart. A subtle shift had occurred in their relationship, a lingering connection without explicit promises or declarations, only a shared understanding. For now, that was enough.

Back on board, the ship's grandeur glowed in the fading daylight, its sparkling exterior towering above them. They stood together, neither ready to let go but knowing it was time to part.

"So," Aidan said, his voice casual but tinged with something deeper, "I'll see you tonight?"

Harper's pulse quickened at the thought of their date. "Seven o'clock," she said, her smile widening. "I'll be ready."

With one last glance, they went their separate ways. Harper walked back to her cabin, a quiet excitement thrumming through her. Aidan's arm around her and their silent, yet powerful kiss remained. As she reached her door, she could no longer mask her smile.

Back in her cabin, Harper set her things down and paused to soak in the stillness. No Paige, no background chatter—just silence, confirming what she already suspected. She smirked, amused by her roommate's strategic headache, a convenient ticket to a private evening with Brody. She undid the straps of her sandals, feeling the pleasant tingle in her feet from the day spent walking around the island, and went to the bathroom to shower and prepare for the evening.

Harper closed her eyes as the warm water cascaded down her skin, dissolving the salt and sweeping away the final traces of the day's tension. Her thoughts drifted back to Aidan, how he'd held her on the tender ride back to the ship, and the soft kiss he'd pressed to her head. She contemplated the indulgence of this transient romance, if only for a short period. The thought filled her with a mixture of exhilaration and nervous anticipation for their dinner later.

Harper heard the cabin door open and close as she massaged conditioner through her hair. Water trickled down her face as she called out, "Paige, you feeling better?" Her voice held a teasing lilt, knowing full well that the so-called headache was a smokescreen.

She heard Paige's playful laugh from the other side of the door. "Oh, much better," Paige responded, her tone dripping with innuendo.

Harper smirked to herself. "Yeah, I'm sure Brody's special brand of medicine worked wonders."

"Oh, you have no idea," Paige shot back, barely containing her laughter. "I think he could open his own pharmacy with those skills."

Harper laughed as she rinsed the conditioner from her hair, imagining the mischief dancing in Paige's eyes. After a few more minutes under the warm spray, she turned off the water and stepped out of the shower, wrapping herself in a plush towel. When Harper emerged from the bathroom, she found Paige sprawled on the bed in nothing but her sports bra and skimpy panties, looking completely unbothered. Her earlier clothes were haphazardly tossed onto the floor, and she wore a satisfied, lazy grin that practically screamed "post-romp glow."

"Wild afternoon?" Harper teased, raising a brow as she sat down at the vanity to get ready.

Paige stretched, her arms rising above her head as if basking in the aftermath. "Let's just say it was worth skipping a couple of cocktails for," she purred, her tone dripping with innuendo.

Harper smirked, shaking her head. "I bet. You two seem to be hitting it off ... pretty intensely."

Paige rolled onto her side, propping her head up with one hand, her smile turning wicked. "Oh, girl! Let me tell you ... Brody's got ... stamina." She shot Harper a slow, knowing wink, drinking in her friend's inevitable cringe like it was the best part of the story.

Laughing, Harper shook her head. "Well, I hope you still have some energy left for formal night. Wouldn't want you falling face-first into your dinner."

Paige waved a hand dismissively, lounging like a satisfied cat. "Oh please, honey, I can rally. Besides," she added with a suggestive grin, "I think I'll be having Brody for appetizer, entrée, and dessert."

"Okay, okay! TMI," Harper laughed, shaking her head as she focused on her reflection. She slipped out of her towel and reached for her underwear, the cool air of the room brushing against her bare skin. "But seriously, don't let him wear you out too much."

Paige snickered as she rose from the bed, gathering her things for a shower. "Trust me, I've got this handled," she tossed over her shoulder before heading into the bathroom.

As the sound of the water flowed, Harper called out through the door, her voice a bit more serious now. "So ... what's going on with you and Brody? Is this just a cruise fling or ... something more?"

The water muffled Paige's response, but she raised her voice just enough to be heard. "I'm not sure yet, honestly! I'm not rushing to figure it out. But I am planning to visit him in Atlanta after the cruise. I mean, Jacksonville's not that far away."

Harper's eyebrows shot up. "Oh, really? Already planning a post-cruise rendezvous?" There was a teasing note to her voice but also genuine curiosity. Harper envied how easily Paige could throw caution to the wind.

"I mean, why not? We're having fun, and he makes me laugh. That's all I need to know for now," Paige said lightly, though there was a flicker of something unspoken in her tone, a rare glimpse of her own uncertainty.

Harper smiled, shaking her head as she started blow-drying her hair. Paige's ability to live in the moment and not stress about the future was something she admired. It was a freedom Harper could never master.

Paige reemerged from the bathroom, towel-drying her hair as she studied Harper. "Alright, enough about me and my escapades. What about you and Aidan? Still keeping things casual, or are we talking sparks here?"

Harper hesitated, running her fingers through her damp hair. "I don't know. It's been really nice. We've kissed a little, and I feel ... comfortable around him, which is rare for me. But ... I'm not sure where it's going."

Paige tilted her head flashing a wry smirk toward Harper. "Comfortable? Wasn't that the dagger that slowly killed your engagement?"

The words landed like a stone in still water, rippling through her. Harper's fingers paused on the zipper of her dress, her stomach tensing as her gaze slipped downward. The unease wasn't new—but hearing it aloud made it impossible to ignore.

Comfortable.

That was the word, wasn't it? The one she had clung to, not realizing it had become the very thing that unraveled them. She had trusted in the quiet certainty of Dan's presence, so much so that she let their relationship drift, assuming it would always be there—reliable, unwavering, enduring. But love needed more than endurance. It needed to be nurtured, prioritized, chosen. And she hadn't chosen it. Work had been easier—tangible, structured, demanding. And Dan? He had been patient. At least, until one day, she looked up and realized he had stopped waiting altogether.

Had she ever really fought for him? Or had she just assumed he would stay?

A flicker of doubt wove through her. Was she doing it again? Trading one version of "comfortable" for another? But with Aidan, there was no quiet settling, no steady predictability. There was a current between them, a spark that made her breath quicken and her body lean in before her mind could catch up. This wasn't familiar—it was electric, untamed, undeniably alive.

And yet, the thought gnawed at her edges. What if comfort wasn't the problem? What if it was her?

Paige let out a dramatic sigh. "Girl, that dress is a weapon, and you better use it. Zip up, strut like you know you're the best thing he's ever seen, and let Aidan burn for you. And please, for the love of Poseidon, do not fight what you both already desire."

With a soft shake of her head, Harper slipped into the sapphire-blue dress, the fabric gliding over her body like a lover's touch. The single strap left her collarbone bare, the low back revealing the graceful line of her spine. A high slit danced along her thigh, offering a glimpse of skin with every shift. As she zipped it up, the dress molded to her shape, the shimmering fabric catching the light and deepening the blue in her eyes. She drew in a breath, letting the sensation settle. Tonight, she didn't just look confident—she felt it.

Yet the word "comfortable" lingered like an unwelcome guest, its presence faint but persistent. Harper straightened her shoulders, brushing off the doubt with practiced care, refusing to let it follow her into the evening.

At the vanity, she fastened delicate sapphire earrings that caught the light as they swayed, then clasped a matching necklace that rested just above her collarbone. The rich blue stones glowed against her skin, a perfect complement to the dress. For the finishing touch, she slipped into silver heels, their soft sparkle adding just the right amount of glamour.

Harper stepped back to study herself in the mirror. The dress clung to her in all the right places, its elegant simplicity accentuating her curves. The lone strap played with asymmetry, drawing attention to her bare shoulder, while the cutout back offered a daring glimpse of skin. With rosy cheeks, warm eyes, and a touch of rose on her lips, her makeup was soft yet sophisticated. She turned slightly, letting the hem sway and glimpsing her bare back in the mirror.

The truth settled over her like a revelation—she was more than deadlines and heartbreak. She was sultry, magnetic, and brimming with untapped fire.

Anticipation thrummed beneath her skin, quick and addictive. She couldn't wait to see Aidan's reaction, to feel his eyes on her in this dress. Whatever doubts had lingered earlier faded into the background. Tonight wasn't about overthinking or holding back. Tonight was about feeling radiant, daring to embrace the moment, and letting the tide carry her wherever it wanted.

With one last glance in the mirror, Harper grabbed her silver clutch and turned to Paige. "How do I look?"

Paige looked her up and down, raising an eyebrow with a slow, teasing grin. "Girl, even I'm turned on," she winked. "If Aidan can't handle you tonight, I might."

Harper laughed, shaking her head at her friend's boldness, though she had to admit—it did add an extra thrill to the night. "Thanks, but I think I'll manage," she said, her voice carrying a newfound confidence that felt good to own.

Paige smirked, leaning back on the bed. "Just saying ... tonight's gonna be something else."

Harper gave her reflection one last nod of approval. "Let's make sure it is."

Fourteen

The atrium shimmered like a dream. Glass and crystal illuminated the space and made it feel alive with possibility. Harper lingered at the top of the grand staircase, her fingertips brushing the cool railing as she took in the scene below. Her heart pounded, a delicious anticipation thrumming through her veins, and then she saw him.

Aidan stood at the base of the staircase, his focus locked on her with an intensity that sent a shiver down her spine. He looked dangerously good in a fitted black suit that molded to his body in a way that made her pulse stutter, the emerald-green tie a perfect complement to the smolder in his eyes. He had cleaned up for the evening—his jaw smooth, his dark hair neatly trimmed—but there was something else, something deeper. There was a quiet power in the way he held himself, a magnetic pull that wrapped around her like silk, like the slow, heady rush of a sip of the finest wine.

Across the atrium, Harper spotted Maude at the bar, her soft, approving smile radiating an almost maternal warmth. It wasn't just encouragement—it was recognition, as if Maude had always known Harper would end up here. Her words from earlier echoed in Harper's mind: *The tide always knows where it's going*. And tonight, Harper was ready to trust its course.

The space between them hummed with unspoken energy, tightening with each step she took. She was aware of every inch of herself, the way her dress clung to her curves, the slit that flirted with her thigh, hinting at more with each stride. Caught in his stare, Harper felt power and anticipation; every inch of her heightened under his attention.

When she reached the last step Aidan stepped forward, his movements slow and reverent, as though any sudden motion might shatter the tension between them. He extended his hand, a simple gesture that felt anything but casual. Harper's fingers slipped into his, and the contact sent a shockwave through her, a spark that ignited a low, simmering ache deep in her core. His hand was warm and solid, his grip firm yet tender, and for a moment, the rest of the world seemed to drop away, leaving only the two of them standing on the edge of something vast and electric.

"You look ..." he murmured, barely above a whisper, as if the words alone weren't enough to capture what he saw, "... incredible."

She couldn't hold back her smile any longer, not with the way his eyes burned into her, drawing her in like a flame licking at the edges of something combustible. The room faded around them, leaving only this breathless, impossible pull between them. She wasn't just stepping into something new, it was something inescapable. She was falling.

Harper's smile widened. "You look pretty slick yourself," she teased, arching an eyebrow as her fingers brushed along his freshly shaven jawline, lingering just long enough to feel the warmth of his skin beneath her touch. "What's the occasion? Special date?"

Aidan's grin was easy, but the flicker in his emerald eyes was anything but. "Maybe. Figured I should clean up if I wanted to keep up with you tonight." He leaned in slightly, murmuring, "Didn't want you thinking I only looked good in an apron."

Harper leaned in just slightly. "Oh, I don't know," she said, her voice laced with pure temptation. "I think you might look good in only an apron." Her gaze was bold, letting the insinuation hang in the air between them, and she felt a thrill as she watched his eyes darken, his lips quirking into a surprised but delighted smile.

Aidan let out a breath of laughter, eyes widening for half a second before he gave a small shake of his head. "Is that so?" he asked, his grin almost sheepish. "Guess I'll have to find an excuse to make that happen sometime."

She arched a brow, her smirk wicked, laced with playful connotation. "Just say the word. I'll bring the apron."

They didn't need to say more as they left the atrium together. Harper's hand was warm in his as they made their way down the ship's elegant corridors toward Ambrosia, the Greek restaurant.

The scent of rosemary and warm pita bread enveloped Harper the moment she stepped inside, mingling with the tang of citrus and the briny aroma of freshly grilled seafood. The transition from the sleek elegance of the cruise ship to the rustic charm of the restaurant felt almost surreal, as if she had been transported straight to a sun-drenched taverna on the Aegean coast.

The restaurant exuded effortless charm—whitewashed walls with strokes of deep blue, the glow of woven lanterns casting an intimate shimmer over tables draped in crisp white linens. Cobalt vases held sprigs of olive branches, their subtle earthiness overshadowed by the mouthwatering fragrance of garlic, oregano, and grilled lamb drifting from the open kitchen. A melody of bouzouki music curled through the space, harmonizing with laughter, the soft chime of wine glasses meeting in toasts, and the lively cry of Opa! as a waiter sent flames leaping from a plate of saganaki.

Harper's eyes lingered on the open kitchen, where chefs expertly turned skewers of lamb and chicken over an open flame, the air thick with the scent of sizzling meat and warm olive oil. Near the bar, a tall glass case displayed bottles of crisp Assyrtiko and deep-hued Agiorgitiko, their labels a mix of old-world charm and modern elegance. Nearby, a dessert cart brimmed with flaky baklava and delicate kataifi, the sticky sheen of honey catching the light, promising a sweet, indulgent finish.

Their table was positioned near a wide window, offering a breathtaking view of the moonlit ocean. The water shimmered with silver light, rippling softly beneath a sky dusted with stars.

Aidan pulled out her chair, a gesture so effortlessly chivalrous that it caught her off guard. *Since when did I get flustered over old-school manners?*

He sat across from her, reaching for his glass of wine just as she did the same. The rich ruby hue of the Agiorgitiko swirled in their glasses, catching the light. Harper lifted hers, the moment stretching between them, charged with something unspoken.

"To new adventures," she said, her voice soft but full of meaning.

"To new adventures," he echoed, his eyes never leaving hers.

The restaurant pulsed, the hum of conversation and the rhythmic clinking of silverware forming an inviting backdrop. Their plates arrived, brimming with roasted lamb, creamy moussaka, and horiatiki salad glistening with plump Kalamata olives and tangy crumbles of feta. She'd never been to Greece, yet in this moment, it felt like a place she had somehow always known.

She took a slow bite of the lamb, the tender meat melting against her tongue, rich with oregano and garlic. As she reached for her wine, the conversation between them unfolded easily, as if they had done this a hundred times before. Aidan spoke of his family's restaurant, his words threaded with an affection. Harper listened, watching the way his eyes lit up as he described the clatter of pots, the fragrant stews simmering on the stove, the life built from flour-dusted countertops and generations of tradition.

She found herself leaning in, drawn not just to his voice, but to him.

"Cooking's in my blood, I guess," Aidan admitted, swirling his wine. "I was practically raised with a wooden spoon in one hand and a ladle in the other. The restaurant has always felt ... natural, you know? Like it was what I was meant to do."

Harper listened, taken by the nostalgia in his voice. "You make it sound like a fairytale," she said, almost wistful. "A life where you know exactly where you belong."

Aidan's focus drifted toward the window, his expression distant as he watched the moonlight ripple across the waves. "Maybe ... but somewhere along the way, it started to feel like a job. Like I was just ... going through the motions, meeting expectations." His fingers raked through his hair, the movement slower this time, almost as if he were trying to work through his thoughts. "I guess I lost the spark some-where. Forgot what it felt like to cook for the joy of it."

"I get that," she responded. "For me, it was advertising. I wanted to work in the creative world, to tell stories, to build things people cared about. But sometimes I wonder if I built my cage instead." She hesitated, opting for another sip of wine. "Do you ever feel like ... you've been running so long, you don't even know what you're running toward anymore?"

"Yeah. All the time." He set his glass down, leaning slightly across the table. "But you're not running tonight, are you?"

She smiled, feeling a flush creep up her neck, though whether from the wine or his words, she couldn't tell. "No," she admitted. "Not tonight."

They lapsed into a serene silence, the hush felt like an invitation, a space where words were unnecessary, and the warmth of the wine blurred the sharp edges of her thoughts.

"So," Aidan said casually, "imagine you could give up work, stress, and all those deadlines—what then?"

She blinked, surprised. "You mean ... like, fantasy-world stuff?"

"Sure," he said with a grin, "let's go with that."

She paused, rolling the stem of her glass between her fingers. "Okay," she said, letting herself think about it. "I think I'd ... open an art gallery. A small, cozy one. The kind with warm lighting, big open walls, and eclectic pieces from local artists. I'd host exhibits, wine nights, and maybe even painting workshops. It'd be more than just a gallery; it'd be a place for people to connect. A place where they can get lost in something beautiful, even if just for a moment."

Aidan tilted his head, his smile deepening. "That sounds like you."

She laughed softly. "Does it? I feel like it's the opposite of everything my life is right now."

"Exactly," he said, his tone easy but full of quiet understanding. "Maybe that's the point."

Harper was surprised by the insight, and realized she was baring pieces of herself she hadn't shared in a long time. Maybe ever. She took another sip of wine, the magic elixir emboldening her.

"What about you?" she asked, tilting her head. "What's the dream?"

He leaned back in his chair, contemplating. "I'd open a tiny restaurant. Just a handful of tables, enough to cook for maybe twenty people at a time. Something intimate, where I could change the menu every day depending on what inspires me." He shrugged. "It'd just be about the food. No pretenses, no business plans. Just ... pure creativity."

Harper smiled at the thought. "I'd eat there."

"Good," he said. "Because I'd save you the best seat."

"To art galleries and tiny restaurants," she pronounced while raising her glass for a toast.

"To art galleries and tiny restaurants," he echoed while his eyes never parted from hers.

As they lingered over the last sips of wine, the warmth of the evening settling between them, Aidan leaned back slightly, studying her with quiet consideration. "Want to take a walk?" he asked, his voice low, unhurried. Harper agreed without hesitation.

The evening stretched ahead like the horizon itself—open, untamed. For once, she didn't feel the need to plan or second-guess. She wasn't running anymore. Not tonight. Tonight, she let herself simply be—here, with him.

Lanterns cast a golden shimmer over the promenade, their flickering light stretching across the polished deck in soft, lazy patterns. Cool night air brushed against her skin, but it couldn't temper the warmth spreading through her every time Aidan's arm brushed hers. She glanced sideways at him catching on the way the light sculpted the sharp lines of his profile. There was something steady about him, unshakable, yet he still managed to spark a giddiness.

Every subtle glance, every unspoken beat between them seemed to add to what had been simmering since they met. She wasn't sure how much longer she could hold it in. It was anticipation, yes—but also something more. Something inevitable.

Breaking the silence, she tilted her head toward him, her tone teasing. "So ... how's life?"

When he chuckled, the sound was low and warm, sending a delicious shiver down her spine. "Life," he murmured, his voice rich with meaning, "at least right now ... feels pretty damn perfect."

The simplicity of his words, paired with the way he looked at her—like she was the only thing that mattered—was unraveling. She felt her breath catch, a longing unfurling deep in her.

"Think we could just ... stay here forever?" she asked softly, the question half-teasing, but with an ache she couldn't quite hide.

Aidan stopped walking, turning to her, and without hesitation, he reached out and covered her hand where it rested on the railing. His touch was warm, solid, and unyielding, a small spark igniting wherever his fingers brushed hers. "If forever looked like this," he said, his voice low, "I wouldn't mind."

The way he said it, the way his thumb brushed over her knuckles as if to reassure her, sent heat rushing through her veins. The air between them thickened, charged with an energy she could barely contain. Her heart pounded as she felt herself lean slightly closer, his presence pulling her in like a tide she couldn't resist.

But even in this perfect moment, doubts flickered. Her attention drifted back to the horizon, the endless expanse of water mirroring the questions she'd been carrying for so long. "Do you ever think about leaving it all behind?" she asked quietly. "Just ... walking away and starting over somewhere?"

Her words hung as Aidan leaned on the railing. The gentle rhythm of the waves filled the pause before he finally spoke. "Yeah," he admitted, his voice quiet. "But there's always something that holds me back—responsibility, family, guilt." He let out a slow breath. "I guess I've always been the one to hold the line, you know? Even when it feels like it's crushing me."

Harper's lips curved into a faint smile, though her thoughts were far away. "I get that," she said softly, her fingers trailing along the railing. "For me, it's fear. Fear of what I'd lose if I left. Fear of what I might not find if I did." She paused, her voice dropping lower. "Sometimes I wonder if the dream I've been chasing all these years is even mine. Or if it's just something I thought I wanted because it looked good on paper."

Aidan turned toward her, steady, as if he could see straight through the walls she so carefully constructed. "So what keeps you from walking away?" he asked gently.

She hesitated, her fingers tightening on the railing. "I keep hoping it'll get better. That I'll find a way to make it work." Her eyes met his, searching his face. "But some days, it feels like I'm just ... surviving. You ever feel like that?"

Aidan's throat worked as he swallowed, and when he finally spoke. "Yeah," he said. "I know that feeling."

Now that the words had been spoken, their struggles no longer felt like something to bear in silence. Instead, they settled as a quiet understanding, something neither had to carry alone—not tonight.

"Do you think we'll ever figure it out?" Harper asked.

"Maybe," he said. "Or maybe we just have to stop trying so hard to figure it out and let ourselves be happy where we are."

His words weren't profound, but they didn't need to be. Their quiet certainty settled the restless inside her. "That's not a bad idea," she murmured.

And then energy shifted.

When she turned to face him, it was there—in his eyes. The longing. The need. The promise that had been simmering between them, waiting to ignite. He took a step closer, his eyes flicking to her lips, and a thrill shot through her, every inch of her suddenly awake, waiting.

When his lips finally met hers, it felt like a release—like something they had both been waiting too long. The kiss started gentle, hesitant, but quickly deepened, the spark igniting into a flame. Harper slipped her arms around his neck, pulling him closer as her body pressed against his, every point of contact a heady mix of warmth and fire.

His hands found her waist, strong and steady, stabilizing her even as her heart raced wildly. She melted into him, her fingers threading through his hair as she kissed him back with all the passion and longing she'd been holding back. It wasn't just desire—it was inevitability, a connection that had been pulling them from the start.

When they finally broke apart, breathless, Harper rested her forehead against his, her lips tingling. The world around them seemed impossibly still, the waves and the stars fading into the background. She didn't feel lost. She felt found.

When they finally pulled apart, both of them breathless, Harper opened her eyes to find him watching her with a look of equal parts awe and hunger. She felt her heart flutter, a delicious thrill settling deep in her, as his thumb traced small circles against her waist as if reluctant to let her go.

"This ..." she whispered, her voice barely more than a breath, "this feels ..."

He didn't let her finish. His lips claimed hers again—deeper this time, more certain—his hands tightening around her. Harper surrendered to it, to the heat spiraling in her, to the way his touch forced the rest of the world to fade, leaving only this.

As they broke apart once more, foreheads resting together, both of them struggling to catch their breath, she felt a quiet certainty.

"Brody mentioned he'd be staying with Paige tonight." He hesitated, just long enough to make her heart stutter, his fingers brushing the small of her back. "So ... if you'd like, you're welcome to stay with me tonight."

Harper didn't hesitate. Instead, she answered him with a smoldering look that spoke louder than words, pulling him into another fierce, intoxicating kiss. Her hands slipped into his hair, fingers tangling as she pressed her body against his, feeling the delicious heat radiate from him. When they finally broke apart, her eyes were sharp, almost daring. "Why are we still standing here?" she asked, her tone playfully impatient.

The words barely left her lips before they were moving, sparking a shared urgency between them as they made their way through the winding corridors of the ship. Every step felt like an eternity, and every glance he shot her made her pulse pound harder.

As they moved through the ship, past the dimly lit lounges and the quiet hum of other passengers retreating to their cabins, Harper's mind spun, her thoughts a tangled blur of anticipation. Aidan walked close enough that she could feel the warmth radiating from him, his hand grazing hers with each hurried step. She risked a glance up, only to find his eyes locked on her—dark, intense, filled with something that sent a shiver down her spine. It was intoxicating—their steps quickening, their breaths shallow—as if they were both chasing a spark already ignited, a collision waiting to happen.

By the time they reached his door, she was practically vibrating with need, her heart pounding as she met his eyes, wordlessly daring him to make the next move. Aidan fumbled with the key card, his hands clearly not as steady as he might have liked, and the sight brought a rush of heat to her cheeks. There was something deeply satisfying about knowing he was just as eager and affected by this magnetic pull. As the door finally swung open, she caught her breath, stepping inside with him.

The door clicked shut, the soft sound echoing in the quiet cabin. Harper slipped off her heels, letting them fall to the floor as she watched Aidan turn to hang the do-not-disturb plaque on the door handle. His actions simple, deliberate nature sent a small thrill through her; he wanted no interruptions. The intensity in smolder when he turned back to her made her pulse quicken.

Without a word, she reached for his tie, fingers curling around the silk fabric as she pulled him toward her, closing the distance between them in one swift, fluid motion. Their mouths met in a fiercer, deeper kiss than any kiss they'd shared before, a tangle of lips and heat that sent sparks skittering down her spine. Her hands moved instinctively, slipping his suit jacket off his shoulders and letting it fall to the floor as they inched closer to the bed.

Aidan's hands slid along her sides, his fingers brushing the fabric of her dress as he reached for the zipper at her side. But his hands were trembling, fumbling, and he let out a low, frustrated chuckle that was both endearing and maddening. She took over with a knowing smile, unzipping the dress and feeling the fabric loosen against her skin. However, it stayed in place, clinging to her frame, teasingly refusing to fall.

Their breathing quickened, mingling as Harper's fingers found the buttons of his shirt. She tried to unfasten them, but her hands trembled, her urgency outweighing her coordination. The first button refused to yield, and with a quiet huff of impatience, she tugged harder—until it finally snapped free, her pulse hammering in response.

Aidan let out a low laugh, his voice rough. "It's okay," he murmured against her lips, his eyes blazing. "I never wear this shirt anyway."

The words were all the permission she needed. She slid her fingers to the following button, then the next, each one giving way with a satisfying pop as she pulled his shirt open, the fabric parting to reveal the hard lines of his chest beneath. She let her hands roam over his bare skin, feeling the steady beat of his heart under her fingertips.

His shirt gaped open, the fabric hanging loose around his frame, his chest rising and falling in shallow, uneven breaths. Their eyes locked as she slipped one arm out of her dress's single strap with a slow, purposeful movement. The fabric finally surrendered, sliding down her body in a silken whisper, pooling around her feet and leaving her standing in nothing but her favorite black thong. The cabin's lighting cast a golden sheen over the curves of her body. His chest rose sharply, his fingers twitching at his sides, as if barely holding himself back.

His gaze moved over her like a sculptor's hands shaping marble, tracing every curve with an unspoken hunger. Harper could feel it—his desire, his restraint, the way his focus carved through the space between them and set her skin aflame. With a languid grace, she crossed one leg over the other and leaned back, her smile a quiet invitation, a study in seduction.

She beckoned him closer, her voice low and inviting. "Are you just going to stand there?"

He lingered, unmoving, he just stared as if he needed to burn this image of her into his memory forever.

Aidan's fingers moved to his belt, unlatching it with a smooth flick before letting his trousers drop to the floor.

Harper gasped, eyes widening as she clapped a hand over her mouth—half in surprise, half in barely contained laughter. For a moment, the silence held, stretching just long enough to make it unbearable, before she let out a bright, delighted laugh, the sound spilling into the room like champagne fizzing over the rim of a glass.

"Unicorns?!" Tears of laughter clung to her lashes as she watched him glance down at his colorful unicorn print boxers. And that was it—he lost it too. His deep, unrestrained laugh crashed into hers, the absurdity of it wrapping around them like a burst of color in an otherwise sultry scene. The last remnants of tension melted away, replaced by something natural. It was silly, unexpected, completely unplanned—but somehow, that made it even better.

"They're my lucky undies," he said, his eyes locking on hers, their playful tone melting into something more primal."

Aidan moved onto the bed, his slow, deliberate approach sending a shiver down her spine. Harper let go, her carefully built walls trembling under the weight of it all. For so long, she had lived behind an image of control—always composed, always untouchable. But with Aidan, she felt raw, open in a way she never had before. Not even with Dan had she felt this bare, this vulnerable. She refused to let thoughts of tomorrow creep in, refused to think about what came next. Right now, all she wanted was this feeling, this exhilarating rush of being seen and desired without hesitation or reserve.

When his lips met hers, she melted into the kiss, her body instinctively arching to meet his, every nerve ending alive and tingling. The kiss was slow and deep, a gentle exploration that quickly built into something more intense, a hungry need that left her breathless. Aidan's hands were warm as they moved down her sides, fingers pressing gently into her skin as though trying to memorize every curve. She let herself respond freely, wrapping her arms around him, pulling him closer, giving in to the sensations swirling inside her with a newfound freedom.

As Aidan kissed his way down her body, Harper let her eyes flutter shut, surrendering to the sensations that rippled through her with every press of his lips. The warmth of his mouth against her skin sent shivers coursing through her, each kiss a spark that ignited a fire deep within. His touch was deliberate, unhurried, and yet it set a thrilling urgency alight in her veins. She had never felt so seen, so cherished, as though every inch of her was a treasure to be discovered and adored.

Her fingers twisted in the sheets as his lips traveled lower, tracing the gentle curve of her waist. The soft brush of his stubble against her skin added a delicious contrast, a fleeting graze of roughness that only heightened the heat pooling at her core. Each lingering kiss felt like a tease, a slow unraveling, and without thought, her body responded—hips tilting, breath stuttering—wordlessly begging for more.

When his hands reached her hips, his fingers skimming the edge of her thong, a sharp intake of breath escaped her lips. Anticipation rippled through her, spreading outward like ink blooming in water. She felt a strange mix of vulnerability and exhilaration. Exposed as she was, she felt unguarded, stripped of every layer she'd ever built, and he still looked at her as if she were something exquisite.

The fabric slid down her legs in a slow, torturous descent, his fingers tracing fire in its wake. Then he looked up, his gaze locking onto hers, and the heat that surged through her was instant and overwhelming. There was nothing hurried in his movements—only a quiet confidence.

Aidan moved between her thighs with deliberate ease, his hands gliding along her skin like a brushstroke over canvas, parting her with the lightest pressure. A shiver rippled through her as the cool air kissed her slick heat, anticipation drawing her taut. But it wasn't until breath—warm, knowing—ghosted over her, sending a shiver through every inch of her skin. She arched into it, helpless to resist, as though her body had been waiting for this moment, for him.

The first glide of his tongue sent a tremor through her, a gasp slipping from her lips as her fingers tangled instinctively in his hair. His tongue moved with languid precision, sliding through her swollen lips and teasing the sensitive bud at the apex of her desire. The wet heat of his mouth was exquisite, each flick another deliberate stroke, a carving of pleasure into her very being.

She was liquid beneath him, waves of sensation rippling outward as his touch sent her spiraling into a haze of light and color. Her thighs quivered, her breaths tumbling from her lips in uneven moans, each one painting the air with the raw honesty of pleasure. Then, without warning, he teased her with just the right pressure, and something inside her broke loose.

A sharp, unrestrained squeal burst from her lips, raw and unchecked, like an artist's boldest, most reckless stroke breaking through careful composition. Heat flared over her skin, her body jerking under his touch, her pleasure too vast, too consuming to contain. And he didn't stop—he only deepened the rhythm, as if taking her response as proof that he was mastering her pleasure, rendering her into something more.

But just as the heat threatened to consume her entirely, her hands tugged gently at his hair, pulling him toward her. She needed more.

His lips moved over her stomach, her breasts, pausing briefly at the curve of her throat where her pulse fluttered wildly against his mouth. Her hands explored the breadth of his back, tracing every muscle, every dip and ridge, marveling at the strength beneath her touch. When their lips met again, her breath caught, the taste of herself mingling with the warmth of his mouth, sending a fresh surge of heat through her.

Her body responded instinctively, her legs shifting beneath him, parting slightly, her hips lifting until she felt him—hard, ready, aching against her. The contact sent a shiver down her spine, setting off a wildfire deep inside. She reached between them, her fingers brushing the heat of his erection, feeling his pulse throb as she wrapped her fingers around his shaft, guiding him where she needed him most.

Their eyes met, and in that instant, the world seemed to hold its breath. The emotion in Aidan's gaze sent a deep, aching pressure through her chest, a feeling as raw and unguarded as the hunger threading between them.

"Aidan ..." she whispered, her voice low and breathless. It wasn't a plea, but an invitation—a silent acknowledgment of their shared need, of everything this moment meant to them both.

He pressed forward, his head teasing the edge of her, testing, coaxing. Harper's breath caught as he sank into her, the stretch both sharp and delicious, a contrast of pleasure and pressure that left her trembling. He moved with agonizing patience, each inch sending ripples of sensation through her nerves, her walls molding around him, pulling him deeper with every heartbeat.

Her fingers tightened against his shoulders, gripping him as he pressed into her fully, the stretch of him sending a shudder through her limbs. She could feel every pulse, every subtle shift of his body, the heat between them so consuming it blurred the lines between where she ended and he began.

He moved, slow at first, each thrust dragging heat across her skin, sending shivers cascading through her. The friction between them was exquisite, a slow burn that built and built, heat rising in waves, consuming her inch by inch.

Every inch of her felt awakened, her body responding instinctively to his—her legs tightening around his waist, her breath catching as he murmured her name against her neck. The feeling of him, of this, was overwhelming in the most beautiful way.

Their bodies moved in perfect tandem. Harper felt her walls flutter and tighten around him, her body reacting instinctively to his every movement. Each thrust brought him deeper, the sensation of his girth filling her, sending jolts of pleasure through her entire being. The weight of his body against hers, the press of his skin, the way he murmured her name against her neck—it was intoxicating.

Harper felt completely free, completely alive. There was no past, no hesitation, only this—only him. Every ache, every unspoken wound melted away, replaced by the quiet certainty they had built together.

As the night unfolded, she let herself surrender fully to him, knowing this was a moment she would carry with her long after the dawn.

Fifteen

Harper woke to the soft rise and fall of Aidan's chest beneath her cheek, his warmth wrapping around her like a blanket. The rhythm of his heartbeat was steady and reassuring, grounding her in the fragile stillness of the morning. His arm rested lightly around her waist; his hand splayed across the curve of her hip as if holding her there was as natural as breathing. She remained still, not wanting to disturb the quiet intimacy that felt too perfect, too fleeting.

This wasn't how she usually woke up. Her mornings in New York were marked by the sharp jolt of an alarm, the relentless ping of emails, and Cierra's cold, dark apartment that reminded her of how tightly she'd wound her life around work. But here, with Aidan's warmth radiating against her and the soft light filtering through the thin curtains, the world outside felt distant and irrelevant. There was no rush, no urgency—just the two of them, cocooned in time that felt borrowed from another life.

Harper tilted her head slightly, her eyes following the soft curves and sharp angles of his face, as if committing him to memory like a portrait she might never see again. He was unguarded—lashes fanned against his upper cheekbones, lips parted just slightly, the slow rise and fall of his chest a quiet rhythm. She wondered what it would be like to wake up like this every morning, to let herself have this kind of tenderness without second-guessing it. The thought sent a pang through her chest, sharp enough to make her breath hitch.

Because this wasn't forever.

The ship would dock tomorrow, and they'd step back into their separate lives—his in Charlotte, hers in New York. She didn't know if they'd find a way to hold on to what they'd started, or if this connection, so powerful and unexpected, would simply fade into a memory once they both went back to reality.

A knot formed in her stomach, a quiet ache that whispered she'd miss this more than she was ready to admit.

Aidan stirred beside her, and she quickly closed her eyes, pretending to still be asleep. His arm tightened around her waist, and she felt the faint brush of his lips against her hair.

"You've got that look," he murmured, his voice still thick with sleep, and she felt her heart twist. Of course, he'd noticed. Aidan had a way of seeing right through her, peeling back the layers she tried to keep hidden.

She hesitated, then gave a slight shrug. "I was just ... thinking about tomorrow," she admitted, her voice quieter than she'd intended. "About how we're supposed to go back to real life."

Aidan's features softened, but Harper could see it—that flicker of sorrow beneath the surface, a quiet understanding that made this moment feel even heavier. It wasn't regret. It was something deeper, something tender and aching all at once. He glanced down, his fingers grazing the tangled sheets as if they might somehow hold the answers neither of them wanted to face. "Yeah. I've been trying not to think about it," he said. "I just wanted to be here, with you. But now ..."

Harper nodded slowly, reaching for his hand beneath the blankets. The weight of reality settled, undeniable and unavoidable, yet she couldn't let go.

"We don't have to figure it all out today," she whispered, her voice steadier now, as if reassuring herself as much as him. "Maybe ... maybe we just focus on today. We still have twenty-four hours, right?"

When Aidan looked at her, the uncertainty seemed to shift—not disappearing, but lightening, as if hope had managed to slip through the cracks. He brought her fingers to his lips, his kiss deliberate, lingering—a silent declaration. "Twenty-four hours," he repeated, his voice soft and resolute. "If this is all we get, let's make it count."

Harper's fingers wandered absentmindedly over Aidan's chest, sketching invisible patterns against the warmth of his skin. The rise and fall of his breath beneath her palm was hypnotic, a quiet rhythm that made everything else fade into the background. She didn't rush. She explored, drinking in the way his body reacted to her touch, thrilled knowing that her touch could unravel him completely.

Her hand trailed downward, a slow exploration of firm muscle and shifting strength beneath her touch. The faint line of hair guided her like a whispered path, her touch teasing along its edge as if testing the boundaries of restraint. She lingered just above where he wanted her, savoring the power in his silent plea. And then, finally, she touched him—a featherlight brush against his throbbing shaft. The sharp, unrestrained breath he took sent a jolt through her, pleasure and control intertwining in a way that made her pulse pound in sync with his.

"Let's not waste any time," she whispered, the heat in her voice matched by the hunger in her eyes. His expression darkened, something flickering—a challenge, an invitation, a surrender all at once.

She shifted gracefully, straddling him with effortless ease, her lips capturing his in a lingering kiss before trailing downward, her mouth tracing a path along his body. She let herself move slowly, savoring every reaction—the way his breath deepened, the way his muscles twitched beneath her touch.

Each kiss followed the rhythm of his breath, her mouth tracing along the steady beat of his heart. The warmth of him, the way his body responded—tightening, shivering, waiting—sent a quiet thrill through her. As her lips brushed over his stomach, she felt the tension coil beneath his skin, his breath stuttering in a way that made her own pulse quicken.

Harper paused, letting the moment settle, like a brush hovering over an untouched canvas. There was something intimate in the stillness. Then, slowly, she wrapped her fingers around him, her touch light at first, testing, teasing. Aidan's quiet groan of approval hit her like a spark to dry kindling. She had him—completely. And as she leaned forward, her pulse quickened, her body purring with a thrill.

The first press of her lips against him was light, almost reverent, a lingering pause before the inevitable descent. As she took him into her mouth, slow and unhurried, she felt each inch glide past her lips, her tongue tracing the subtle curves and ridges, painting delicate strokes of sensation against heated flesh. His pulse was a steady, insistent beat against her tongue, a rhythm that matched the erratic pounding of her own heart. The heat of him, the sharp exhale of breath above her, the way his fingers flexed in her hair as if resisting the urge to pull her closer—it was intoxicating, powerful, addictive.

Her mouth worked over him in a steady, consuming rhythm, each flick of her tongue, each slow descent designed to pull another groan from his lips. The sound sent a thrill rushing through her, a quiet, potent affirmation of just how completely she had him unraveling beneath her touch. As she took him deeper, her hands explored—tracing up his tense thighs before cupping his jewels, kneading gently. She felt his fingers tighten in her hair, his encouragement urging her forward, and she responded instinctively, increasing the tempo, the intensity.

Harper felt unbound—as if she had stepped outside the frame of the life she had so carefully painted for herself. The morning's intimacy, the quiet trust between them, unfurled like a masterpiece in motion, each brushstroke breathtaking—the way they fit together, as seamless as color blending into canvas, as if they had always belonged to the same composition.

When she finally lifted head, her lips still warm from her worship of him, she spotted an intensity in his eyes left her breathless. There was something raw and vulnerable in his expression, a reflection of her own emotions. It echoed inside her, as if they were two pieces of the same mural, painted in matching hues of desire. The thought sent a delicious shiver through her, the line between physical and emotional dissolving into something more.

Aidan's touch was steady, reassuring as he guided her upward, his hands skimming along her arms before settling at her hips. Harper moved with him, instinctively attuned to his silent request. They didn't need words—this was understanding, trust, desire, all intertwined in the press of skin against skin.

As she straddled him, the velvet heat of his erection nestled between her slick folds, sending an anticipatory tremor through her. Her breath caught as she wrapped her fingers around him, guiding his swollen shaft into her. The first press of his head against her entrance sent a jolt through her, the mingling of their heat setting every nerve alight. Slowly, she took him in, the stretch of him both overwhelming and intoxicating. A soft gasp escaped her as her body yielded, accepting the fullness of him, their bodies pressing together in an intimacy that felt deeper than flesh.

Her nails dug into his shoulders as she sank lower, taking him deeper, her body molding around him in a way that felt inevitable. For a moment, they were motionless, clinging to the intimacy of the moment, to the overwhelming weight of this—not just the physical, but everything it meant.

Harper moved with a slow, sensual grace, each shift of her body a clear invitation, each motion layering pleasure upon pleasure, deepening the masterpiece they were creating. Her hands wandered over his chest and shoulders, feeling the tension in his muscles, the way they flexed beneath her touch, the way his breath stuttered in response to every roll of her hips.

She savored the way his hands slid down to grip her, his fingers pressing into her flesh, guiding her as they found a rhythm that was entirely their own. She needed this, needed the release, the rawness of it, the way it stripped her down to something unguarded, something real.

And then it hit—like the final, breathtaking stroke of a masterpiece, complete and undeniable. Her body clenched around him, release crashing over her like a wave against the shore, unstoppable, undeniable. She clung to him, gasping, trembling, the aftershocks leaving her weightless, undone.

Aidan's arms wrapped around her, anchoring her as they both came down from the high, their bodies still tangled, their breath mingling in the quiet. Harper pressed her forehead to his, a slow smile curving her lips as the warmth of him settled around her. In the quiet stillness, she felt something settle inside her—a warmth, a belonging, a moment she would carry with her like the most vivid painting in her collection, a piece of art she never wanted to let go of.

Tomorrow could wait. Wrapped in Aidan's arms, with his heartbeat thrumming against her cheek, Harper let herself sink into the quiet rhythm of now.

Harper lay draped across Aidan, listening to the steady pulse of his heartbeat, a rhythm as steady as the tide. But morning had arrived, sunlight cutting through the room, reminding her that they couldn't stay tucked away in this dream forever. With a sigh, she propped herself up, her hand tracing a gentle line along his chest before she slipped out of bed, gathering her things.

Only then did she realize—she had brought nothing else to wear. She looked around, almost laughing at her oversight, just as Aidan caught her eye, his expression amused yet affectionate. Without missing a beat, he sat up and rummaged through his drawer, pulling out a clean blue T-shirt and gym shorts.

"Here," he said, handing them to her with a grin. "It's not exactly high fashion, but ..."

Harper laughed, gratefully taking the offered clothes. She pulled the oversized T-shirt over her head, adjusting it until it draped just right. Then, with a playful smirk, she tied a knot at the side, cinching it at her waist. Next, she pulled on the gym shorts, tying the drawstring and giving them a little fidget until they settled into a surprisingly cute, almost skirt-like shape around her hips.

She did a mock twirl, striking a pose. "Who knew your wardrobe had so much potential?" she teased, grinning at him over her shoulder.

Aidan shook his head, clearly charmed. "Look at you," he said, unable to hide his admiration. "Better than I could've ever imagined."

With that, they slipped out of the cabin, Harper's hand finding its way into Aidan's as they strolled through the ship's corridors. She could feel a lightness in her step, a warm, giddy sensation bubbling up inside her that felt as bright and easy as the morning sun. An undeniable, almost domestic comfort emanated from how they moved to breakfast, hand-in-hand, softly laughing as they passed other guests. It felt like they were in their own little world, a world she wasn't ready to let go of just yet.

The buffet was already bustling, with passengers grabbing coffee and loading plates with fresh fruit, pastries, and steaming omelets. Aidan guided her through the crowd, spotting Brody and Paige sitting by a window overlooking the ocean. They made their way over, Harper still holding Aidan's hand, her heart fluttering at the casual intimacy of it all.

As soon as they reached the table, Brody looked up, his eyes lighting with a knowing smirk. "Well, well, well," he drawled. "Wasn't sure if the two of you would come up for air."

Aidan rolled his eyes, though he couldn't quite keep the grin off his face. "Good morning to you, too," he replied, grabbing a chair as Harper slipped into the seat beside him. She felt her cheeks warm, but she was too happy, too relaxed to care about the teasing.

Brody continued to smirk, tossing Aidan a wink before turning attention to Harper. "Nice outfit," he remarked, his voice laced with amusement. Paige elbowed him, but she was smiling, too, clearly entertained by the situation.

Paige shook her head, still grinning, and turned to Harper. "Is that Aidan's shirt?"

Harper laughed, adjusting the knotted fabric at her waist with a shrug. "Turns out his wardrobe has a little versatility," she quipped, her eyes meeting Aidan's with a lighthearted glint. She loved the easy banter between them, the way she could joke about borrowing his clothes as if this were a routine morning.

They settled into conversation, the four recounting last night's adventures, laughing about the little details and mishaps filling their time aboard the ship. Harper listened as Brody recounted a clumsy attempt at karaoke, complete with dramatic gestures. Paige rolled her eyes, half embarrassed, half amused.

Harper stole glances at Aidan throughout breakfast, marveling at how natural this felt. She envisioned a future of mornings like this: shared laughter, comfortable silences, and intimate glances. But just as quickly as the thought arrived, she felt a pang of sadness. Tomorrow, everything would shift. Their individual lives awaited them as the cruise drew to a close.

As breakfast wound down, Harper could feel a bittersweet tension settle over their little group, an unspoken awareness that the end of their time together was drawing near. She looked around the table, taking in Paige's animated expressions, Brody's casual smirk, and Aidan's quiet intensity. Bathed in the golden rays of the morning sun, they seemed frozen in time, a scene from a captivating story she was loath to interrupt.

Brody leaned back in his chair, stretching. "Alright, we can't just let this end tomorrow and never see each other again," he declared, looking each of them in the eye. "Promise me we'll stay in touch, alright? If nothing else, we're booking another cruise together one day."

Paige nodded eagerly, raising her coffee cup in a mock toast. "Absolutely. Good friends—and good travel buddies? They're hard to find. We can't let this go."

Harper felt excitement at the idea, a flicker of hope that maybe this wasn't the end of their little family. She glanced from Paige to Brody, then finally over to Aidan. "Agreed," she said, her voice soft but filled with conviction. "We'll need another adventure to look forward to."

Harper saw through Aidan's smile—it was a mask disguising the storm beneath. She could feel that ache of goodbye already tugging at her, a preemptive sadness over the inevitable return to their separate lives. They had been living in a world separate from reality, but the illusion was slipping. Once they stepped off this ship, everything would change. The little bubble of time they'd shared would pop, and she couldn't see a way to keep it intact.

While she yearned for another cruise and the thrill of new adventures, Harper knew that what she and Aidan had wouldn't last once they returned to everyday life. She had her career and responsibilities in New York; he had his family and restaurant in Charlotte. Their separate worlds, anchored by commitments, left little space for impulsive adventures or long-distance love.

But today wasn't over yet. They still had one last day and night to enjoy together, one more day to make memories before they all went their separate ways.

As they pushed their chairs back and stood up, Aidan moved beside her, slipping an arm around her waist as they fell in step with Brody and Paige. She leaned into his warmth, feeling that familiar thrill as he held her close. On impulse, she reached around and slipped her hand into his back pocket, giving him a playful squeeze that made him laugh, a deep, soft sound that rumbled through her.

"You're thinking too much," she murmured, her gaze steady and warm as she looked up at him. In his eyes, she saw a reluctance she recognized in herself; she yearned to make things easier, granting them the freedom to simply exist.

Aidan met her eyes, and sighed. "You're right," he said, his voice quiet but filled with gratitude. His hand tightened slightly on her waist, pulling her closer. "Let's just enjoy today."

Her heart swelled at his words, and together, they turned to follow Brody and Paige through the bustling corridors of the ship. Their arms remained wrapped around each other as they walked, a quiet but constant reminder of the connection they'd built, each step carrying them into the shared adventure of this last day.

Harper, Aidan, Paige, and Brody set out to enjoy this final day. Tomorrow could wait; today was theirs to savor.

With Aidan's arm around Harper and her hand resting on his back, they felt they were exactly where they were meant to be.

Sixteen

The morning light filtered softly through the cabin's curtains, painting the room in a golden hue that belied the bittersweetness of the day. Harper zipped her suitcase and glanced around, ensuring she hadn't left anything behind. The room felt empty now, stripped of the laughter and memories it had held all week. This trip had been a brief escape, a reminder of what it felt like to truly live. But now, reality beckoned, pulling her back to New York.

Across the room, Paige hummed cheerfully as she tossed clothes into her suitcase, her energy as vibrant as her neon pink bra straps peeking out from under her tank top. "Guess where I'm heading next weekend?" Paige teased, a roguish sparkle in her eye.

"Atlanta, I'm guessing," Harper smiled, rolling her eyes.

"Bingo." Paige grinned. "Brody invited me. He's got a plan to show me around and cook for me. And honestly?" She shrugged, her expression softening. "I want to see where this goes."

Harper smiled, happy for her friend but unable to ignore the ache it stirred within her. Paige and Brody were like two magnets, drawn together effortlessly. Their lives fit. Harper and Aidan ... they'd been something else entirely. Something more profound but less practical. Two ships that met in the middle of the ocean, offering each other sanctuary before sailing in separate directions.

Paige's voice pulled her from her thoughts. "What about you? Any plans to visit Charlotte?"

Harper shook her head. "No. We knew what this was. He has his life there, and I have mine in New York. It wouldn't work."

Paige gave her a sympathetic smile, squeezing her hand. "But it was still worth it, wasn't it?"

Harper nodded, her chest tightening. "Yeah. It was." She thought of their nights under the stars, how he'd looked at her in that sapphire dress as if she were the only woman in the world. "He made me feel seen. Like ... like I mattered in a way I haven't felt in a long time."

Paige's smile turned wistful. "Some of the greatest connections are the ones that are beautifully temporary."

Harper offered a hesitant nod, though doubt whispered at the edges of her thoughts. She slipped on the blue T-shirt Aidan had lent her, tying a knot at the side as she had before. The fabric, worn soft from years of washing, still carried the faintest trace of him—a quiet comfort, a reminder of warmth and belonging. With the shirt draping loosely over her sports bra, she was set for the journey ahead. as she traced the fabric with her fingertips, a hollow ache spread. This shirt might be the last thing she had to hold onto, a quiet keepsake of their fleeting time together.

Harper scanned the cabin, the once-vibrant space now quiet, stripped of the life and laughter it had held all week. She hesitated in the doorway, memories settling over her like the final hues of a sunset—soft, fleeting, impossible to hold onto.

Her hands hovered as she shut the suitcase, a hesitation she hadn't expected. This had always been temporary, a fleeting escape from reality. She had tried to savor every moment. But now, standing at the brink of goodbye, the ache felt deeper, heavier—more real than she had expected.

Just as she took a steadying breath, her phone buzzed, pulling her out of her thoughts. She glanced down at the screen, expecting a notification from the airline or a text from Aidan. Instead, she blinked in surprise at the name that appeared.

Dan.

A name she hadn't let herself dwell on in days. And yet, as she stared at the message, it felt like looking at a past self she barely recognized. He was reaching out asking to meet for coffee—saying he wanted to apologize for how things had ended.

The old Harper would have felt a pang of anxiety, an urge to overanalyze, to pick apart his words for hidden meaning. But now... she only felt stillness. Whatever she and Dan had shared belonged to another version of herself, one who had clung so tightly to the idea of comfort and stability that she hadn't realized she was coasting, letting the relationship exist without truly tending to it.

Maybe she had been unfair to him, expecting certainty without offering real vulnerability in return. Maybe, in her search for safety, she had stopped seeing him at all.

She exhaled, glancing around the cabin, her thoughts drifting back to Aidan, to the easy laughter, the late-night conversations, and the way she had felt so present with him. *Was that the lesson in all of this?*

Maybe she hadn't needed an escape so much as a chance to look at her life from the outside and see what she had been missing.

She slid her phone back into her pocket, knowing that meeting Dan wouldn't change what she had found here. But for the first time, she wasn't afraid to face what she had left behind.

Paige zipped up her suitcase with a flourish, snapping Harper out of her thoughts. "Alright," she said, slinging her bag over her shoulder and grinning with excitement and mischief. "One last morning on this ship. Ready to face the real world again?"

Harper took a deep breath, glancing around the cabin one last time. "As ready as I'll ever be."

They hit the buffet for a quick breakfast, gossiping and giggling over the week's best parts: Paige's hilariously lousy karaoke, their Grand Cayman sunburn, and the romantic moments that made the cruise dreamy.

As they passed through the bustling hallways, Harper noticed others saying goodbye and friends exchanging numbers and promises to stay in touch. She and Aidan, however, had made no such promises. They knew this week was one of those perfect moments that only happened once, a beginning and an end.

Paige nudged her, breaking her thoughts. "Hey. You okay?"

Harper nodded, "Yeah. I think I am."

Paige and Harper stepped off the ship together, the hum of disembarking passengers buzzing around them as they descended the gangway. The bright Miami sun beat down relentlessly, its heat bouncing off the pavement and driving home the reality of their trip's end. The week had passed in a blur, fleeting as a dream, and as her feet met solid ground, a quiet heaviness settled in.

It was over.

The terminal bustled with activity as they collected their bags, a swirl of laughter, chatter, and the scrape of suitcases rolling over tiled floors. Near the entrance, Brody stood waiting, his signature cocky grin lighting up his face as soon as he spotted Paige. Harper caught the way Paige's face lit up in return, and something softened inside her. Their effortless connection made you want them to be happy. As much as she teased Paige, Harper truly hoped it would last. They just seemed to fit.

Paige turned to Harper, her bright eyes carrying both excitement and the quiet ache of goodbye. "I'm gonna miss you, roomie," she said, pulling Harper into a tight, full-bodied hug. "Promise me we're doing this again someday."

Harper laughed, squeezing her back with all the affection she felt for her vibrant, free-spirited friend. "Oh, we're definitely doing this again. And you have to come visit me in New York soon. Brody can't have you all to himself."

Paige pulled back flashing a wink and a playful grin. "I think I can manage a trip to the Big Apple. Maybe I'll even drag Brody with me. I'll text you once I've got dates in mind."

"Perfect," Harper said, her smile widening. "I can't wait to take you out on the town."

With one last shared grin, Paige turned and bolted toward Brody, who greeted her with open arms, sweeping her up in a playful twirl that made her laugh. Harper watched from a distance, her heart lifting and aching at once. There was a lightness to them, a sense of tomorrow woven into their embrace. And while Harper regretted nothing about her time with Aidan, she couldn't stop the longing that came with knowing her own goodbye, which likely wouldn't hold the same certainty.

As Harper stood at the curb, her suitcase in hand, she spotted Aidan across the way. Their eyes met, and the world seemed to still. She lifted her hand, blowing him a silent kiss, and he smiled, raising his hand in a quiet goodbye. No words could capture what they had, they didn't need them. Some things stay, even when people don't.

As the taxi pulled away, Harper leaned back in her seat, fingers brushing the hem of Aidan's shirt. She closed her eyes, letting the memories wash over her. Could Paige have been right? Some relationships are lovely, precisely because they're temporary, like the last rays of the sun before it dipped below the horizon, no less vibrant for their brevity.

She let herself savor the warmth of those memories, carrying them like treasures as the taxi wove through Miami's streets. Aidan had reminded her of something she hadn't realized she'd lost: the courage to be open, even without guarantees.

It was a pleasant memory, but she knew it was just a quick romance on the ocean. And yet, it had felt so real, meaningful. Aidan reminded her of what it felt like to be open and let someone in, even briefly.

Lost in thought, her phone buzzed, jolting her back to the present. She glanced down and saw a text from her sister, Helen.

Helen

> Hey! How was the cruise?? Can't wait to hear all about it. Call me asap?

Harper smiled, a warm rush of affection filling her. Helen was overjoyed when Harper took a break to escape work and experience a change. Harper could already picture her sister's excitement, how she'd demand every detail, especially with Aidan.

She typed back a quick reply, fingers moving quickly over the screen.

Harper

OMG. It was … amazing. So much to tell! I'll call when I'm back in NY. Luv ya

She hit send and glanced out the window, watching the Miami skyline pass.

Maybe that's the magic—when time is fleeting, you skip the slow unraveling and go straight to the heart. Aidan saw parts of her that people she'd known for years had never glimpsed. It was liberating, a kind of honesty you only find when you stop needing guarantees.

She remembered Paige's words: *Sometimes, those are the best connections … beautiful because they're temporary.* Paige was right.

Harper smiled softly, feeling the ache in her chest lighten just a little. She didn't need a promise of forever to know this was worth something. She'd carry this week, a pocket of warmth to turn to on lonely days. It was a reminder that moments of connection and kindness were waiting somewhere out there if she stayed open to them.

For now, she let the warmth of Aidan's shirt and the memory of his touch carry her forward like the steady rhythm of the waves guiding her home.

Seventeen

The sky outside Cierra's apartment was a dull, oppressive gray, with clouds hanging low over the city. The tiny, dirty windows let in barely any light, casting a lifeless radiance over the cramped space. It felt like a world away from the endless blue skies and warm Caribbean sun Harper had soaked in just days before.

Harper slumped on the pull-out sofa, the scratchy cushions digging into her back. A thin throw blanket hung over her shoulders, doing little to ward off the damp chill that clung to the apartment. Her laptop screen flickered on the coffee table, but no email! She was still waiting to hear about coming back early from her sabbatical. Three days back, she hadn't left the apartment. She wasn't even sure what she was waiting for anymore.

Her thoughts drifted, unspooling like threads from a world that now felt far away: the heat of the Caribbean sun, the way the turquoise sea glittered under a boundless sky, barefoot walks on powder-soft sand, laughing and dancing under the stars, letting herself feel alive. And then there was Aidan. *God, Aidan*.

His rich laugh echoed in her mind, filling the silence of the apartment. She could almost see him—his crinkled smile, the steady way his eyes held hers, making her feel cherished and safe, a comforting feeling washed over her. His touch was so gentle, yet sure. She still remembered his shirt that morning, that woodsy, warm smell clinging to it.

Her eyes fluttered closed as the vivid and consuming memories enveloped her. His stare, burning like a wildfire, sent her pulse racing, her skin flushed. With a tenderness that stole her breath, his hands moved over her skin, his touch lingering long after he'd finished. The electricity of his touch, each brush of his fingers sending waves of heat and tingling across her skin.

A shiver rolled through Harper as her fingers traced from her collarbone, skimming lower, drawn by the lingering ghost of his touch. Her hand flirted with the waistband of her shorts, anticipation building—until a noise at the door ripped her back to reality.

Her eyes snapped open, the dim, gray apartment rushing back into focus. Gone was the golden light of the Caribbean, the heat of Aidan's touch, the intoxicating thrill of that world. She was here, back on Cierra's pull-out sofa, a blanket draped over her shoulders and her laptop glowing faintly with the same unanswered emails.

The door creaked open, and Cierra stepped in, her hair pulled back into a loose ponytail and a takeout bag swinging from her hand. Seeing Harper curled up and dazed on the sofa, she arched a skeptical eyebrow.

"Hungry?" Cierra asked, shaking the takeout bag with a grin.

Harper tugged the blanket tighter around her shoulders and nodded. "Yeah, I guess." Her voice sounded thin even to her own ears.

She was trying to stay positive, to remind herself that the cruise had been just a break, a fleeting escape, not a permanent detour from her real life. But in Cierra's dim apartment, everything felt ... smaller. Confining.

Cierra plopped the bag on the coffee table, glancing at Harper. "So, how are we doing?" she asked, settling onto the edge of the pull-out sofa.

"I'm ... trying," Harper said, smiling as she hugged her arms around herself. "Trying to stay positive, trying to find the light in things. But honestly, everything just feels ... flat. Like I'm back to square one."

Cierra gave her a sympathetic pat on the knee. "Flat is fine! Flat is normal. Isn't that what you wanted? To feel like yourself again?"

Harper hesitated, glancing at the surrounding walls. The low ceiling and cramped space pressed in, and the dim light filtering weakly through the windows only worsened it. "Maybe. It's just ..." She paused, her smile tilting into something wry. "Maybe it's the apartment. I mean, your place is ... cozy."

"Cramped? Dark?" Cierra teased. "It's okay, you can say it. I know it's not exactly a luxury yacht."

Harper laughed a little more sincerely this time. "It's not that. It's just ... different from what I'm used to." She thought briefly of the spacious, light-filled apartment she'd once shared with Dan. Her old life had been predictable, orderly, and, above all, stable. And maybe, after everything, that's what she needed now. Something familiar.

Her attention dropped to her phone on the cushion beside her, Dan's name staring back at her from her list of contacts. He'd texted a few times since she got back, suggesting coffee. She'd ignored him at first, telling herself there was no point in dredging up the past.

But now, sitting in Cierra's apartment with its tangled cords and mismatched furniture, saying yes didn't feel so unthinkable.

Dan was safe, steady—the kind of certainty she had once shaped her life around. With him, there was no guesswork, no messy unknowns. Just a path that had always been clear: a wedding, a shared home, a future laid out like a checklist. If she hadn't taken him for granted before, if she hadn't let herself get lost in everything else, maybe she wouldn't be wondering now if she even deserved another chance.

Aidan, though. Aidan had been none of those things. He'd laughed too loudly, kissed her recklessly, and left her spinning, untethered from everything she thought she knew. His excitement was as brief and thrilling as the Caribbean experience. She'd lived fully in his world for one golden week, but it had been a fantasy. A beautiful one, but not built to last.

She stared at Dan's name, her thumb hovering over the screen. Aidan had been the dream. Dan was real. Maybe what she needed now wasn't the spark of something unpredictable. Perhaps she needed the steady flame that didn't burn out.

Her thumb lingered. Connecting with Dan could remind her of who she was before the cruise, before Aidan, before everything had felt so complicated.

She thought she should just return to her old life, pressing her lips together as something restless curled inside her. Before the cruise, she had convinced herself that working late and sacrificing weekends made her reliable, but that wasn't true. She hadn't been dependable—just stuck in a pattern of neglecting what mattered, always assuming Dan would wait.

Her breakdown at work, the one that had led to this forced sabbatical, seemed like a distant, embarrassing memory now. The quiet giggles of her coworkers about Harper's collapse echoed in her ears; *the dependable one, broken*. She'd been fragile, unraveling. But Dan had always been steady. He didn't unravel, at least not until he could no longer hold on.

The woman she'd been on the cruise felt too far away to hold on to. Aidan had been intoxicating, yet that feeling of being seen, alive, and free, couldn't be real. A man like him, a life like that was destined to be savored only in passing. Aidan belonged to warm nights under the stars, the hum of the ocean, and golden mornings that stretched forever.

Golden mornings were an illusion. Real life was muted skies, predictable rhythms, and quiet nights spent on a couch that had never quite fit, much like the life she had built around it. Dan had been part of that world—steady, uncomplicated, the kind of certainty she might have held onto if she had been paying attention.

Safe wasn't thrilling. Safe wasn't Aidan. But it had been Dan. And maybe, after everything, it was time to stop chasing fleeting moments and return to something she could count on.

She shook her head, pushing Aidan from her mind. His touch and laugh all felt too good to be true. She'd been foolish to think someone like him could ever be more than a fleeting chapter. The cruise had been a beautiful, impossible escape, but it wasn't her real life. This gray, predictable world was.

Or was it?

As Harper sat curled up on Cierra's sofa, something inside her resisted. A small, quiet voice whispered that maybe she deserved more than just "normal." That incredible woman from the cruise might have been real. But how could that version of herself survive here, in New York, under these gray skies?

She sighed, frustration bubbling up. The cruise already felt like it had happened to someone else, like it belonged to a story she'd loved and left behind. She was Harper from New York—the one who made steady, pragmatic decisions. The one who was reliable, predictable, and safe.

The Harper from the cruise? She'd been on vacation. It was time to let her go.

A week ago, the idea of coffee with Dan would've been unthinkable. She had been too involved in the sun-soaked thrill of the cruise and the ache of something new and reckless. But now, in Cierra's dim apartment, her phone felt heavy, almost as if it were pulling her back to earth.

Dan's life, neat and orderly, was something she understood. He must have reached his last nerve when he ended things because he used to be safe. maybe she needed that again, and how he made her feel before the breakup. *Could we even get that back?* Their apartment had been orderly, filled with matching throw pillows and framed photos of weekend getaways. They always ate Italian on Fridays and read the paper with coffee on Sundays. It hadn't been exciting, but it had been comfortable.

Maybe this was what maturity looked like: letting go of fantasies and accepting that love didn't need to feel like fireworks. Dan wasn't perfect, but he was reliable. He knew her coffee order and how she liked to sleep with the window cracked, even in winter.

Aidan hadn't seen those parts of her, the messy edges. Beside him, she blossomed into the woman she aspired to be: brave, passionate, and unrestrained. But could that version of her exist here, in the real world?

The message came quickly, almost too easily:

Harper

Sure, let's do coffee … tomorrow?

The words felt hollow, even as she typed them. But they also felt familiar. Saying yes to Dan didn't feel like moving forward or backward. It felt like standing still. And maybe standing still was what she needed.

She paused, remembering Aidan's laughter, touches, and kisses beneath the stars. The way he'd made her feel free. But then she thought of Dan, of mornings filled with routine and the stability that once felt like enough.

She let out a breath and pressed send.

The message disappeared into the void, taking with it the last trace of Aidan. That door was shut now, and she wasn't sure she had the strength—or the desire—to reopen it.

Harper's phone buzzed beside her, breaking through the fog of resignation she'd been sinking into. She thought it might be Dan responding to her coffee invitation, but when she glanced at the screen, Paige's name flashed instead.

Paige

Hey girl, let's catch up!

Harper smiled, warmth bubbling up. Paige had been one of the best parts of the cruise, with her wild stories, infectious laugh, and constant nudging to let loose. She hesitated, thumb hovering over the call button. Talking to Paige would mean revisiting the cruise—the freedom, the spark, the version of herself she'd been trying to ignore. But before she could overthink, she tapped the screen.

Paige picked up on the first ring. "Harper!" she squealed, her voice bright and bubbly, cutting through the dimness of the apartment. "Oh my god, it's so good to hear from you!"

"Paige," Harper said, laughing. The sound felt good like sunlight breaking through clouds. "You're not pregnant with Brody's kid already, are you?"

"Gawd, Harper! Rude!" Paige laughed, mock outrage in her voice. "Just because I'm head over heels doesn't mean I'm reckless. I've got some self-control, thank you very much!"

Harper laughed again, the tension in her chest easing. It felt like they were back on the Elysian Serenade, teasing each other and talking late into the night as if they'd been friends forever.

"Seriously, though," Paige said, her tone softening. "Brody and I ... it's just easy, you know? I've never felt this way before." Harper could hear the thud of a suitcase being tossed on a bed. I'm busy packing now to see him in Atlanta this weekend. Just ten days ago, I didn't even know he existed, and now I'm driving five hours to see him. Is that insane?"

"It's not insane," Harper said, though a wistful note crept into her voice. "You're following your heart."

"Exactly!" Paige exclaimed, her excitement bubbling through the line. "Life's too short, right? After the cruise, I just decided I'm done waiting for things to fall into place. If I want something, I'm going for it."

Harper pulled the blanket tighter around her shoulders. "I wish I had that kind of courage," she murmured.

"Harper, don't sell yourself short," Paige said. "You opened up. You let yourself be free, even if it was just for a week. That wasn't nothing. Don't go back to 'normal' just because it's easier. You deserve more."

Harper swallowed, her throat tightening. "I know. But it's different now. I'm back in New York, and Aidan's ... well, he's probably back at Murphy's, doing his thing." She tried to sound casual, but the hollowness in her voice betrayed her. "I'm trying to get back to normal. Dan and I are meeting for coffee tomorrow."

"Dan?" Paige's tone dropped in exasperation. "Seriously, Harper? I thought we agreed he was an ex for a reason."

"It's just coffee," Harper said defensively, though she didn't quite believe it. "He wants to apologize. Yeah, maybe I need to finish that chapter and get it over with. Maybe it'll make it easier to move on."

Paige sighed but didn't push. "I get it. Closure is important. Just promise me you won't lose yourself in 'normal,' okay? You're more than that."

Harper closed her eyes, letting the words sink in. She'd been clinging to the idea of "normal" like a lifeboat, convincing herself it was what she needed. Something about Paige's voice rekindled a feeling she'd been trying to suppress since her return.

"Yeah," Harper said finally, her voice soft. "I'll try."

"Good," Paige replied, her tone brightening again. "And hey, who knows? Aidan might surprise you. Hey, if I drive five hours to see Brody, the least Aidan could do is try ... if he feels the same way about you."

Harper forced a laugh, though the mention of Aidan left a familiar ache in its wake. "Yeah. Maybe."

They chatted a little longer, trading cruise memories and laughing, Paige's voice a dose of sunlight in Harper's gray apartment. But as the call ended, the brightness faded, and the weight of the room settled back in.

Harper set her phone on the coffee table, her gaze drifting to the screen. Dan's name hovered above her last message: Sure, let's do coffee ... tomorrow.

The words felt heavier now, like a choice she couldn't entirely take back.

The words on the screen felt small yet heavy. It was done. She'd committed to seeing Dan, to revisiting that version of her life. Safe, familiar, practical Dan. The man who didn't ask her to risk anything, just wanted to be part of her world.

Harper exhaled, Paige's voice echoing: *Don't return to 'normal' just because it's easier.* But wasn't that why she'd sent the message? Wasn't normal what she needed?

Her gaze shifted to the suitcase still by the door, unopened since she returned. Somewhere inside, buried under sand-dusted clothes, was her memories. She'd meant to unpack it, but the thought had felt ... too final, too much like goodbye.

She momentarily imagined being back on the cruise, carefree, dancing barefoot, kissing Aidan, believing anything was possible.

But the image dissolved, like sea foam washing away on the shore. In its place was the gray stillness of the apartment and the weight of the choices she'd made.

Eighteen

It started with coffee. Just coffee, she had told herself. A simple, neutral meeting to talk things through, to see if the distance between them was something they might be able to cross. But one coffee turned into dinner the following week. Dinner became a weekend movie night, and before she knew it, she was there again—back in Dan's meticulously neat apartment, unpacking her toothbrush and telling herself this was the right thing to do. Familiarity. Comfort. Predictability. Those were the things she had been chasing, weren't they?

And yet, sitting here now, poking at lasagna on a plate from Mario's, she couldn't shake the hollow feeling that had lodged itself deep in her. She was back with Dan, but part of her felt like she had left herself behind somewhere else entirely.

"You still like the lasagna from Mario's, right?" Dan asked, glancing over with a small, comfortable smile. "We always used to order it."

Harper forced a smile, nodding as she took a bite. "Yeah ... it's still good." The words felt as bland as the food. She chewed slowly, telling herself she was tired and that adjusting back to normal life after her sabbatical was bound to feel strange.

Dan chuckled softly, setting his fork down. "Do you remember the first time we tried Mario's? You spilled red sauce all over that off-white top you loved so much. You were so mad at me for laughing about it."

Harper blinked, the memory rising in her mind: sitting in the cramped little restaurant, laughing awkwardly while blotting at the stain with club soda. At the time, she'd been equally frustrated and amused by Dan's teasing grin.

"Yeah," she said lightly, giving a small laugh. "I think I ended up throwing that shirt away."

"You were so upset." Dan's smile widened, his voice warm with nostalgia. "But you were cute, too. You kept insisting it was my fault because I bumped the table."

Harper smiled politely, but the warmth in his tone didn't quite reach her. The memory should have evoked fondness, a sense of connection, maybe even a little joy, but it didn't. Instead, it felt flat and distant, like she was watching it through a fogged window.

Dan turned back to the TV, still smiling to himself. "I figured, why mess with a good thing, right?"

"Right ... why mess with it?" Harper murmured, her words automatic. But inside, something twisted. The monotonous routine—the same takeout, the same show, the same comforting silence—felt suffocating. This was safety, wasn't it? Exactly what she'd once thought she wanted.

Dan glanced at her, his brow creasing slightly. "You sure you're okay? You seem a little ... off tonight."

Harper forced a smile. "I'm fine. Just tired."

He hesitated, his fingers brushing the edge of his plate. "It's just ... you've seemed tired a lot lately." His voice was softer, almost cautious as if testing the waters.

"I guess it's just work," Harper murmured, forcing the words out as she avoided his eyes.

Dan nodded slowly, his fingers tapping lightly against the plate. He opened his mouth as if to say something, but stopped, his jaw tightening. Instead, he turned back to the TV, carefully resuming his meal.

Harper caught the subtle drop of his shoulders, a silent plea in the way his lips pressed together. It was as if he was waiting for her to return to him, to return to the version of herself he remembered. Frustration swiftly followed a pang of guilt. She didn't know how to bridge the space between them—and she wasn't sure she wanted to.

There was an almost imperceptible sigh as he returned his focus to the TV, his face again calm, composed, perfectly familiar. But something unguarded remained—a small crack in a wall she hadn't known was there.

It made her wonder, for a moment, if he was feeling trapped too.

She studied his profile in the soft glow of the TV. His face was calm, his attention fully absorbed in the storyline unfolding on the screen. There was no tension between them, no discomfort ... and no spark. She searched her memory, trying to recall the last time she'd felt a genuine thrill in his presence. Perhaps that was stability: knowing each other so well, the silence felt fine. Maybe this was what she'd been trying to return to.

And yet, part of her couldn't help but compare this moment to those wild, unguarded nights she'd spent with Aidan, laughing until her sides hurt, feeling his touch leave trails of warmth and excitement on her skin. The memory rose unbidden, an unwelcome reminder of a version of herself that felt light-years away from this living room.

Her mind drifted to the work she'd been doing lately. Every day, she delivered exactly what her clients wanted: safe, predictable campaigns that didn't challenge or excite her. The days bled together in a repetitive cycle of work, each one a paler reflection of the previous.

She looked back at Dan, wondering if he got it or was just saying what she wanted to hear. Racking her brain, she couldn't remember when they'd last had a genuine, substantial conversation.

After dinner, Dan stood, stacking his plate on top of hers before heading to the kitchen. Harper stayed on the couch, her legs curled under her, absently scrolling through her phone. The familiar sounds of dishes clinking and water running barely registered—just another piece of a routine she knew by heart.

Dan reappeared, passing through on his way to the bedroom. At the doorway, he hesitated, his hand resting on the frame, caught in a moment of quiet indecision.

"I'm heading to bed," he said, his voice laced with hesitation. He glanced at her, his lips parting like he wanted to say more. For a fleeting second, he looked almost vulnerable, like he was about to ask her to come with him. But then his fingers twitched against the doorframe, and whatever he had been about to say slipped away.

"Goodnight," he said instead, his tone neutral but tinged with something Harper couldn't quite name.

"Goodnight," Harper replied automatically, barely looking up from her phone.

Dan stood there a beat longer, hesitation woven into the silence. It felt like he was waiting—for a word, a gesture, a sign that the distance between them could still be crossed. But when Harper didn't move, he nodded to himself, almost imperceptibly, and turned away.

She heard the soft creak of the bedroom door as it closed behind him, and the apartment seemed to grow quieter, heavier in his absence. A trace of guilt surfaced, light and passing, but it slipped away just as easily, leaving only the weight of everything unspoken.

She sank into the couch, wrapping the blanket tighter around her shoulders. She didn't know if she wanted him to say something or if the space he was giving her was exactly what she needed. Or maybe she just didn't want to think about it at all.

Her phone buzzed, jolting her out of her thoughts. Paige's name flashed on the screen, and Harper smiled despite herself. It had been weeks, but seeing her name again felt like a familiar hand reaching through the distance.

"Paige!" Harper answered, her voice lifting.

"Harper! Oh my God, it's been forever!" Paige's voice sparkled with energy. "How's life in the big city?"

Harper forced a cheerful tone. "It's ... good. Same old routine, you know. Work's keeping me busy."

"Same old, huh?" Paige teased. "That sounds ... safe." Her voice had humor, but Harper caught a thread of understanding beneath it.

Harper hesitated. "Yeah. Safe."

"But enough about me," she added quickly. "What about you? How's Brody?"

"Oh, Harper, it's insane," Paige gushed. "We're actually talking about moving in together! It's like one big adventure with him; I'm always surprised, and I love that feeling."

Harper's heart twisted, equal parts happiness for her friend and envy. "That's ... amazing, Paige. I'm so happy for you."

"And you deserve the same, Harp," Paige said gently. "Don't settle for the illusion of 'safety.' You deserve someone who makes you feel alive."

Harper's throat tightened, and she laughed softly, hoping Paige wouldn't hear the strain beneath it. "Yeah ... maybe. We'll see." She hated how hollow her words sounded, how small they felt against the certainty in Paige's voice.

They chatted longer, sharing memories from the cruise and laughing about the antics of their fellow passengers. But even as Harper laughed along, she felt a growing hollowness settling in her. Each story and memory felt like a distant echo, a reminder of a version of herself she could barely touch anymore. The woman who'd danced barefoot under the stars, kissed Aidan with abandon, felt the thrill of possibility humming in her veins ... that woman felt like a stranger now.

After they hung up, Harper sat silently, staring at her phone's screen until it faded to black. The apartment around her felt dim and heavy, the quiet pressing down like a weight. She thought of Paige's laughter, of the way her friend's voice had shimmered with excitement and purpose, as if life were something to be seized and savored, not merely endured.

A surge of restlessness rose, sharp and insistent. She recalled Aidan's intense look, a feeling of profound understanding and a newfound vibrancy she hadn't known she craved. She remembered the nights they'd spent together, the freedom and thrill that had pulsed between them like a heartbeat. It was reckless. It was intense. But it felt real.

And now, sitting here in this quiet apartment, Harper felt the absence of that thrill like a dull ache. She glanced toward the bedroom's closed door, where Dan was already asleep. Dan, who was kind, dependable, and safe. Dan, who would never surprise her, never challenge her, never make her feel as if her life were anything other than a predictable series of days stretching into the future.

But yet, she desired more.

Stability was supposed to be her anchor, the thing she had been searching for—so long as she didn't let herself drift from it again. Dan is a safe harbor. But as she sat alone in the living room, Paige's words echoed: *Don't settle for the illusion of safety.*

A tiny, defiant voice stirred, whispering that perhaps safe wasn't enough. Perhaps she wanted more than predictability, routines, muted colors, and the unassuming comfort of "normal."

But she pushed the thought away, telling herself she was being foolish and unrealistic. Life wasn't a vacation in the Caribbean. Real life was practical, responsible, and steady. And Dan, with his neatly arranged apartment, steady job, and careful plans, was everything she was supposed to want—everything she'd once convinced herself she wanted.

Harper curled tighter on the couch, wrapping the blanket around herself as if she could ward off the creeping sense of dissatisfaction. She tried to convince herself that this was enough, that she could be content with this version of "safe." But the hollow feeling persisted, gnawing at the edges of her resolve, whispering that perhaps "normal" had become a prison she'd willingly walked back into.

The night stretched on, the apartment silent, as Harper sat there, caught between the weight of her choices and the faint, persistent pull of something more.

Harper slipped into bed beside Dan, careful not to disturb him. He'd already fallen asleep, his breathing deep and even, his face turned away from her. She lay on her back, staring at the ceiling, her hands folded on her stomach. The room was silent, save for the faint hum of traffic from the street below, but the silence felt heavy, almost suffocating.

Dan was always a constant and reliable presence in her life. She used to find comfort in his quiet company, knowing that he was beside her, offering stability. But stability required effort, and maybe, in her search for something more, she had neglected what was already hers. Now, instead of reassurance, his presence felt oppressive, like a shadow creeping in. They hadn't even kissed goodnight. No lingering touches, no whispered words before bed. Just the familiar stillness of two people sharing a bed but living separate lives.

She closed her eyes, telling herself that this was what she'd wanted. Stability. Security. A relationship she could rely on, something that didn't shift beneath her feet. She'd craved the calm that Dan brought into her life, the promise of a steady and secure future.

Don't settle for the illusion of 'safety,' Paige's words echoed in her mind, refusing to let go. The spark of restlessness they'd ignited was still there, flickering like a pilot light waiting to catch.

As long as she stayed with Dan, she had security. A stable job. A home. The New York life she had spent years working toward.

It was everything she had planned for. *So why does this feel like something is missing?*

Dan's soft breaths lulled her, yet her thoughts returned to Aidan, to the joy of his laughter and the revitalizing warmth of his presence, a feeling she hadn't known in years. She could almost feel his hand in hers, how he'd looked at her as if she were fascinating, someone worth knowing deeply. That memory tugged at her, an ache she couldn't quite shake. It had just been a vacation, she reminded herself. Just a week of sun and freedom and wild possibility. An illusion, she insisted, trying to force the thought away.

But the ache remained ... stubborn and insistent.

Harper took a slow, deep breath, trying to steady herself. But as she lay in the dark, she couldn't escape the quiet, unsettling truth pressing on her: Dan was supposed to feel like shelter. So why did it feel like she was slowly suffocating?

Nineteen

Harper sat at her desk, staring blankly at her computer screen. Her office's muted tones and sterile neatness felt more like a cage than the creative haven she'd once envisioned. Years ago, she'd dreamed of crafting bold, inspiring campaigns. Now, every client request blurred together: polished, predictable, and utterly dull.

She skimmed through her emails, each one requesting the same safe ideas with no room for risk. They always greeted her pitches with polite nods and the inevitable refrain: "Let's stick with what we know works, Harper."

Her fingers hovered over the keyboard, her reflection faintly visible in the darkened screen. The spark she once had for her work had long since faded, leaving behind tired eyes and an emptiness she couldn't ignore. *When did I become this person?* The question settled in her chest like a stone.

Her eyes fell on her to-do list: finalize edits, review client notes, and prepare a report. Tasks that once gave her purpose now felt suffocating, their weight pressing down until she could barely breathe. *Is this what I moved to New York for?*

She sighed, glancing at the clock. Almost six. Dinner with Dan: predictable, quiet. Stable, she reminded herself. A stable job, a stable relationship, a stable life. This was supposed to be the dream. So why did it feel so heavy?

Her phone buzzed on the desk, cutting through the office's hum. She glanced at the screen, expecting a text from Dan confirming their dinner plans. Instead, another name appeared.

Aidan.

Her breath caught. His text was simple:

Aidan

> Hey … how's life?

Two words, casual and unassuming, but they stopped Harper in her tracks. It had been three months since the cruise, and she'd spent most of that time convincing herself Aidan was nothing more than a fleeting memory. Yet here he was, pulling her thoughts back to warm nights on the deck, his easy laughter, and that unspoken connection that made her feel truly seen.

Her thumb hovered over the keyboard. She wanted to tell him everything: how her job had dulled into a monotonous grind, how she felt trapped by the very life she once dreamed of, and how she missed the person she'd been when she was with him. But she stopped herself. Aidan didn't belong in this world of muted offices, endless deadlines, and predictable dinners with Dan. He was part of a different chapter, one that felt miles away from her current reality.

She typed a response, deleted it, tried again, and deleted that too. Finally, with a frustrated sigh, she locked her phone and slipped it into her bag. But his question lingered. *How's life?*

Harper looked around her office, noticing the carefully arranged furniture and spotless desk. This was the life she'd worked so hard to build: a steady relationship, a polished career, the New York dream she'd once longed for. Yet it all felt hollow. The fire that once fueled her had flickered out. And Aidan's text made her see it clearly.

She needed something more than safe.

The clock struck six, pulling her back to the present. She grabbed her bag and coat, heading to meet Dan for dinner at their usual spot. Stability is good, she reminded herself. This is the life you chose.

But Aidan's words stayed with her as she walked toward the elevator. *How's life?*

By the time she pushed open the door to the small Italian restaurant, she understood—she needed something new to bring back her joy. The dim lighting and warm wood tones, once comforting, now seemed like a reminder of how predictable everything had become. Mario's had been their spot for years, but the excitement of those early dates had long since faded into routine.

Harper found Dan at their usual table, eyes fixed on his phone, his expression blank. The moment he noticed her, he set it aside and gave her a polite, practiced smile.

"You're right on time," he said as she slid into the seat across from him, draping her coat over the back of her chair.

"Yeah, traffic wasn't too bad," Harper replied, picking up the menu, even though she knew it by heart. For years, they frequented

Mario's, finding solace in the predictable comfort of their favorite lasagna and linguine.

Looking up from his menu, Dan spoke to her casually but distantly. "So, how was work today? Busy as usual?"

"Yeah. Same old," she said with a faint shrug. "Nothing exciting, just the usual rounds of meetings and emails."

He nodded, looking back down at his menu. "Well, at least it's stable, right? Nice to have some consistency."

She forced a smile. "Right. Consistency is ... good."

There was a lull in the conversation, the kind that had been creeping in more often. Harper glanced around the dimly lit restaurant, noticing the other couples sharing quiet laughs or leaning close over candle-lit tables. She and Dan, in contrast, sat like two people playing assigned roles, going through motions they'd rehearsed a hundred times before.

Dan cleared his throat, setting down his menu. "I think I'm going to try the chicken parm tonight."

Harper looked up, startled by the break in routine. "Not the lasagna?"

He gave her a small, self-conscious smile like he was testing the waters. "I thought ... you know, something different might be nice. Shake things up a little."

"Oh," she said, trying to summon enthusiasm but unable to muster more than a polite nod. "That sounds ... good."

Dan leaned back in his chair, folding his hands together. "You should try something different, too. They have a risotto special tonight. I remember you said you liked risotto when we went to that place in Brooklyn ... a while ago."

Harper hesitated, glancing at the menu she hadn't bothered to open. "Maybe," she murmured, her fingers absently twisting the napkin in her lap.

Dan's smile faltered slightly, though he recovered quickly, lifting his water glass and taking a sip. "Just thought it could be fun to change things up, you know? A little variety never hurt anyone."

She forced a small smile. "Right. Variety."

But the word felt distant, as if it belonged to someone else. Across the room, couples leaned in close, laughter bubbling between them, hands reaching for each other instinctively. She and Dan weren't like that. They were comfortable, familiar, predictable. And maybe that was exactly the problem.

Harper's attention shifted back to Dan, who was now scrolling through his phone, absently flicking his thumb across the screen. He looked up, as if sensing her eyes on him. "What?" he asked lightly, though a faint crease in his brow gave him away.

"Nothing," she said quickly, shaking her head and looking away.

But it wasn't nothing. A wave of frustration bubbled up, sudden and unexpected. *Is this it?* she thought, staring across the table at Dan, his face familiar but distant, like a photo she'd seen too many times to still feel anything for. She knew every line, every expression, every phrase he would use. There was comfort in that, she supposed. But sitting here, listening to him talk about risotto and chicken parm like they were the answer, she felt a pang of something close to grief.

He was trying. She could see that. Switching up his dinner order ... it was an effort. A small one, but an effort nonetheless. But it was like adding a single drop of water to a well that had already run dry.

Harper inhaled sharply, something rebellious stirring inside her. Dan, still scrolling through his phone, didn't notice.

Before she could second-guess herself, she reached across the table, taking his hand and pulling him closer. Dan looked up, surprised, just as she leaned in—a kiss meant to shake them both from their slumber, to remind them that once, long ago, this had been something alive.

His lips felt warm but hesitant, responding gently rather than eagerly. When she pulled back, he looked at her with quiet confusion. "What was that for?"

Harper swallowed, the spark fading, replaced by a deep, aching emptiness. "I don't know," she said softly, managing a faint, sad smile. "I just ... thought it might help."

Dan chuckled awkwardly, reaching for his water glass. "Help with what?"

Her eyes dropped to the table, the truth settling over her like a heavy fog. She swallowed, then lifted her eyes to his. "Dan ... what are we doing?"

He blinked, his expression shifting. "Having dinner?"

Her lips pressed together, and she shook her head, her voice low and heavy. "No, I mean ... what are we doing?"

Dan's realization shifted as he leaned back in his chair, exhaling slowly. "Oh."

The noise of the restaurant dulled, fading beneath the reality of unspoken truths. Dan stared at the table momentarily, his fingers tracing the edge of his napkin. "I don't know," he said finally. "I guess I thought we were just ... staying the course. Being comfortable."

Harper nodded faintly. "Comfortable. Yeah. But is that enough? Are we enough?"

Dan sighed, his shoulders slumping slightly. "I thought so. Isn't that what long-term relationships are supposed to be? You find a rhythm, and you build routines. It's ... safe."

The word landed between them like a stone. Safe. It was what she had always relied on, what had made life feel steady and predictable. And maybe that was the problem. Safe had been so easy, so unquestioned, that she had let it lull her into complacency. She had neglected them, assuming they would always just be. But now, she knew what it felt like to want—to crave something that lit a fire inside her.

She swallowed hard. "But what if it's not enough?" she asked softly, almost to herself. "What if safe feels ... empty?"

Dan looked at her then, and for the first time in months, his guarded calm cracked, revealing a flicker of sadness. "I had a feeling," he admitted, his voice quiet. I guess I was hoping it was a phase—that you'd ... settle back in."

Harper's throat tightened. "I tried. I thought that if I returned to normal, everything would feel right again. But it doesn't, Dan. It just doesn't."

He nodded slowly, his eyes dropping to the table. "I don't want to be someone you stay with just because it's comfortable. You deserve more than that."

She reached across the table, resting her hand on his. "You weren't just comfortable—you were my constant, my safety. But maybe ... maybe that's not enough anymore. Maybe we're not enough."

Dan's eyes lifted to hers, his expression filled with a bittersweet understanding. He gave her hand a gentle squeeze. "Maybe we're both holding on because it's familiar. Because it's what we thought we were supposed to want."

Harper felt something shift inside her, like the final piece of a puzzle clicking into place. That was it. She had spent so long convincing herself that stability was the same as happiness, that love was measured in routine and reliability. And for a while, maybe it had been enough. But now, she knew better. Love wasn't just something you settled into—it was something that set you on fire. Something that made you feel alive.

Harper felt a wave of clarity settle over her, a sense of certainty that had eluded her for so long. "I think it's time I start being honest with myself," she said, her voice steady despite the ache in her chest. "I've been trying to fit back into this life, but ... I don't think it's what I really want anymore."

Dan studied her, the sadness in his eyes shifting into something almost proud. "Good for you, Harper. Really. You deserve to find what makes you feel ... whole."

She felt a mixture of sadness and gratitude, and she gave him a small, wistful smile. "Thank you. For everything."

For never making her feel unsafe. For giving her a place to land when she needed one. For being the kind of love she thought she needed—until she learned she needed more.

Dan stood, and after a quiet beat, he pulled her into a hug. They didn't fight or drag it out; there was nothing left to say. Just the quiet, mutual understanding that this was right.

"Take care of yourself, okay?" Dan said, his voice warm and affectionate.

"You too," Harper replied softly. "Goodbye, Dan."

Stepping outside, Harper was met by the warm embrace of the summer night. The city buzzed around her—the hum of traffic, laughter drifting from sidewalk cafes, and the distant melody of a street performer. A warm breeze played with her hair, and she stood still, letting the sounds and movement flow through her, as if waiting for something to take shape.

She pulled out her phone to call a cab, imagining herself heading to Cierra's apartment for the night. Her phone buzzed just as she was about to get in the vehicle.

She froze as her phone illuminated. A message from Paige filled her screen: a photo of Paige and Brody, beaming in front of a mountain backdrop. Paige proudly displayed her new engagement ring, a stunning sparkler, on her raised hand. The caption read:

Paige

> I said YES!! Can you believe it?!

Harper felt a rush of happiness, a warmth of pride in Paige's bravery, and a flicker of her own exhilaration. Paige had gone after what she wanted with her whole heart. Harper stared at the photo for a moment, her lips curving into a smile. She typed out a quick reply:

Harper

> Congrats, Paige! So happy for you. You deserve this.

Harper thought of Paige and Brody, who had fallen into each other like they'd been waiting their whole lives to meet. Three months later, they were still going strong. Meanwhile, Harper felt like she'd been treading water, stuck in a life she didn't recognize.

Looking back at the cab, Harper hesitated. She could picture herself sitting in the quiet car, heading straight to Cierra's apartment, but the thought felt stifling. She stepped back, lifting her hand to wave the driver off. "Never mind, I'm going to walk."

She needed to move, to walk, to let the city remind her of why she'd come here in the first place.

Adjusting her bag on her shoulder, Harper set off toward Cierra's. She was just gonna stay there until she could get her own place, a new beginning to build her own life. She'd text Dan tomorrow to arrange to pick up her things, but tonight was about something other than loose ends. Tonight was about moving forward.

The city pulsed with a vibrancy Harper hadn't felt in years. She let herself sink into its rhythm—the low murmur of voices, the chime of clinking glasses, the warm flow of music drifting through open doors. With every step, something inside her loosened. She thought of Paige's unfiltered joy, the fearless way she had chased what she wanted, and Harper felt the spark of that same courage flicker inside her.

Stopping at a crosswalk, Harper tilted her face toward the sky. City lights blocked the stars, but their presence was strong. The part of her that yearned for excitement—not just security—was finally breaking free.

She didn't know exactly what lay ahead, but she wasn't afraid of the unknown. And that was exhilarating.

With the city buzzing around her and the warm summer air on her skin, Harper walked forward into the night, her heart wide open to whatever came next.

Twenty

The conference room was oppressively quiet, and the soft hum of the projector was the only sound as another slide flickered onto the wall. Beyond the glass walls, the hum of the office carried faintly—phones ringing, keyboards clicking, and snippets of muted conversations. Overhead, fluorescent lights cast a pale, artificial glow, making the gray interior feel even colder.

Harper sat at the head of the table, her notebook and pen neatly placed in front of her, surrounded by the faint but familiar aroma of stale coffee. Around her, the team shifted in their chairs—Jason rubbed his temples, his face etched with exhaustion. At the same time, Sarah, the junior designer, flipped through a stack of sketches, her movements sluggish and resigned.

On the screen, a pastel-colored logo floated cheerfully above the tagline: **Adventure Starts Here!** It was the campaign for Trailblaze, a hiking and camping brand meant to inspire people to connect with nature. However, the projected images of sanitized backyard camping and smiling families felt strangely lifeless. Adventure, packaged in pastels.

Harper cleared her throat. "Alright, let's walk through the campaign. 'Family Adventure' is broken into three themes: Beginner's Bliss, Weekenders, and Backyard Explorers. Each one targets families looking for simple, approachable outdoor experiences."

Jason snorted, slouching deeper in his chair. "So ... people who like thinking they're outdoorsy but never actually leave their driveways."

Harper shot him a sharp look, but said nothing. Sarah quietly clicked to the next slide, revealing social media concepts: pristine campsites, immaculate tents, and slogans like 'Find Your Adventure ... Close to Home!' and 'Take the First Step (But Just One!).' She winced, her hand hesitating over the mouse.

Harper felt the weight of their frustration pressing against her. "This is what the client wants," she said, her voice tighter than intended. "Something accessible. Family-friendly."

Jason's usual sarcasm was laced with weariness. "And not remotely exciting."

Sarah spoke softly, her eyes fixed on the table. "My ideas focused on creating a gritty visual style, featuring muddy boots, rain-soaked trails, and the raw feel of the wilderness. They said it was 'too rugged.' Too intimidating for the average consumer."

Harper's eyes drifted to the glass wall, where Sam, her boss, stood laughing with another team. He thrived on delivering precisely what clients expected. Nothing risky, nothing bold. She turned back to her team, her own frustration smoldering.

"Look, I know this isn't what we wanted," she began, the words dragging as she spoke. "But this is what they asked for. Safe sells."

Jason's pen dropped to the table with a clatter. "Yeah, but do we have to treat the outdoors like an IKEA catalog? This is an adventure brand. Shouldn't we actually be selling adventure?"

Harper opened her mouth to respond but stopped, the spark of something unfamiliar. She looked over Sarah's sketches again—the raw, untamed energy of boots sinking into mud, of hikers grinning through storms. She thought of the excitement that first drew her into advertising, the thrill of creating something that moved people. That spark flared, sharp and undeniable.

She leaned forward, her voice steady. "Let's do it both ways."

Jason and Sarah froze, their heads snapping up. "What?" Jason asked, the word laced with suspicion.

"Two versions," Harper said, her voice gaining momentum. We'll give them the squeaky-clean campaign they want. But we're also going to create something bold. Raw, honest, untamed. The campaign that makes people feel adventure."

Sarah blinked, the edges of her frown easing. "You mean ... actually show them what's possible?"

"Yes." Harper nodded, her tone firmer now. "No constraints. Sarah, I want you to take the lead. Mud on boots, rain-soaked trails, wild colors. Push it as far as you can."

Jason leaned forward, a grin spreading across his face. "Now that's what I'm talking about."

The energy in the room shifted, the tension melting away as Jason and Sarah exchanged excited glances. Jason scribbled ideas into his notebook, muttering slogans under his breath. At the same time, Sarah flipped to her sketches, her hands moving faster, her eyes brighter.

Harper watched them with quiet pride, the buzz of excitement filling her chest. This wasn't just about the client anymore. It wasn't even about the campaign. It was about taking risks and refusing to settle for safety.

Sam's laughter drifted into the room through the glass wall, oblivious to the quiet rebellion brewing inside. Harper didn't care. She felt like she was breaking free.

Harper closed the conference room door behind her, unable to hide her joyful demeanor as she walked back to her office. She felt an unfamiliar lightness in her step, a subtle buzz still running through her from the burst of energy in the meeting. Finally, she'd done something bold. She'd given her team permission to break free from the constraints smothering their creativity for weeks, and watching them come alive had reminded her why she'd gotten into advertising in the first place. This was the spark she'd been missing.

As Harper returned to her office after the meeting, she paused in the doorway, her eyes drawn to the bridesmaid dress hanging by the tall window. She'd picked it up during her lunch break, squeezing in a quick trip to her dry cleaners in between back-to-back client calls. Dusty pink and soft as a whisper, the dress looked oddly out of place in her otherwise professional, muted workspace.

As Harper leaned back in her chair, a rare lull in her workday, her phone lit up with Paige's name. Paige's calls were always energetic, starkly contrasting the carefully ordered chaos of Harper's office life.

"Paige!" Harper greeted. "I was just thinking about you. The dress is here, safe and sound."

"Oh, thank God!" Paige's voice practically sparkled. "Can you believe it, Harp? Two weeks! I'm getting married in two weeks!"

Harper laughed. "Are you in full bride-mode chaos yet?"

"Absolutely," Paige said, breathless. "But it's worth it. We're getting married, and it'll be amazing—everyone we love will be there. Nothing boring, nothing predictable."

Harper leaned back, her voice warm. "Okay, spill. What's the big plan?"

"A mountain lodge surrounded by red and gold trees," Paige said, her voice soft with excitement. "The ceremony will be outdoors, with leaves all over the place and pine scent in the air. It's like autumn come to life."

Harper closed her eyes, letting the vivid image bloom in her mind. "That sounds perfect, Paige."

"And the colors!" Paige continued. "Black and white with pops of red and pink. Just wait until you see it."

Paige's unrestrained happiness made Harper's heart flutter. Paige's boldness, fearlessness, and ability to create a life full of vibrancy and meaning made Harper's carefully controlled world feel even smaller.

Paige lowered her voice, conspiratorial now. "Guess who Brody's best man is?"

Harper froze. "Not ... Aidan?"

"Yes!" Paige squealed. "We met because of Aidan, so it's only right. He's practically the reason this wedding is happening."

Harper's breath caught. *Aidan.* Just the thought of him brought back laughter under the stars, the kind of effortless joy she hadn't felt since returning to New York. It wasn't quite true that Aidan had introduced Paige and Brody. But Paige was radiant, caught up in the moment, and Harper saw no reason to correct her.

The thought of seeing him again sent a rush of excitement through her, but it was tangled with something deeper—something closer to fear.

"Harper?" Paige's tone was laced with quiet concern. "You okay?"

"I'm fine," Harper said quickly, masking her emotions. "Just surprised, I guess. I hadn't thought about seeing him again."

"Well," Paige said gently, "I know that week meant something to both of you. Maybe this is your chance to reconnect."

Harper glanced at the bridesmaid dress hanging by the window, the soft pink fabric catching the fading light. It looked like an invitation to something unknown, a path she hadn't dared to walk since the cruise. The earlier spark of daring returned, this time a bit unsure but determined.

"Maybe," Harper murmured, her voice quieter now. "Right now, I'm just excited to celebrate with you. This is your big day."

Paige laughed, bright and joyful. "Trust me, Harp, this will be one for the books."

As the call ended, Harper stared at her phone, Paige's excitement still ringing in her ears. The contrast was undeniable—Paige ran toward what made her happy, while Harper, until recently, had spent years playing it safe, carefully avoiding anything that might shake the foundation of her predictable life.

Paige's words echoed in her mind: *Nothing boring, nothing predictable. Everything we love.*

Harper shifted with a quiet determination. Maybe it was time to stop clinging to safety and start chasing what truly made her feel alive.

As the office started to wind down for the evening, Harper noticed Sarah still at her desk, illuminated by her computer screen. She was hunched over her keyboard, focused in as she worked on the first mockups for the new pitch. Most of the team had already trickled out, but Sarah's focus remained unshaken.

Harper leaned on the edge of Sarah's desk, folding her arms with a small, encouraging smile. "Burning the midnight oil?"

Sarah glanced up, startled for a second, then relaxed, offering a quick smile. "Yeah, I just ... I really want to nail this. It's exciting to finally try something bold, you know?"

Harper nodded, feeling a surge of pride. "That's exactly why I wanted you to take the lead. You've got that spark, Sarah. You have an eye for detail and a fantastic sense of style. This project—it's your chance to really let loose. Show the client what you can do when you're not stuck following the usual formula."

She leaned forward, her voice steady with conviction. "I know we've pitched bold ideas before, only to have them shut down before we could even get started. But this time, we're not holding back. I want us to go all in—no second-guessing, no playing it safe. Let's show them what happens when we create without limits."

Sarah's face brightened slightly, but hesitation flickered in her expression. "I just ... I don't want to mess it up, you know? It's one thing to come up with ideas, but pitching them feels different. The client could reject the whole thing, and then ..." She trailed off, her fingers fidgeting with the edge of her notebook.

Harper reached out, placing a reassuring hand on Sarah's shoulder. "Listen, I've been there. I know how easy it is to let that fear hold you back, but don't give it too much power. We'll give them two options—safe and bold. If they want to play it safe, they'll have that.

But the bold version? That's where you can really shine. Don't hold back."

Sarah glanced down at her keyboard, her fingers tracing the keys absent mindedly. "It's been a long time since I've felt like I had permission to do something like this," she admitted softly. "I got used to following the formula. And sometimes I wonder if I even remember how to be bold."

Harper smiled knowingly. "I get it. This industry can grind you down, make you doubt yourself. But trust me, you've still got it in you. You just need to take the leap."

As she spoke, Harper felt her own words push down on her, like an echo of a lesson she hadn't yet fully embraced.

Sarah's eyes met Harper's, a spark of determination flickering behind the doubt. "Thanks, Harper. It means a lot that you believe in me."

"Believe in you?" Harper laughed softly. "Sarah, I see so much potential in you. This project—it's just the beginning. Swing for the fences. If there's ever a time to take a risk, it's now."

Sarah's smile started small but grew, lighting up her face with each passing word. Confidence replacing hesitation. "Okay. I'll do it. I'll give it everything I've got."

"That's what I like to hear." Harper gave her shoulder a supportive squeeze. "And hey, if the client doesn't appreciate what you bring to the table, that's on them. But I have a feeling you're going to blow them away."

Sarah nodded, her shoulders straightening as a newfound confidence settled in. "I'll make you proud, Harper."

"You already do," Harper said warmly. "Now go home, get some rest, and come back tomorrow ready to unleash that creativity. I want to see your wildest ideas on those mockups."

Sarah laughed, gathering her things and standing. "Alright, boss. Thanks again ... for everything."

Harper watched as Sarah's silhouette disappeared down the hallway, her steps lighter and more assured than when the day began. It was gratifying to see that spark rekindled, to know that taking risks could ignite something not just in others, but in herself too.

Leaning back in her chair, Harper's thoughts drifted to her call with Paige. Her friend's unrestrained excitement still buzzed in her ears.

Her fingers drifted to her phone. Paige's encouragement echoed in her mind as she scrolled to Aidan's name. His text history stared back at her, frozen in time—a conversation that had fizzled out months ago. Paige had mentioned he'd be at the wedding, but the thought of waiting two more weeks to see him made her restless. Should she reach out now?

She tapped into the blank text box, her thumb hovering over the screen. *What would I even say?* The cursor blinked, expectant and unrelenting. Her heart picked up speed as she considered her words, imagining his reaction. Would he welcome the message, or would it feel intrusive after all this time?

Then, three little dots appeared at the bottom of her screen.

Her breath hitched. Aidan was typing.

Butterflies erupted in her chest, her mind racing with possibilities. Was he thinking about her too? Wondering the same things she was? The idea that he might break the silence first filled her with a sudden thrill, her pulse quickening with anticipation.

And then the dots disappeared.

Harper stared at the screen, her excitement deflating as quickly as it flared. No message came through. She waited, but the silence stretched on.

Maybe he'd changed his mind, second-guessed himself the way she so often did. Or maybe he wasn't ready. The silence wasn't a rejection, but it left her suspended, unsure of where they stood.

With a sigh, she locked her phone and set it gently on the desk, taking a steadying breath. In two weeks, she reminded herself. She would see him at the wedding. Maybe then, face-to-face, they could say the things neither of them seemed able to put into words now.

Standing, Harper's eyes drifted to her desk one last time. The carefully stacked papers and spotless surfaces had once symbolized success, proof that she'd made it. Now, they felt like relics of a life that no longer fit.

Harper glanced at the clock on her computer. It was nearly seven, the office floor outside her door already quiet. She stretched, her chair creaking faintly, and looked back at the dress hanging by the window. She couldn't leave it here overnight—she needed to pack it when she got home, along with the rest of her things for Paige's wedding weekend.

With a sigh, she grabbed her phone and bag, then carefully draped the dress over her arm. The fabric whispered against her jacket as she headed for the elevator.

Twenty-One

Harper's apartment, still feeling more like a work-in-progress than a home, was in its usual state of semi-chaos. She'd moved in a couple of months ago after a short stay with Cierra, and though she loved the airy windows and cozy layout, she still hadn't fully settled. Her open suitcase spilled onto her bed, clothes draped over the footboard, and shoes and jewelry scattered around. She held up two dresses before her, debating which one to pack for Paige's rehearsal dinner. Just as she was about to toss one onto the "maybe" pile, her phone buzzed.

Helen. Perfect timing.

Harper hit the green button, putting her on speaker. "Hey! Just the person I need."

"Oh, good, because I'm definitely the person who can solve all your problems from my couch," Helen said, voice warm with its usual mix of sarcasm and sisterly affection. "What's going on?"

"Hold on," Harper said, fumbling to prop the phone up on her dresser. "I need eyes on this. Let me switch to video."

She tapped a few buttons, and suddenly, her sister's face appeared on the screen. She was lounging comfortably in her living room. Helen had piled her hair in a wildly messy bun, wrapped in a fuzzy purple robe, and held a **Best Mom Ever** mug in one hand.

Helen squinted at the screen, adjusting herself slightly. "Oh, look at you, New York glamour queen, with your big city wardrobe crisis."

Harper rolled her eyes, grinning. "Yes, because nothing says 'glamour' like a suitcase that won't close and me trying to figure out if I need three pairs of shoes or four."

Helen snorted, taking a sip from her mug. "Four, obviously. Just in case you break a heel doing something dramatic."

"Like running away from a wedding, I'm not even in?" Harper laughed, holding up a black dress in front of the phone. "Help me out here. I'm trying to decide what to wear to the rehearsal dinner."

Helen raised an eyebrow. "Why are you so nervous? It's not even your wedding, Harp."

"Funny," Harper replied, ducking into the bathroom to change. "I'm just ... excited. It'll be nice to see everyone, that's all."

There was a brief pause before Helen's voice drifted in, dripping with playful suspicion. "This wouldn't have anything to do with a certain someone being there, would it? You know, tall, dorky, and handsome?"

Harper reemerged in a plain black sheath dress, ignoring the flutter in her stomach. "This is not about Aidan," she insisted, smoothing the skirt. She turned for her sister to see.

"Uh-huh," Helen said, her eyes twinkling with amusement. "Sure, it's just a 'coincidence' that you're stressing over dresses right now ... Yeah, that one's a snooze-fest; it's way too work-appropriate. Next!"

Harper sighed, rolling her eyes but smiling as she returned to the bathroom. "We haven't even talked since the cruise, Helen. It was just a fling."

She could almost hear Helen's eyebrow go up over the phone. "A fling that you called me about the minute you got off the ship, swooning like a schoolgirl. 'He's so funny, Helen! And his laugh ...'"

"Okay, okay!" Harper laughed, reaching into her closet for the next option. "Fine, I may have been a little excited back then. But he's Brody's best man, and I'm Paige's bridesmaid, so it'll be nice to see him again. Nothing more."

Harper slipped into the deep sapphire-blue dress, the fabric hugging her curves and catching the light in an undeniably striking way. She adjusted the strap, then stepped back, catching her reflection in the mirror. The dress ignited a fleeting recollection of her cruise with Aidan, a romantic night they shared, dining and strolling the promenade beneath a star-filled sky, the vast ocean surrounding them.

As she smoothed down the dress, a memory surfaced, clear and sharp.

She could almost feel the warmth of his hand in hers, the way his thumb traced absentminded circles as they talked for hours under the stars. That night, they'd shared dreams and secrets, the quiet intensity of his eyes making her feel truly seen.

That night, flirtation turned to passion, leaving this glimmering sapphire dress pooled on the floor of his cabin.

The fabric was cool beneath her fingertips, but in her mind, it was warm—still carrying the ghost of his touch. Six months hadn't dulled the memory of that night, of the way he made her feel like she was the only thing in the world that mattered.

Helen's voice broke through, pulling her back. "Harper! Are you gonna show me the dress or admire yourself all night?"

Harper gave a little laugh, brushing off the flush of nostalgia that had crept up her cheeks. "Sorry! Got lost for a second." She stepped into view, doing a little twirl.

Helen's eyes widened when she saw the dress. "Oh my god, Harper, is that the same dress you wore on that fancy cruise dinner with Aidan?"

Harper froze. "Maybe ..."

"Oh, sure, it's totally not about him," Helen teased. "Wearing the exact same dress you had on for your date with him? Not suspicious at all, sis." She exaggeratingly winked. "Yeah, too much glitter would be a no-no. You don't want to outshine the bride."

Harper groaned. "You're probably right." She turned back toward the bathroom to try on her next option.

"So," Helen said as Harper slipped into a fun purple dress with a playful ruffle at the hem, "how's work going, anyway? Think you're ever going to tire of big-city life and move back home?"

Harper emerged in the purple dress, doing a little twirl. "If I moved home, you'd just make me babysit Channing every weekend," she joked, striking a mock pouty pose.

"Damn right I would," Helen laughed, but the sound carried a weariness Harper hadn't noticed before. "I'm just saying we all miss you around here. Mom and Dad would love to see you more. And, honestly, I could really use the help. Channing's three, a whirlwind of climbing, endless 'whys,' and a crumb-finding superpower I didn't know was possible. A lot of this stuff just ... falls to me."

Harper paused mid-turn, catching something unspoken in her sister's voice. Helen kept her tone light, but her words had an underlying heaviness: exhaustion that went beyond just chasing after a toddler.

"Still," Helen continued, her smile back in place as she waved her mug in the air, "I'm just saying it wouldn't be the worst thing in the world if you traded your glamorous big-city life for a quieter one with your adorable nephew as your sidekick."

Harper chuckled, glancing in the mirror to study the purple dress. It was cute, but ... it didn't feel quite right. "I know. I miss you guys, too. But I don't know if I'm ready to leave New York just yet."

"Not even if I promise you endless quality time with your favorite nephew?" Helen teased, but her tone was softer this time, as if she were offering Harper something she couldn't quite refuse.

Harper rolled her eyes, heading back to try on her last option. "Tempting, but I'll hold out a little longer."

"Fine, fine, stay in the big city," Helen replied with an exaggerated sigh. "Don't forget, Harp, it's Mom and Dad's anniversary next month? We're still going in on a gift together ... yes?"

"Of course! We'll figure something out," Harper called from the bathroom. She slipped into the last option, a stunning emerald-green dress, its cut hugging her waist and flaring slightly at her hips. The fabric shimmered subtly and showed just the right amount of skin. She stepped out, looking at her reflection—feeling good.

Helen's jaw dropped on the screen. "Harp. That's the one."

Harper turned to give her sister the full view. "You think?"

"Oh, I know," Helen said, nodding firmly. "It's sexy, but still classy. That color really makes your eyes stand out! Plus, if a certain someone notices ... well, let's just say you won't be disappointed."

Harper blushed, but she couldn't hide her smile. "Alright, alright. Green it is." She headed back to the bathroom to change, hearing Helen's laughter echo through the phone.

As she slipped out of the dress, Helen's voice floated through the speaker, rich with knowing amusement. "And don't forget to pack some, you know ... sexy lingerie. Just in case."

Harper gasped, clutching the dress to her chest. "Helen! Do you talk like that in front of Channing?"

Helen laughed. "He's three, he won't remember. Come on, you know I'm right. Go for it. You might be grateful in the end."

Harper shook her head, chuckling as she folded the green dress into her suitcase. "Fine, maybe I'll bring something a little ... special. But it's only because I want to feel confident, not because I'm planning on, you know, anything."

"Uh-huh. Keep telling yourself that, sis." Helen's voice was teasing, but her tone shifted more sincere. "Seriously, though ... Aidan sounds like a good guy, based on everything you've told me. Are you really okay with just letting that go?"

Her fingers lingered on the suitcase, memories unfurling like a slow-burning flame. Aidan's smirk, the playful challenge in his eyes, the way he'd drawn her in without hesitation. Their nights together had been intoxicating, filled with whispered promises and the kind of passion that left her breathless.

But then reality had set back in. Returning to New York, her job, and Dan, she attempted to persuade herself that her life was perfectly alright.

"Helen ... I don't know," she admitted, finally. "It was such a ... surreal week, you know? And I haven't seen him or talked to him since. What if he's moved on?"

"Well, there's only one way to find out," Helen said, her voice warm and encouraging. "Sometimes you have to take a leap, Harp. See where you land."

Harper zipped her suitcase shut, amusement playing in her expression. "Yeah. Maybe you're right."

Silence settled, comfortable and unspoken, bridging the miles that separated them, holding them together.

Then Helen broke the silence with a laugh. "And hey, if it doesn't work out, you can always come home and be the world's best aunt. I'll even let you borrow my Best Mom Ever mug."

Harper laughed, rolling her eyes. "Oh, lucky me! The ultimate prize."

"Hey, don't knock it till you've tried it. Besides, you'd look cute pushing a stroller around Myrtle Beach."

"Stop," Harper said, but she was smiling. She took a deep breath, as a restless energy swirled inside her, caught between eagerness and hesitation.

"Alright, go pack your fancy underwear and get some sleep. You're going to have an amazing weekend," Helen said with a warmth in her voice that only a sister could manage.

"Thanks, Helen. Love you."

"Love you too, sis. Go knock 'em dead—and bring me back some juicy stories!"

Harper ended the call, looking around her apartment with a new clarity. She thought back to the whirlwind months after her second breakup, moving from Cierra's pull-out couch to this space that now felt like hers. The apartment wasn't perfect yet—half-finished touches and unpacked boxes hinted at the transition still in progress. But it represented a fresh start, a space that finally felt like hers.

And now, another potential fresh start loomed on the horizon—one that had nothing to do with furniture or paint colors. More than a wedding weekend, it felt like an opportunity to break free from the past and find her true self. A chance to leap, and maybe, just maybe, finally catch the life she'd been holding back from.

She would not let the opportunity pass her by—not this time.

Twenty-Two

I f Harper smoothed the front of her dress one more time, Paige was going to swat her hand away.

"Would you relax?" her friend teased, nudging her with an elbow. "It's a wedding, not a battlefield."

Harper exhaled, forcing a small laugh. She knew she was being ridiculous. She'd been to several weddings, and yet, as she scanned the cozy ballroom, her nerves prickled with something unfamiliar. It wasn't the setting or the crowd.

It was the knowledge that Aidan was somewhere in this room.

She hadn't seen him since the cruise, hadn't allowed herself to linger on the way he'd made her feel. At least, not consciously. But in the quiet hours of the night, her mind always seemed to return to those quiet conversations under the stars, the ease of being around him, the spark that had felt so real. But she'd convinced herself to leave those memories in the past. After all, they'd each returned to their separate lives, jobs, and routines that had nothing to do with moonlit conversations or whispered secrets.

And yet, standing here tonight, she couldn't shake the feeling that maybe those memories weren't content to stay buried.

A ripple of excitement moved through the ballroom as Brody entered, the groom's arrival drawing cheers and applause.

But Harper? Her attention was elsewhere.

Her focus was locked on Aidan.

He was just as she remembered—yet there was something different now, something rooted in the way he carried himself. His suit fit him perfectly, broad shoulders filling out the sleek cut, his hair perfectly undone in that effortlessly confident way. His eyes moved through the room, scanning faces, searching. And Harper found herself holding her breath, waiting to be the one he found.

The urge to slip into the background gripped her, just until her pulse steadied. But she'd spent too much time stepping aside. Tonight, she wanted to celebrate Paige. To stay present. To let herself feel something real.

She steadied herself, shoulders squaring as their eyes met. His face lit up, a slow, easy smile spreading. He moved toward her, unhurried but intentional. She could feel a magnetic pull—subtle but undeniable—as if gravity itself was pulling him closer.

"Aidan," she greeted, her voice cracking. The sparkle in his eyes told her he remembered it all.

"Harper," he replied, his voice rough, like he was holding back emotions. He paused, almost reaching out to touch her, as if needing to feel her there.

"You look ... amazing," he added, a little breathless. There was something raw and unfiltered about him that made her heart do a flip.

She felt a flush rise in her cheeks. "Thanks," she said, laughing softly to hide her nerves. "You're not looking too bad yourself."

They shared a quick laugh, and the tension eased a little, though Harper could still feel it humming under the surface. It was as if all the unsaid things, the moments they'd left unfinished, waited to be acknowledged.

After a beat, Aidan gestured to a quieter corner. "Want to catch up for a bit?"

She nodded, her pulse kicking up. Together, they drifted from the crowd, finding a secluded alcove at the edge of the ballroom. A wall sconce illuminated a pair of comfortable chairs, crafting a space that felt like a quiet retreat from the lively party.

"It's good to see you," she began, her voice sincere. "It's been ... a while."

"Yeah ... it has. And I've been wondering ..." He paused, his eyes searching hers. "I guess I just wondered how you've been after ... you know."

Harper glanced down, her fingers brushing against her dress. "Well," she started slowly, "it's been ... a strange few months. I went back to New York and got back together with Dan." She looked up, observing his reaction. There was a hint of disappointment, or maybe sadness, in his eyes. "But that didn't last," she added, a hint of humor. "Turns out ... I was just comfortable. Not happy."

The words felt heavier than she'd expected. Saying them out loud made her realize she'd been settling and using comfort as an excuse.

Her voice softened. "Actually ... it ended the night you sent that text. 'Hey, how's life?'" She chuckled, shaking her head. "It sounds silly, but it kind of jolted me awake. Made me realize I was trying to go back to something that didn't fit anymore."

Aidan's shoulders tensed, his eyes dipping downward for a beat. "Harper ... I didn't know."

She shrugged, offering a small, self-deprecating smile. "Neither did I. I think ... sometimes we don't realize what's wrong until something outside us reminds us of what we're missing."

"Ever since the cruise," he murmured, his voice low, "I haven't been able to shake this feeling that something's missing. Like I had a glimpse of something real, something alive, and then it was just ... gone."

Harper felt a pang of recognition, understanding his words all too well. "Is it the freedom?" she asked gently. "Or just the change of scenery?"

He let out a light laugh. "Maybe both. Or maybe it's the realization that I could feel ... I don't know ... more alive. That there's a world outside of Murphy's and Charlotte."

Harper's fingers traced the rim of her glass, a wistful smile playing on her lips. "The cruise had a way of making things feel different, didn't it?"

"Yeah," he murmured. "But sometimes I wonder if it was real or just some dream we all had together."

She shook her head, reaching out impulsively to place a hand on his arm. "It was real. For me, at least. Maybe just a different version of real than what we're used to."

Aidan's eyes lowered to where her hand met his arm, his breath hitching just slightly. She felt a strange, comforting sensation in the contact, a reminder of their shared connection that had never really faded.

"I'm glad we're here together this weekend," she said, breaking the silence. Her words felt charged with a depth she couldn't quite explain.

"Me too," he replied. "More than you know."

They remained in their isolated space, content to be near each other, the hum of the wedding rehearsal nothing more than background noise. Harper could feel her pulse steadying, as if something long buried was finally starting to make sense.

Just then, Paige waved to them from across the room, her face alight with joy. Aidan noticed and nudged Harper gently. "Looks like we're being summoned."

Harper laughed softly. "Looks like it. Meet the parents?"

Aidan grinned. "Guess we're getting the full wedding experience."

Before they moved, though, he paused, turning back to her. "Hey, before we go ..." He took a breath, his eyes locking onto hers. "Can we promise to spend some more time together this weekend? Really catch up?"

A smile spread across Harper's face. "I'd like that. Let's make it happen."

Harper returned to the crowd, the fire's crackle and scent of pine encompassed the room as candlelight danced against rough-hewn beams. And yet, the quiet thrill of Aidan's presence remained.

She was caught up mingling with a bridesmaid when a gentle hand touched her elbow. She turned, surprised to see none other than Maude standing beside her, her face alight with that familiar, serene smile.

"Maude!" Harper exclaimed, her surprise melting into delight as she leaned in for a quick hug. "I didn't expect to see you here."

"Well, Paige and Brody insisted," Maude said, her presence effortless, as if fate had simply placed her here at just the right time. "And I'm never one to turn down an invitation from my favorite cruise kids."

Harper shook her head. "Of course they did. That sounds exactly like something Paige would do. They really seem happy."

"If you want to create waves, toss something larger than a pebble into the ocean. They fearlessly tossed an enormous boulder over the cliff, creating waves felt miles away." Maude gave a soft laugh, her gaze warm but knowing as she looked Harper up and down. "Speaking of ripples, I caught sight of you and Aidan earlier, cozy in the corner. It's good to see the two of you together again, talking like that."

Harper felt a blush rise in her cheeks, her attention instinctively flicking toward Aidan, who was across the room, deep in conversation with Brody. She tried to play it off with a casual shrug. "Oh, we were just catching up. It's been a while, that's all."

"Hmm." Maude's smile took on a knowing glimmer. "Well, sometimes 'just catching up' is exactly where magic likes to sneak in, isn't it?"

Harper started to answer, but Maude interrupted, quickly removing a bracelet from her wrist. It was a simple but gorgeous bracelet with blue and teal beads and little seashells. She took Harper's hand and pressed the bracelet into her palm, closing Harper's fingers around it.

"For you," Maude said, her soft and serious tone. "This has been with me for a while, and I think it's time it found a new home."

Harper looked down at the bracelet, then back up at Maude, eyebrows raised. "Thank you ... but are you sure? This looks special."

"Oh, it is," Maude replied, her voice rich with the echoes of ages past. "Those stones? They're not just any stones. The gods, in their wisdom, sculpted a colossal statue to capture the essence of passion—raw, unyielding, eternal. But as their chisels struck the stone, fragments fell into the sea, scattering across the tides until they washed upon the shores of a small island near Greece. The mortals who found them swore they carried whispers of fate, stirring hidden desires and granting the strength to follow them."

"Maude," Harper bit her lip, trying not to laugh. "That sounds a little ... convenient, don't you think?"

Maude snickered, unfazed. "Maybe so. But magic is just belief dressed in possibility." She shimmered, as if she carried ancient wisdom from her travels. "Strength is not always loud or obvious. Sometimes, it waits in the quiet, waiting for us to remember it's been there all along. And when it calls, we must follow."

Again, Harper glanced at the bracelet, running her fingers over the cool, smooth stones. Convenient or not, something about the story resonated, sparking a flicker of resolve. She slipped the bracelet over her wrist, feeling a strange calm.

"Listen to the tides, Harper," Maude murmured, her hand moving as if she were smoothing ripples in the air. Harper followed the almost hypnotic gesture, her heart skipping as her eyes found Aidan, lost in easy laughter beside Brody.

When she turned back to thank Maude, the older woman was gone. Harper blinked, glancing around, but there was no sign of her. She stood alone, the faint scent of the sea seeming to linger where Maude had been only moments before.

Harper looked down at the bracelet, smiling to herself. Maybe the story was far-fetched, but Maude's words rang true nonetheless. She felt her hand drift to the bracelet, tracing over the beads as she watched Aidan. *Listen to the tides* ... maybe it was time she did precisely that.

At dinner, Harper sat across from Aidan at the wedding party's table, watching as he shared jokes with Brody's groomsmen, his laughter unguarded. A strange ache, a deep longing to see him often in this easy, joyful state, settled in her heart; it felt like a physical need.

As the night wore on, Brody stood to make a toast, his voice uncharacteristically serious. "We just want to say how grateful we are to everyone who came out to celebrate with us," he began, glancing around the room. "To our family, friends, and everyone who somehow thought it was a good idea to spend a weekend in the middle of nowhere with us."

The guests laughed, raising their glasses in response. Harper smiled, feeling a wave of genuine happiness for her friend. She'd known Paige for only a few months, and seeing her so radiant and free was a reminder of what genuine love looked like.

Brody's attention bounced between Harper and Aidan. "And a special thank you to these two matchmakers over here," he winked. "Even if they don't admit it, we know they had a master plan, orchestrating this whole setup. Couldn't have done it without you two!"

The crowd laughed, raising their glasses to Harper and Aidan, who exchanged a slightly embarrassed smile —both of them aware Brody wasn't accurate. They could have set the record straight, but why bother? Brody, like Paige, had crafted his own version of events. After all, this weekend wasn't about the details—it was about celebration, and sometimes, it was nice to let the story be bigger than the truth.

Brody continued, turning to Paige, his voice lowering. "And, of course, to my beautiful Paige ... my partner, my compass ... my life is better because you're in it, and I can't wait to keep making memories with you." His voice caught, and then he laughed, clearing his throat. "And, uh ... well, as a wise woman once said, 'When the tide wants you ... it'll ... uh, find you ... or you'll find it!' ... never mind ... cheers, everyone!"

"Cheers!" everyone echoed, lifting their glasses.

Harper's eyes locked onto Aidan across the table as she sipped her champagne. *When the tide wants you, it'll find you.* The phrasing wasn't quite right, but the sentiment clung to her thoughts. Maybe this weekend was the beginning of something she'd been waiting for all along.

Twenty-Three

The wedding was only hours away, but the world outside the lodge felt untouched by the rush. Harper stepped onto the forest path leading to the ceremony site, her breath curling in the cool late-morning air. Mist wove through the trees, droplets clinging to crimson and gold leaves like tiny jewels.

She had come outside for fresh air, for a moment to clear her thoughts. But no amount of crisp autumn stillness could quiet the memory of last night—the way Aidan had looked at her, the spark she thought she'd buried but now knew was still alive.

She'd previously dismissed their connection as a brief, magical shipboard encounter. Surely, it won't hold up under the weight of reality, she had convinced herself. However, last night, seeing him laugh and look at her, it felt too real to just forget. And now, as she walked down the forest path, she felt that spark still quietly flickering, stubborn, and alive.

Ahead, the trees opened to reveal the ceremony site. Rows of chairs lined a natural aisle carved out of the forest, the ground beneath them soft and damp. Tiny droplets clung to the edges of leaves, catching the morning light in a way that made them shimmer like prisms. The setting felt beautiful, intimate, and unreal, as if a dream had produced it, complete with the sounds of trickling water and rustling leaves.

Harper paused, letting it all settle around her—the beauty of the scene, the quiet hum of anticipation. And yet, underneath the beauty of it all, one question refused to fade: Had the spark she'd felt last night been waiting for her to finally notice it?

"Hey, Harper." Joe's voice broke her from her reverie. She turned to see her aisle partner, one of Brody's football buddies, giving her an appreciative smile. "You look beautiful."

"Thank you, Joe," she replied, smiling back as they took their place together. "You're not looking too shabby yourself."

They waited in companionable silence, listening to the gentle music filtering through the trees. Harper's fingers drifted to the floral embroidery on her dress, tracing the patterns absently as she tried to settle her nerves. She glanced down the aisle, catching sight of the groomsmen lined up at the front. And there, amid them was Aidan.

Seeing him again stole the breath from her lungs. He looked effortlessly put together, his dusty pink jacket—echoing the bridesmaids' dresses—lending an easy charm. But she knew better. Beneath that relaxed expression, there was something else—a flicker of restraint, a quiet tension. And when he caught her staring, his smile—gentle, knowing—made everything else disappear, if only for a heartbeat.

They began the walk down the aisle, and Harper focused on keeping her steps steady, her head held high. The soft fabric of her dress brushed against her calves with each step. She knew her face showed only calm, but inside, she felt she was unraveling. This day, with its rich tapestry of earthy scents from the damp leaves, the comforting weight and warmth of her shawl, and the occasional heart-stopping glimpses of Aidan, was leaving her with a longing too profound to ignore.

When they reached the front, Harper and Joe parted, each joining their respective sides. She fell in line with the bridesmaids, but her focus drifted—pulled even—back to Aidan. He stared at her again. She saw it. She couldn't tell what he was thinking, but that thing between them? He felt it, too. Her pulse kicked up, heat rising in her cheeks.

She turned her attention forward as the music changed, and Paige appeared arm-in-arm with Brody's father at the end of the aisle. A vision of beauty, Paige moved gracefully, her short dress swirling, her red heels a striking accent. She wore a tiara of wildflowers in place of a veil, a fitting touch for someone so unapologetically herself.

Harper's eyes stung, an unexpected swell of emotion rising as she watched her friend walk toward the love of her life. Paige was radiant, her joy almost tangible. Harper's eyes landed on Brody; the adoration and wonder in his eyes as he looked at Paige resonated with her, a deep, flustering feeling.

As the vows began, Harper tried to focus, absorbing the love and sincerity in each word. But beneath it all, a quiet ache stirred. This kind of connection, this certainty, was something she had spent years keeping at arm's length, even while she was engaged with Dan. How many times had she chosen stability over passion, comfort over courage? How often had she convinced herself that safe was enough?

Paige's voice rang clear and confident.

"Brody, I vow to love you endlessly," she said, "even after completely obliterating your 'all-star' fantasy football team last week." A ripple of laughter passed through the guests, but Paige's smile remained steady. "I vow to be your loudest cheerleader and your toughest opponent, because love isn't about going easy on each other—it's about striving for greatness, pushing boundaries, and making every day feel like a championship game worth playing."

Harper swallowed hard, Paige's words striking deeper than she expected. Love wasn't about playing it safe—it was about choosing someone, repeatedly, even when it meant stepping into the unknown.

She let her focus drift to Aidan once more, feeling the quiet tug of possibility between them. It was undeniable, like a promise just at the tips of her outstretched fingers.

For now, she let herself be swept up in the ceremony, hoping her own path was finally beginning to reveal itself.

The ceremony ended with a cascade of cheers and applause as Paige and Brody shared their first kiss as husband and wife. The newlyweds walked back up the aisle hand-in-hand, their faces glowing with a joy that seemed to radiate to everyone gathered. Guests rose from their seats, chatting and laughing as they returned to the lodge for the reception.

Harper didn't rush off, instead choosing to enjoy the ambiance. The chairs were emptied, and the natural aisle dappled with sunlight streaming through the trees. She stayed rooted, watching the leaves shimmer with droplets from the morning's mist. The world felt still.

She exhaled slowly, her fingers brushing absentmindedly against the embroidery on her dress. Paige and Brody's wedding vows left her with a strange ache, a longing she didn't understand. Their love had been so unapologetically bold, so unflinching in its honesty. It made Harper question the choices she'd made in her own life, the ways she'd kept herself guarded, choosing safety over risking her heart.

The stillness around her felt like comfort and a challenge, as if the forest asked her to step forward and take her own leap. Could she ever let herself be that open? That vulnerable? The thought both thrilled and terrified her.

"Harper?"

She turned at the sound of his voice, her heart slightly jolting. Aidan stood a few feet away, hands in his pockets, his posture easy, but his expression unreadable. His dusty pink jacket caught the soft afternoon light, and the forest seemed to fade momentarily, leaving just the two of them.

"They're calling for you," he said, gesturing toward the direction Paige and Brody had gone. "Bridal party photos. We need all hands on deck."

Harper laughed softly, shaking her head as she broke from her reverie. "Of course. Can't keep the bride waiting."

As Aidan walked closer, she felt the weight of his presence next to her. He wasn't rushing her; instead, he simply stood there, taking in the empty aisle and the canopy of autumn leaves above.

"You okay?" he asked, his voice quieter now.

Harper hesitated, glancing at him out of the corner of her eye. Something about how he asked made her feel like she didn't have to answer with platitudes. "Just ... taking it all in," she admitted, her voice soft. "It's a lot to process."

He nodded. "Yeah. Days like this tend to do that."

They stood there while the faint murmur of distant laughter and music drifted through the trees. Harper paused, wondering if she should add something. *What should I say?* But Aidan extended his arm with a crooked smile before she could decide.

"Come on. Let's not give Paige another reason to hunt us down."

Harper couldn't help but laugh, slipping her arm through his as they walked back toward the lodge. The path was lined with scattered petals, their soft hues a gentle reminder of the beauty they were leaving behind and the celebration that awaited them ahead.

Each step brought them closer—not just in distance, but in something deeper. Harper allowed herself lean into it, to welcome the quiet pull of his presence and the quiet possibility of the night ahead to guide her.

By the time the reception began later in the afternoon, the lodge had transformed into a glowing haven of celebration. Inside the cozy hall, warmth and laughter filled the air, with guests gathering at round tables draped in autumn-colored linens.

Harper found a seat near the front, her shawl draped over the back of her chair, and took in the scene. She saw Aidan moving through the crowd confidently, stopping to shake hands and share a few laughs. The way he carried himself, relaxed but purposeful, drew her attention. She watched as he brushed a hand down the front of his dusty pink jacket, a small, habitual gesture, and felt a flicker of pride when his eyes briefly found hers.

"You're going to do great," she'd whispered to him earlier, just outside in the crisp, fading afternoon air. He paused, and they stared at each other. A silent understanding—like a secret—zipped between them. He'd nodded, the corner of his mouth tilting into a half-smile before stepping back inside.

Aidan took the microphone, and Harper saw it—the quiet shift, the spark of focus sharpening in his eyes. The room hushed in response, the murmurs fading to a hush as Aidan looked around the room and his smirk spread, as if he knew how to win the crowd.

"Now, if there's one thing to know about Brody," he began, his voice carrying an effortless charm, "it's that subtlety has never been his strong suit."

The crowd chuckled, and Harper felt herself relax, her own laughter joining in. Aidan let the moment hang for a beat before adding with mock seriousness, "I mean, just look at those pants! Red like his love for Paige, I guess."

The laughter swelled, rippling through the room, and Harper couldn't help but beam. He exuded a magnetic confidence—a genuineness that felt undeniably him.

She watched Brody and Paige, their love bold and consuming, a wildfire that burned without hesitation. Harper felt a sudden mix of admiration, envy, and longing. Their connection was fearless, unguarded, everything she'd always held herself back from. Things with Aidan were slower and quieter, like waiting for embers to blaze. Yet, as her focus returned to him, she wondered if she was finally ready to let herself burn without fear.

Aidan continued, his tone growing softer. "I first met Brody on a cruise that neither of us expected much from. I figured, at best, it would be a week of sun and drinks. But then ... Brody met Paige."

Aidan's concentration shifted to Paige, grinning beside Brody, their fingers intertwined. "Their fire roared hot and fast from the very start."

Harper's heart fluttered as she reminisced about the fun times on the ship with Aidan and their unspoken connection. She looked up, catching Aidan's eye as he spoke, and felt a rush of warmth. Did he still feel it, too, that same bond that had remained, even as they'd returned to their separate lives?

"Honestly, I didn't think it'd survive the week," Aidan admitted, shaking his head with a smile. "But here they are. And somehow, I'm not surprised anymore." His words went beyond Brody and Paige as if he were speaking to something implicit, a recognition that some connections don't fade, even with time and distance.

Harper's fingers tightened slightly around her champagne flute, her heart thudding. She realized she had been restraining her emotions, preventing herself from openly expressing desires like Brody and Paige did for each other—she had been settling for safety, maintaining a distance from Aidan and herself. But watching Aidan speak, she felt her walls crumble, a daring invitation to risk, feel, and desire.

As Aidan lifted his glass to Brody and Paige, his eyes found hers once more. "To Brody and Paige," he said, raising his glass, "may you always keep that fire going. Cheers!"

The room erupted in applause, glasses clinking all around her, but Harper barely noticed. She joined in the cheers, raising her glass, but her eyes were fixed on Aidan. She felt the anticipation build, an undeniable sense that the spark between them wasn't just a memory. It felt intensely real, vibrantly alive, and the potential reward pulsed with a risky allure.

The applause died down, and Harper spotted Aidan slipping through a side door, his glass still in hand. His steps were steady, his posture strong, but something about the way he moved felt heavier than usual. He disappeared onto the balcony, and without thinking, Harper grabbed two champagne flutes from a passing waiter. Her pulse quickened as she followed him into the night.

The night air was crisp, and the faint scent of pine carried on the breeze. Harper stepped onto the balcony, the golden light from inside spilling out just far enough to illuminate Aidan's silhouette. He leaned on the wooden railing, his back to her, his glass dangling loosely in one hand as he gazed out at the darkened forest.

"Aidan Murphy, hiding away already?" Harper said softly, holding out a glass as she approached.

Aidan turned, his expression shifting from surprise to a warm, amiable smile. "You caught me," he teased, taking the glass from her hand. "Needed some air."

Harper smiled back, stepping beside him to rest her elbows on the railing. "I was afraid you forgot your champagne."

He raised his glass to clink it gently against hers. "Good call."

"That was a great speech," she said. "You had the entire room eating out of your hand."

Aidan chuckled, the sound low and soft. "I don't know about that. I was trying to get through it without tripping over my words."

"Well, you nailed it," Harper replied. "You always seem to know exactly what to say."

He turned his head toward her, their eyes locking together. "Not always," he said. "There has been plenty of times I didn't say what I wanted."

Harper's looked down at her glass, her fingers tracing the rim. "And what do you want, Aidan?"

The breeze picked up slightly, and Harper shivered, the thin fabric of her dress doing little to shield her from the chill. Without a word, Aidan shrugged off his jacket and draped it over her shoulders. The soft, woolen fabric held his cologne's faint, lingering scent; a comforting embrace against her skin.

"Thanks," she murmured, pulling the jacket tighter around herself.

Aidan leaned against the railing, his body angled toward her now. "I guess ... I want to feel alive. I want to wake up excited about what I'm doing every day. The kitchen used to make me feel that way, but now ... now I feel like I'm not making progress. Keeping everyone else happy and forgetting what I actually want."

"I know what you mean," she responded. "Doing something because it's what's expected ... because it's safe or comfortable. It's hard to pull yourself out of that."

But then Aidan's question landed a little too close to home. "What about you?" he asked gently. "Are you ... comfortable?"

Harper dropped her shoulders slightly as she hesitated, debating how much to disclose. "I'm ... comfortable," she admitted. "But not in a way that makes me feel alive. Work is fine. Stable. Safe. But it's like every ounce of creativity, every spark I used to have, has been stripped away. I spend my days making small tweaks to things I don't even care about anymore."

Her voice wavered, cracking under the truth she hadn't fully admitted, not even to herself. "I thought I wanted this. I thought stability was what I needed. But now I just ... I just feel stuck. Like I'm playing it small because it's easier than taking the risk of doing something bold, something real. And I hate it. I'm tired of safe. I'm tired of ... comfortable." She let out a nervous laugh, unsure if she'd shared too much. "I don't even know if that makes sense."

He didn't speak, didn't try to fix or soften her words. Instead, he just listened, letting the silence between them become something steady, something safe. His quiet attention—unwavering and patient—urged her forward.

Harper swallowed as she locked eyes with Aidan. "I'm ready to be done with comfortable, Aidan. Give me more than that. I'm not sure what's next, but I know I can't stay here. Not anymore."

Aidan stepped closer, his touch featherlight as his fingers trailed down her arm before he wrapped her in his embrace. Again, he didn't offer reassurances, didn't tell her things would be okay—he simply held her, steady and unwavering, as if letting her know she wasn't alone.

Harper leaned into him, resting her head against his chest, feeling the quiet strength of his embrace. Then, slowly, she looked up, meeting his eyes. "Aidan," she whispered, "kiss me."

He didn't hesitate. Their lips met in a kiss that was unhurried but certain. There was no urgency, no desperate grasping. Just the quiet certainty of something worth exploring.

As they pulled apart, their foreheads remained pressed together, neither speaking as the night stretched endlessly. It felt sacred.

Aidan's hand traced a slow, deliberate path down her spine, his voice quiet, intimate. "Come back to my room with me tonight?"

Harper gave him a teasing smile, her fingers lightly running down his arm, but before either could say more, the balcony door creaked open. They both turned to see Paige's maid of honor stepping out, her expression apologetic but urgent.

"There you are! They're about to do the bouquet toss," she said, glancing between Harper and Aidan. "You're needed inside."

Harper exhaled, her expression caught between exasperation and amusement. "Duty calls," she said, her smile teasing but reluctant as she met Aidan's eyes.

He nodded, his own smile warm but knowing. "We'll finish this later," he promised.

"Deal," she whispered, her hand finding his as they turned to make their way back inside.

Back inside, Harper waited by the edge of the crowd of single women gathering for the bouquet toss, arms loosely folded as the more enthusiastic bridesmaids jostled for position. She wasn't precisely avoiding the tradition, but wasn't diving in.

Paige, full of theatrics, twirled the bouquet in her hands. "Ready, ladies?" she called, her voice teasing. With dramatic flair, she turned her back and flung the bouquet.

Arcing high, it bounced off a hand, then another, before falling directly into Harper's arms. She blinked, stunned, as the crowd whooped and applauded.

"Really?" Harper thought, clutching the bouquet like it might combust. Of course.

From across the room, Aidan caught her eye, his grin downright smug as he mouthed, "Fate."

Harper shot him a playful glare, shaking her head as if to scold him. She tried to fight the smile, but it was useless. She was falling—completely, irreversibly, and far too fast.

Before she could process it, Brody bounded forward with over-the-top glee. "Gentlemen, it's showtime!" he announced, vanishing beneath Paige's dress like a magician's assistant mid-act. The fabric quivered with exaggerated movement until Paige, giggling uncontrollably, smacked him in mock protest.

Seconds later, Brody resurfaced, grinning like he'd just conquered a great feat, the garter clutched triumphantly between his teeth, Paige's laughter still trailing in his wake.

A reluctant huddle formed among the single men, except for Aidan, who kept his distance. He took a deliberate step back, then another, raising his hands. "I'm just an innocent bystander," he called, leaning casually against a column to signal his complete detachment from this ritual.

Brody grinned wickedly. "Oh, don't worry, Aidan. I got you."

With an exaggerated flick of his wrist, Brody sent the garter flying. It careened wildly off course, missing the huddled players by a mile, and landed, with a soft plop, directly at Aidan's feet.

The room erupted with laughter as Aidan stared at the garter, arms still crossed, as though debating whether picking it up would ruin his life. Finally, he picked it up gently, as if it were cursed.

"Seriously?" he deadpanned, holding it up for everyone. Harper laughed, her cheeks aching from smiling.

He turned toward her, the garter dangling from one finger. His grin was wry, yet his eyes sparkled with humor and an additional, more profound emotion. He gave her a playful shrug as if to say, *Well, look at that.*

Harper clutched the bouquet a little tighter, her heart skipping a beat. First the bouquet, now the garter. Was the universe really this cheeky?

The music shifted, and the crowd pulled back onto the dance floor, drawing Harper into its orbit. She danced, she laughed, but her eyes kept drifting to Aidan. Their exchanged looks carried the spark of a shared joke—one neither of them had said out loud yet.

The evening continued in a wonderous, joyful blur, with laughter and dancing filling the cozy reception hall. Harper was surrounded by friends and strangers, swept into spins on the dance floor, stealing cake bites and clinking glasses with newfound ease. The cake cutting was a sweet moment, Paige and Brody playfully smearing frosting on each other's noses before laughing and sharing a kiss. Their happiness is infectious. Harper laughed along with everyone, feeling the warmth of community, of celebration. Every glance exchanged with Aidan ignited another spark, a thrilling current impossible to ignore.

The laughter and music of the reception blurred into the background as she watched him, her heartbeat thrumming with a mix of excitement and vulnerability. Tonight felt different—charged, significant, as if something was about to shift.

Finally, as the last song wound down, Aidan leaned close, his hand finding hers. "What do you say we make a getaway?" he whispered in her ear.

His breath sent a ripple through her, a whisper of static trailing in its wake. Harper tilted her head toward him, her answer filled with reckless ecstasy. "I thought you'd never ask."

As they made their goodbyes, Paige pulled Harper in, gripping her shoulders as if delivering sacred wisdom. "Ride that man like a mechanical bull after three tequila shots."

Harper choked on her laugh, eyes wide with faux horror. "Oh my God, Paige!" She punctuated it with a sharp smack to Paige's ass before pushing her away. Paige only cackled, entirely unrepentant.

"Good luck with this one," Harper teased, squeezing Brody's shoulder. "She's yours now. No refunds, no exchanges, and unquestionably no returns."

The night air wrapped around them, cool and crisp—but inside, Harper was burning. Her fingers curled around Aidan's, urgent and demanding. Each step toward his room fed the slow-burning embers that had smoldered for six long months, until at last, they ignited, raging into an unstoppable inferno.

When they reached his door, Aidan paused, his grin playful as he slipped the garter over the doorknob, a small, teasing act that drew a laugh from her.

"Think they'll get the message?" His voice was quiet, teasing, but his green eyes betrayed him—burning with heat, with hunger.

Harper didn't answer. Words felt slow and unnecessary for the rush she felt building within. Instead, she stepped forward, giving him a gentle but insistent push through the doorway. The soft click of the door shutting was the last sound she registered before her lips found his.

Her kiss was urgent, hungry, consuming. Six months apart, six months of separate lives, and yet, when their lips met, it was as if no time had passed at all. Her hands found his chest, her fingers curling into the fabric of his shirt as she pressed herself against him. His arms circled her waist, pulling her in as their kiss deepened, and Harper felt her control slip entirely.

They stumbled through the room in a frenzy of need, their movements frantic and uncoordinated. Aidan's jacket hit the floor near the lamp, her shawl slid from her shoulders like liquid silk, and Harper's bouquet fell from her hand, forgotten in a corner. Each kiss grew hotter, fiercer, until they were tugging at buttons and zippers; their fumbling fingers betraying their desperation. The sound of fabric tearing filled the room, mingling with their quickened breaths, and Harper couldn't bring herself to care.

When Aidan's hands gripped her hips, his touch firm and possessive, a jolt of desire shot through her, sharp and all-consuming. Her breath hitched as he pulled her against him, the hard line of his arousal pressing into her stomach. Her body responded instantly, her pulse pounding in her ears as the heat rose.

The sudden feeling of his hands sliding down and gripping her ass, lifting her as though she weighed nothing, stole the breath from her lungs. She let out a soft, startled laugh, but it quickly dissolved into a low, needy moan. Wrapping her legs tightly around his waist, she clung to him, her nails digging into his shoulders as he carried her toward the bed. The sheer strength of him, the way he held her so effortlessly, sent a wave of carnal hunger rushing through her that left her dizzy.

By the time they reached the bed, she was trembling, her body alight with sensation. Aidan lowered her onto the mattress with a gentleness that belied the intensity of their need, his weight pressing her into the soft sheets as he settled over her. Harper arched beneath him, her hips rising instinctively to meet his, craving the contact she'd been denied for so long.

Her hands roamed over his shoulders and down his back, her nails scraping lightly against his skin as his lips found her neck. She gasped, her body arching as his mouth worked its way down her throat, each kiss igniting a fresh spark of fire.

When their bodies finally joined, Harper let out a cry that was equal parts relief and ecstasy. He filled her completely, the sensation overwhelming in the best possible way. She tightened her legs around his waist, her hands gripping his back as she held him to her, her body instinctively moving with his.

Every thrust sent a wave of pleasure rippling through her, each one building on the last until it felt like her body was burning from the inside out. The pressure coiling deep within her grew unbearable, a relentless, delicious ache that had her clinging to him, desperate for release.

Her nails dug into his shoulders as she arched against him, her breaths coming in short, shallow gasps. His pace grew urgent, his movements deep and relentless, like stoking embers into an unstoppable blaze.

Pleasure tore through her, molten and all-consuming. Her head fell back, her body tightening, her breath breaking into a shattered cry. Heat roared through her, licking at every nerve, leaving her raw, aching, alive.

Aidan wasn't far behind. With a sharp, shuddering breath, his grip on her hips tightened as he lost himself completely, his final thrusts erratic and deep. A guttural groan ripped from his throat as he spilled inside her, his body locking against hers, rigid with pleasure.

Harper gasped against his shoulder, her body still pulsing around him, unwilling to let go just yet.

Aidan collapsed onto the mattress beside her, neither of them moving, their breaths the only sound in the hush of the room. Harper's body hummed with the aftershocks, each slow inhale pulling her further from the high.

With her eyes fluttering shut, she let her fingers rest lightly against his chest, fixated on the steady pulse beneath her touch. Aidan's arm curled around her waist, drawing her closer, and she melted into him, her cheek finding its place against him.

Neither of them spoke. There was no need for words. The air around them was warm and still, wrapping them in a cocoon of intimacy that felt both fragile and eternal. Harper's breaths slowed, her body softening as exhaustion crept in, and she let herself drift, the steady rhythm of Aidan's heart lulling her into a peaceful haze.

Woven together in the hush of the night, they let go of the months spent apart. Slowly, her thoughts quieted, and she drifted into sleep, Aidan's presence anchoring her even in her dreams.

Twenty-Four

Soft kisses skimmed over her bare shoulder, each one more insistent than the last. Aidan's lips curved against her skin as he murmured, "Good morning."

Harper stretched with a satisfied sigh, her smile lazy. "Yes, indeed."

She rolled onto her side, fingers trailing lazily down Aidan's stomach, dipping lower before skimming along his thigh in a slow, teasing glide—just enough to make him tense beneath her touch. Then, just as effortlessly, she slipped away.

With a sly smirk, she slid from bed, the sheet sliding from her skin, pooling at her feet like an afterthought.

She didn't rush. She wanted him to watch.

Cool air kissed her skin as she padded toward his open suitcase, every step measured, but the real heat was behind her. She didn't need to turn to know—Aidan's stare was relentless, searing into her like a touch without contact, stripping her bare in a way the air never could.

Aidan groaned behind her. "Oh, hell no. You don't just get to walk away after a night like that."

She glanced over her shoulder, biting back a smirk. "Catch me first."

She didn't rush. Didn't need to.

A pulse of heat chased her across the room as Aidan's hunger grabbed hold like an invisible tether that she had no desire to sever. She reveled in his eager restraint as she reached for his suitcase, her fingers gliding over the fabric inside as if she had all the time in the world.

Behind her, Aidan shifted, the rustle of sheets barely audible over the thick silence between them. "Looking for something?"

She hummed in response, letting her fingers trail idly over the soft fabric of one of his shirts. "Just ... a souvenir."

She knew exactly what she was doing. The arch of her back, the slow spill of her hair over one shoulder—it was all intentional. And if the quiet hitch of his breath was any indication, it was working.

Finally, she plucked a faded green tee from the pile, holding it up with a grin. "Mind if I borrow this?" she asked sweetly—already slipping it over her head before he could answer. The fabric was soft and slightly oversized. She tied a knot at her waist, letting the shirt hang loose around her hips, and looked over her shoulder again, catching Aidan's smile.

"If you're going to keep stealing my clothes, I'll need to invest in more shirts," he said, his voice filled with admiration.

"How about a trade then?" She raised an eyebrow, her lips curving as she bent down again to retrieve her discarded thong from the floor. Without breaking eye contact, she slipped it into the side pocket of his suitcase, pressing it down with her fingertips. "Just a little souvenir," she said with a wink.

A low chuckle escaped him, his eyes gleaming—part teasing, part hunger, all-consuming—and her heart tripped at the look he gave her.

The teasing edge faded as she returned to the bed, folding her legs beneath her as she sank into the mattress beside him. She took his hand, lacing her fingers through his, and the atmosphere shifted—no longer teasing, but more tender.

"You know," she began, "being here with you ... seeing Paige and Brody so happy ... reminded me that I've been settling. Holding back, hoping things would change on their own." Their eyes locked as her words carried an honesty she could no longer hold back. "But being here with you has reminded me that I can't keep waiting. I deserve to be happy, Aidan. We both do."

He nodded, his hand tightening around hers. "I know what you mean," he murmured. "I keep telling myself that things will improve at Murphy's, that I'll find a way to make it work. But I feel like I'm just going through the motions, trying to keep everyone else happy."

She squeezed his hand, her thumb tracing circles over his knuckles. "You deserve more than that, Aidan. You deserve to wake up every day excited, doing what you love."

With a gentle, teasing smile, she leaned forward and gently kissed his cheek. "So ... let's make a promise," she whispered, her tone serious but hopeful. "When we go back, no more settling. No more playing it safe. We go after what we want."

He looked at her, something fierce and resolved in his expression. "No more running in place," he agreed. "It's time to live the life I want."

Satisfied, Harper stood, gathering her dress and shoes from the floor; her confidence reignited. She moved with a sense of freedom, a quiet thrill in the way her hips swayed just enough to tease. Aidan's eyes never wavered from her figure. She draped her dress over her shoulder and peered back at him with look that was nothing short of a slow, sultry seduction.

Her hand paused on the doorknob as she noticed the garter still hanging there—a final scandalous souvenir from the night before. With a daring smirk, she swiped it, twirled it lazily around her fingers, then lobbed it into his lap. "Don't lose that, Murphy. I'm not done with you yet," she teased, winking before slipping out, his sheepish grin the last thing she saw before the door swung shut behind her.

Harper tried to stifle a laugh as she made her way down the hallway.

There she was, sneaking through the quiet lodge in nothing but Aidan's oversized T-shirt. One stray breeze, and the entire lodge would get an intimate lesson in her personal landscaping choices.

But she didn't care. She was on a high from the previous night and felt invincible.

The night before was insane, and she still rode that high of disbelief and joy. She clutched her bridesmaid dress and heels over her shoulder, glancing around every few steps, praying no one else was awake.

Every step was a delicious reminder of her recklessness.

Just as she neared the safety of her door, a voice broke through the hallway's morning silence. "Harper?"

"Shit!"

She froze, turning slowly to find Paige standing there, arms crossed, eyebrows lifted, and a grin spreading across her face. "And where exactly are your pants?" Paige asked, looking her friend up and down with exaggerated judgment.

"Oh, for the love of ..." Harper cut herself off with a laugh, yanking Paige into her room before anyone else could witness her walk of shame. "I didn't know the decency police were patrolling this early," she whispered, half-scandalized, half-amused.

Once the door clicked shut, Harper tossed her dress onto the bed and pulled a pair of leggings from her suitcase. "Honestly, Paige," she muttered, slipping the leggings on, "I'd just about made it when you decided to announce my lack of wardrobe to the world."

Paige threw herself onto the bed, still grinning. "Oh, please. You loved it. I haven't seen you this ... glowing in ages." She gave Harper an exaggerated wink. "You're welcome, by the way."

Harper rolled her eyes, unable to suppress her smile, as she folded a few things into her bag. "Fine, yes, I'm ... happy," she admitted. "More than happy, actually. Last night with Aidan ..." she trailed off, a dreamy look in her eyes. "It was everything I didn't know I was still hoping for."

"I knew it!" Paige exclaimed. "You and Aidan just have ... something. It was like the two of you were in your own world the whole weekend."

"Well, it feels like it," Harper said, laughing as she shoved a sweater into her bag. "But, of course, we now have to go back to our separate lives. It feels almost exactly like leaving the cruise—except ..." She looked at her friend, but Paige wasn't buying it. "This time, it doesn't feel like goodbye. Not really. We promised each other we'd stop holding back."

Paige reached over and squeezed Harper's hand. "Good. Because I'd make you pinky swear if you hadn't said that already."

Harper grinned, squeezing her friend's hand back. "Speaking of romantic promises, though ... why aren't you off somewhere with your new husband? Aren't you supposed to be participating in honeymoon-type activities?" She wiggled her eyebrows playfully.

Paige snorted. "Believe me, Brody's just fine. I wanted to make sure I actually had a chance to catch up with you before we disappeared. Between the wedding chaos and you being swept away by Mr. Murphy, I barely saw you all weekend!"

Harper wrapped her arms around Paige. "I'm so glad I was here for all of this. Seeing you and Brody so happy ... it makes me feel hopeful. Maybe there's a real chance for that kind of happiness for me, too."

Paige pulled back, her eyes shining with pride. "There is, Harper. And I'll be here to remind you of that every step of the way." She stood up, brushing imaginary dust from her dress. "Now, pack up your stuff and promise me you'll follow that spark. Don't let life drag you back into the 'safe' lane."

Harper nodded, feeling that familiar swell of determination rising. "I promise." She looked at her half-packed bag and beamed, imagining the possibilities. She and Aidan might be returning to their own lives, but the path ahead was clear this time.

Paige paused at the door, giving Harper one last playful look. "And remember—go get some, girl," she whispered with a wink before slipping out, leaving Harper laughing and feeling completely alive.

As soon as the door latched behind Paige, Harper collapsed onto the bed, her body sprawling over the bridesmaid dress still draped across the comforter. She let out a long, contented sigh, her smile unfurling freely as she stared at the ceiling. Last night exceeded her expectations; it was passionate, intense, and tender.

After gathering her thoughts, she reached for her phone on the nightstand, untouched since the morning before. She unlocked the screen, scrolling absently through missed calls, messages from friends and family, and work emails. But then, near the top of the screen, one message stood out.

It was from Aidan:

Aidan

> Hey, how's life?

He'd sent it yesterday, right during the wedding ceremony. It was a simple question, but the sight of it stirred something inside her. She felt her heart flutter as she thought of how he'd stood across the aisle, watching her just as she had watched him, feeling that familiar pull even after so much time apart.

She sat up a little, staring at the message, her fingers hovering over the keyboard as she debated what to say. Part of her wanted to type out something playful, "Life's better when you're around," or something flirty, "Thinking about last night." Perhaps even something bolder, "My kitty is still so wet ..."

No ... no, no.

Every time she typed something, she hesitated, pressing backspace and starting over, unsure how much to reveal.

Then, as she scrolled up in the chat, she came across the last time he'd asked her that exact question months ago.

Aidan

> How's life?

She read again, the words a bittersweet echo of that distant afternoon. She vividly recalled that day. It was the day she left Dan. She'd been feeling raw, a strange mix of relief and melancholy, like she was finally letting go of all the parts of herself she'd outgrown.

Her response had been simple: a single smile emoji. She recalled typing it out and accepting it was the first honest smile she'd felt in a long time—a quiet acknowledgment that she was moving forward in search of something real, something passionate. That response, so understated yet final, had somehow captured all the messy, complex emotions swirling within her.

Harper selected a smiley face emoji. Like before, her response conveyed everything she wanted to communicate, "I'm happy."

With a soft smile, she hit send. She didn't need him to respond; the feeling of peace that settled over her was enough. She knew she was exactly where she was supposed to be.

Twenty-Five

H arper stood at the head of the conference table, her pulse thrumming as she scanned the team's eager faces. Today, that sterile room felt charged, like the air before a storm. Jason tapped his notepad with restless energy while Sarah's fingers played along the edge of her laptop, her excitement barely contained. Outside, the sky-scrapers pulsed with New York's relentless energy, echoing Harper's urgency.

This wasn't just another pitch. This was her team's moment—a chance to present something bold, unfiltered, and authentic.

Harper took a steadying breath, fingers brushing the pitch deck emblazoned with Trailblaze: Unleashing True Adventure. The first slide showed a lone hiker on a rugged cliff, wind whipping through their hair, eyes fixed on the horizon. She envisioned the brand as raw, honest, and powerful.

"Today," she began, her voice steady, "I'm showing you two cam-paigns. The first one is precisely what you requested: family-friendly, familiar, and safe." She clicked to a slide of pastel images: smiling families at manicured campsites, children playing in tents.

She paused, letting the undercurrent of disappointment in her tone hang in the still room. They all knew the real pitch was still coming.

"But," Harper continued, her voice sharpening with conviction, "let me show you what Trailblaze could really be." She clicked to the next slide, and the screen came alive: stormy skies, muddy boots, a lone woman scaling a jagged cliff. The tagline read: No Boundaries. No Limits. No Fear.

Harper scanned the room, seeing the executives straighten in their chairs, their polite interest shifting to rapt attention. Sarah's eyes gleamed with pride as her designs commanded the spotlight, while Jason leaned forward, his fingers drumming with restrained excitement.

"This campaign," Harper said, her voice rising, "is about real adventure. It's not about looking outdoorsy; it's about being outdoors and getting lost, getting dirty, feeling the grit of the earth and the exhilaration of the unpredictable. It's for people who crave authenticity—not the illusion of nature, but the real thing. They want challenges that push them past their limits. This campaign isn't safe, and it's not sanitized. It's fearless. And so is Trailblaze."

She paused; the room crackled with energy. Then, her voice steady but full of fire: "If you're ready to take that leap, we're ready to lead the charge. My team has everything in place—visuals, ad placements, and social media rollout. If you agree to this strategy, we can go live today."

Harper leaned in with conviction. "Tonight, Trailblaze could make headlines for their new take on courage and authenticity! All it takes is a 'yes.'"

Silence stretched through the room, and Harper held her breath, her heart pounding as she let the vision linger. She could see the sparks of interest, like tiny embers, igniting in the clients' eyes, and almost hear the quiet click of their minds processing the daring proposal. Their exciting proposal, filled with innovative ideas, was the golden ticket for her and her team. She came to New York for this. This was why she had endured all the late nights, the soul-crushing rejections, the endless compromises.

The lead client, Tom, shifted in his seat, folding his hands as he leaned forward, his expression unreadable. "Harper," he said, his tone contemplative, "I have to admit, this is … impressive. It's clear you and your team put a lot of heart into this." He looked down at his notes, the silence amplifying the frantic beat of Harper's heart, an icy dread replacing the thrill as she braced herself for the inevitable rejection. "But,"

There's the 'but.' Harper's stomach plummeted already mentally preparing for the 'safe' words to come next.

Tom locked eyes with Harper before continuing, "This is a creative gamble we just cannot afford."

Harper cleared her throat ready to defend her work, but Vivian, Tom's sharp-eyed financial analyst, interjected with a clipped tone before Harper could say anything more. "We've run the numbers," she said, "and the budget simply can't accommodate a risk this uncertain. There's no guarantee this bold campaign will resonate, and we're not in a position to gamble on something that might not work."

Harper straightened her posture, not ready to surrender just yet. "Not in a position to gamble?" she questioned, her voice unwavering. "This isn't a gamble—it's an opportunity. The risk you take now could multiply your investment tenfold. People don't connect with 'safe.' They connect with an authentic boldness. If you trust us to do what we do best, this campaign could redefine Trailblaze and make you the standout leader in your industry."

Vivian didn't waver, her calm demeanor unmoved. "Even so, Trailblaze is not in a position to take that level of risk, not when a safer approach ensures stability."

"Exactly," Tom interjected, nodding toward his colleague. "We appreciate the vision, Harper. It's fresh, it's creative, but at the end of the day, we have a brand to protect. Familiarity sells, and our core audience expects consistency. We just can't stray too far from what works."

Harper leaned forward, her voice quickening, almost pleading. "But that's the problem! Familiarity doesn't inspire loyalty—it breeds complacency. If Trailblaze wants to stand out and grow beyond the competition, you need to lead, not follow. This campaign does that. It's exactly what your audience needs to see."

Tom glanced at his watch, a subtle but pointed gesture. He exhaled, his tone polite but final. "I respect your passion, Harper, and I admire the effort you and your team have put into this. But we've made our decision. We'll be moving forward with the family-friendly approach."

"I look forward to continuing to work with you." He stood, smoothing his tie, and briefly nodded to the room. "Thank you again for your time."

With that, he exited the room, leaving an oppressive silence in his wake.

Harper's fingers curled around the edge of the table as she stared at the laptop in front of her. The bold images from the campaign still glowed on the screen, mocking her with what could have been. The room had changed—Sarah sat hunched over her laptop, her expression unreadable in the cold screen light, while Jason's stiff posture radiated frustration. The energy that had once fueled them had collapsed into a suffocating silence.

She turned toward the glass walls and caught sight of her boss, Sam, chatting easily with another client. His confident smile radiated the complacency she had grown to resent. Her jaw tightened. They put in so much effort only to play it safe.

This was not what she had come here for. Not this.

Harper couldn't bring herself to speak. The weight of the team's collective disappointment pressed down on her like a physical thing, heavy and oppressive. She could feel it in the silence, frustration mingled with the shattered hopes they'd all carried into that pitch room. They thought this campaign would finally make them stand out and show what they could do. The campaign that would finally prove that they were more than just another agency churning out soulless, predictable ads.

Jason let out a long, frustrated sigh, breaking the silence. "I knew it," he muttered, his voice low and bitter. "I knew they'd never go for it. We took a risk, and for what? They don't want bold. They never did."

Sarah looked up, her voice barely above a whisper. "But we gave them everything. We showed them something real, something that meant something. And they just ... tossed it aside." Her fingers traced the edge of her laptop as if still feeling the energy of the rejected work. "It's like ... what's the point?"

Harper took another look around the room. Kevin, their strategist, stared blankly at the wall, his jaw tight, as though he'd been punched.

Marissa, typically the team's pragmatist, shook her head slowly, her eyes clouded with disillusionment.

"It's like we're just here to fill in the blanks," Marissa muttered, bitterness creeping into her voice. "They want placeholders, not ideas. Something safe that ticks all the boxes but says nothing. They tell us to be bold, to 'push boundaries,' but the second we do ..." she trailed off with a sharp exhale. "We should've just thrown up a stock photo of a happy family by a campfire. That's all they want."

The sting of Marissa's words hit Harper hard. Mediocrity's reward felt suffocating within the system. But this campaign had been different. They'd dared to reach for something bold, something meaningful. Now, watching her team deflate, Harper felt a surge of protectiveness. She couldn't let it end here.

Sarah let out a bitter laugh, rubbing her eyes. "Why do we even bother? We worked ourselves into the ground for this. I put everything into those designs, and for what? So some executive could pat us on the head and call it 'impressive' before tossing it aside?"

Harper felt a burning rage toward the clients, her boss, and herself for letting her team invest so much in something bound to fail. Their spark was stifled by safe, uninspired work. Once so excited, her team looked deflated after getting rejected.

Her fingers brushed against the bracelet Maude had given her at Paige's wedding. *If you want to make waves in the ocean, you'll need something larger than a pebble.* The words echoed in her mind, their meaning deepening now. Maude had meant love, but they felt just as true here.

Harper determined her team wouldn't accept defeat and feel undervalued. It stopped being about the campaign. It became about their work, the very reason they were all there. This was about creating waves, not ripples.

Harper took a deep breath, her heart pounding, and she felt a surge of clarity. It was time she stopped playing by the rules and wasn't scared of the consequences.

"Fuck it," she said, her voice vibrating with fierce resolve. One by one, she locked eyes with each team member, daring them to stand with her. "We're releasing the bold campaign."

The team stared at her, stunned into silence. Harper saw their shock slowly melt away, replaced by a hesitant hope, a spark of rebellion that ignited like a tiny flame in the dark. For too long, they'd been keeping their heads down, afraid to rock the boat or reach for anything more than what was safe. But now, in the silent room, she felt the energy thrumming, vibrating, and finally breaking free.

Jason blinked, stunned. "Harper ... you're serious?" His voice cracked between awe and apprehension. "If we do that ... if you do that ..."

"I know," she said. "But fear will no longer drive my decisions. I'm done letting them put our creativity in a box and call it 'safe.' We didn't come here to be safe, right?" She paused to observe her team nodding in agreement. "We came here to create, take risks, and make something worth discussing. And we did that with this campaign. So, let's show the world what Trailblaze could be. If it costs me my job ... so be it. It's time to release the kraken!"

A hush fell over the room. Sarah was the first to smile, a shy little smile that got wider as she looked around at the other team members. "Let's do it," she whispered, unsure if anyone else would follow.

Yet, the spark was contagious. Excitement rippled outward, hesitation melting as the team caught on.

Kevin's grin turned wicked, and his usually cautious demeanor was completely abandoned. "Fuck, yeah!" he shouted, slapping the table with a resounding crack. The sound jolted everyone like a starter's pistol.

Sarah didn't even look up, but with a slow, practiced motion, she slid the swear jar across the table. "That's a dollar," she said, deadpan.

Kevin didn't even pause, yanking a crumpled bill from his pocket and tossing it in with flair. "Worth it," he declared, his grin spreading as the energy in the room hit a fever pitch.

The team sprang into action as if an invisible fuse had been lit. Harper watched, pride swelling, as determination swept through them like wildfire. Gone were the slumped shoulders and hollow stares. In their place was a focused, kinetic urgency—every movement cracked with purpose.

"Listen up!" Harper called out over the hum of furious clicking and brainstorming. Her voice was firm and commanding, but lit with excitement. "This campaign is us. It's fearless, bold, everything we came here to do. This is why we show up. It's what happens when we push past the limits they try to put on us. And today, we finish it."

Jason shot her a quick thumbs-up as he raced through captions, his usual snark replaced with razor-sharp focus. "I'm on it," he called, fingers flying over the keys. Across the table, Sarah adjusted images swiftly, her face glowing with the fire of someone finally doing work that mattered. "These designs are going to hit," she muttered, a fierce grin tugging at her lips.

Marissa and Kevin were deep in the weeds on strategy, rattling off adjustments with military-like efficiency. "Shift the rollout to peak hours," Marissa ordered. "And make sure the adventure vloggers get tagged immediately."

"Already on it," Kevin replied, grinning as he flipped through their media schedule. "This is going to blow up."

Harper moved between them like a conductor in a symphony of controlled chaos, the thrill of rebellion humming in her veins. The room buzzed with the energy of a team fully aligned, hearts and minds chasing the same daring goal.

"Ready?" Harper called out as she stood at the center of it all, her voice cutting through the noise. The team turned to her, faces lit with anticipation. Harper's hand hovered over the keyboard, her pulse pounding as she took a deep breath.

"Let's do it," she said. And with one final click, the campaign went live.

The room erupted into cheers, fists pumping and laughter echoing off the walls. For a moment, they didn't care about what came next. Right now, they were soaring. They had fought for something real, something fearless, and it was out there for the world to see.

Whatever the fallout, they had done the impossible. Together.

Harper barely had time to bask in the thrill of her decision before her phone vibrated on the table, Sam's name flashing ominously across the screen. She took a deep breath anticipating the tumultuous storm brewing just offshore.

"Harper!" Sam was fuming. "Get in my office. Now."

Moments later, she stood across from him in his glass-walled corner office, the city skyline sprawling behind him. Sam's expression was stormy, his lips pressed into a thin line. "What the hell do you think you're doing, Harper?" he demanded, each word razor-sharp. "I just received a call from Trailblaze, and they are furious. Do you have any idea how far out of line you are?"

Harper met his eyes, daring him to challenge her. "I know exactly what I'm doing, Sam. And so does my team. But do you?" She didn't give him a chance to answer before continuing. "Instead of fighting for work that's fresh, and bold, you're acting like we should be ashamed of it. Why? This campaign is the best work this team has done in months—maybe years. It's authentic, it's fearless, and it's exactly what Trailblaze deserves. My team didn't just create a campaign; they built a statement. And I won't let that be watered down or buried in corporate fear. Not when we have a chance to do something great. And instead of backing us, you're hesitating. If you actually encouraged creativity instead of stifling it, we'd be unstoppable."

Sam's face darkened, a flush of anger rising to his cheeks. "That wasn't your decision to make. We had an approved direction—a direction that the client explicitly signed off on. And you went rogue, Harper. You ignored the client's wishes, disregarded protocol ..."

"Yes, I know," she interrupted, unflinching. "I understand exactly what this means for me. I know I've signed my own termination notice. But I'd rather walk out of here with my integrity intact than stay and watch great work be buried under fear. I won't sit here and pretend to regret my decisions." Her voice didn't waver, not for a second. "This team proved what they're capable of, and I refuse to let that be ignored. And if Trailblaze can't see that, then it's Trailblaze that's failing—not me."

Sam stared, his eyes narrowing, disbelief mingling with contempt. Then he let out a harsh, humorless laugh. "You really don't get it, do you?" He shook his head, his voice icy. "This isn't some art school passion project. This is business. Clients want results, not risks. And if you don't get that or don't wanna cooperate, then you're in the wrong place."

Harper felt his words land like stones, each one heavy with finality. But she stood firm, refusing to flinch. She knew the risks, knew the price, and was ready to pay it.

"For once, Sam, I think you're right," she said quietly. A strange, unexpected calm settled over her, like the first deep breath after a storm. "I'll pack my things."

Sam's jaw tightened, his eyes hardening. "Yes," he replied, his tone clipped and dismissive. "Do that."

As Harper left his office, the pressure of the past few years, with all the late nights and everything, started to ease up. She didn't look back. Each step brought more freedom, even though she still felt the loss.

She'd fought for something real. She'd given her team a moment of boldness, a glimpse of their capabilities. And she'd stood by her convictions, even knowing it would cost her everything.

Back in her office, as she packed up her belongings, a calm resolve filled her. No more cage! She was free to follow her dreams.

She packed her belongings and texted her sister.

Harper

I'm coming home.

No more New York City dreams.

The city didn't care. As Harper stepped out of the skyrise for the last time, New York roared around her, busy, relentless, unmoved by her exit. People hurried past, voices clashing, a siren wailing somewhere in the distance. For years, she had seen herself as part of that rhythm, another ambitious dreamer lost in the pulse of Manhattan.

New York had once held the magic of a love letter. She envisioned herself as part of the city's romantic narrative, reminiscent of films like, *You've Got Mail*. In her mind, New York had been a place of possibility, an enchanted backdrop where lives transformed, love bloomed, and dreams came true under the city lights. She'd imagined herself as a protagonist, just like Kathleen Kelly in that movie, walking down these very streets with a heart full of ambition, on her way to something grand and meaningful.

But now, as she looked around, she felt only a hollow detachment. New York's reality had stripped away the magic—the compromises, the endless grind, the dream slowly crushed under corporate bureaucracy. It wasn't the story she'd once believed.

And yet, she hadn't crumbled.

For a change, Harper felt clear-headed, unburdened. She was no longer tangled in the city's chaos; she was breaking free from it. She'd left that job behind, finished chasing dreams, and was ready for the real thing. With a determined stride, she felt like she was finally on the right path.

As she turned onto the crowded sidewalk, she wasn't leaving. She was arriving.

Twenty-Six

S ix months had passed since Harper left her New York agency for the last time, trading the city's relentless grind for a slower, quieter life in Myrtle Beach.

She'd spent years imagining New York as the as the setting for her grand story, her own romanticized dream, a place where she'd finally "make it." But reality was different. The city's pulse, once intoxicating, had turned relentless, leaving her exhausted and creatively stifled.

Now, she was starting over in Myrtle Beach, where the rhythm was slower, the air softer, and the horizon endlessly open. She went from fancy conference rooms to working in a corner of her sister's little guest room. But there was a charm to its simplicity, a sense of honesty that felt right for this chapter of her life.

The morning sun filtered through the blinds, creating soft stripes of light across her workspace. Harper's laptop sat open on a rickety wooden desk she'd scored for $10 at a local thrift shop, surrounded by a growing mess of notepads, pens, and sketches for her new clients' campaigns. In this coastal town, each client was a small, local business, like an art gallery, surf shop, or family bakery, seeking to establish its unique identity. These clients couldn't pay for a fancy NYC agency and wanted something unique.

Above her desk hung a handmade Blue Horizon Creative sign, a gift from her three-year-old nephew, Channing. His crayon letters were endearingly messy, and he'd decorated it with seashells they'd collected together on the beach. A smile played on her lips each time she glanced at it; it was a constant reminder of the inspiration behind "Blue Horizon." Like the endless ocean, her new job felt full of limitless opportunities, way beyond her old life. Here, "safe" and "predictable" were no longer limitations.

The room, a chaotic and charming blend of guestroom, office, and storage, overflowed with papers, suitcases, and half-packed boxes, creating a unique atmosphere. The guest bed? A crazy, inspiring mess of drawings and plans—just like her life, chaotic. The faint scent of the ocean drifted in from an open window, mingling with the slightly burned aroma of her sister's coffee.

It wasn't the sleek, minimalist office Harper had once envisioned, but it had a warmth that surprised her. It didn't have to be fancy, just practical. It felt more like home than her fancy NYC office ever did.

Here, Harper was crafting something real. Each campaign she created for local businesses was bold and personal, alive with creativity and purpose. It wasn't perfect, but Blue Horizon was hers, and that's what mattered.

Channing's excited giggles echoed down the hallway, followed by a crash when he "accidentally" pushed her door open. Harper smiled.

"Aunt Harper!" he whispered, as if he were sharing a secret only they would understand. "Are you working?"

She chuckled, motioning him in. "Just a little, buddy. What's up?"

He shuffled in, clutching a toy dinosaur in one hand and a piece of paper in the other. "I drew you something!" He thrust the paper toward her with all the enthusiasm a tiny human could muster. The drawing was a blur of green and blue scribbles, with a few shaky letters that Harper recognized as his attempt at spelling Blue Horizon.

"It's perfect, Channing," she said, her heart swelling as she took in his earnest expression. She hugged him, breathing in his familiar scent of peanut butter and cheesy crackers. "Thank you for helping me make my office look awesome."

He giggled, clearly pleased with himself, before bounding out of the room, his dinosaur clutched tight. The door banged shut, and Harper was alone again, her heart warmed by his visit. She could still hear him in the hall, chattering to his toys as he stomped them across the floor, their tiny roars filling the quiet.

Harper leaned back, stretching her arms over her head as she let out a slow breath. Six months ago, she would have been in a sleek, silent conference room, brainstorming for clients who never truly saw her. Now, she was in a cozy, slightly chaotic guestroom, but she was building something real, something hers. *Blue Horizon Creative.* She let the name roll through her mind, savoring its significance.

Just as she began losing herself in work again, her phone buzzed. She glanced down and saw Sarah's name flashing on the screen. She picked up, instantly hit by nostalgia, as Sarah's familiar, bright voice filled her ear.

"Harper! I've been meaning to call for a while," Sarah said, her words tumbling with excitement. "The Trailblaze campaign? The one you insisted on, even when the client rejected it? It's a massive hit!

They've finally realized what they had, and now they're thrilled—already asking for more work like it."

Harper's chest swelled with pride and a bittersweet pang of nostalgia. She could picture her old team's faces, their eyes lighting up as they brainstormed those bold ideas. "That's amazing, Sarah. I'm so proud of you all. I always knew the team could pull it off."

"Honestly, Harper, none of this would've happened without you." Sarah replied. "You believed in us when no one else did. You refused to settle for 'safe,' even when the client doubted the vision. You didn't flinch, and that made all the difference."

Harper smiled. "You all made it happen, Sarah. I just held the door open."

Sarah's laugh carried a mix of gratitude and emotion. "Well, you did more than that. You showed us what it means to stand by our ideas, even when it felt risky. You showed us what it means to lead." She paused, leaving the line quiet before her voice returned. "You showed me what it means to lead. I ... well, I wanted you to know I got promoted. I'm in your old position now."

A single tear traced a slow path down her cheek, catching on the curve of her smile. She let it stay, embracing the emotion. "Sarah, that's incredible. I couldn't think of anyone better for the job."

Sarah paused before saying, "Sam said he, uh, wants you back. He said he'd give you more creative freedom this time. If you ever ... you know, wanted to come back."

For a fleeting instant, Harper glimpsed her former self, the one from six months prior who would have seized the opportunity. But as she glanced at the colorful Blue Horizon Creative sign above her desk, she felt an unexpected peace. She'd changed, and the allure of those glass conference rooms was gone.

"Sarah," she began, her voice resolute, "that's your team now, and you're going to do amazing things with it. I'm so proud of you." She paused, choosing her following words carefully. "But my path is here. My agency helps small businesses build authentic brands and strong communities. It's not the big-city agency life I once dreamed of, but it feels ... right. It feels like home."

Sarah exhaled, a mix of understanding and admiration in her tone. "I get it, Harper. And honestly? I'm glad you've found something that feels like that. We miss you, though. Just know that."

Harper smiled. "Thank you, Sarah. That means a lot. But you're the leader now, don't forget. Trust your instincts. Push for the bold ideas. Your team is worth the effort."

Sarah hesitated, then laughed softly. "I think you're right where you're supposed to be, Harper. And I'm so glad you found it."

After sharing a few more words of encouragement, Harper ended the call with a promise, "You know where to find me if you ever need anything."

As she hung up, a quiet sense of closure settled over her. She'd left New York but hadn't left behind the best parts of herself. What she was shaping in Myrtle Beach wasn't just hers—it was something real, something that mattered.

She recollected everything that led to this. In New York, she was hooked on the city's dream of success, just like in movies she grew up romanticizing. She believed big city success meant self-discovery and becoming the person she'd always dreamed of. But the reality had been a far cry from those expectations. New York had turned out to be less of a romantic comedy and more of a marathon, a relentless grind that left her weary and creatively drained.

She was still amazed at how different life felt, but it was all hers. Every morning, she woke up with a new sense of purpose.

Harper leaned over her notebook, her pencil flying across the page as she sketched ideas for a local surf shop's campaign. She was in the zone, imagining ways to tell their story and create something that felt as authentic and bold as the ocean they lived by. Helping these small businesses find their voices had become more than work—it reflected her own journey. She was building something meaningful, one story at a time.

After a while, Harper paused and stretched, reaching for her phone to take a quick break. She scrolled through her clients' social media pages, double-checking their recent posts. She scrolled past minor updates, such as new gallery items and a bakery promotion, until she saw Aidan's name and froze.

The page wasn't one of her clients, but his personal one. Her breath caught as she tapped the post. There it was: Emerald Tide, Aidan's food truck, parked under the South Carolina sun with its vibrant turquoise and emerald paint gleaming in the light. The Celtic knot designs traced elegantly around the logo, while a subtle wave graphic along the side gave the impression the truck was riding the tide. The caption read, **Catch Emerald Tide Food Truck this weekend at the Myrtle Beach Food and Art Festival! Bringing Irish flavors to every shore.**

Harper stared at the post, her heart skipping. She knew Aidan had been driving his food truck around the Southeast, but hadn't known he was coming to Myrtle Beach. A rush of excitement washed over her as she reread the caption. He pulled it off! That crazy bold vision of his, just like he said he would.

His photos, all tasty-looking blends of Irish and Southern food, showcased his dad's "Seamus Specials" and shared stories about his family and the legacy he was keeping alive. The authenticity and passion radiated from every post, and Harper smiled, deeply proud.

Watching him thrive fueled her own passion. Their bond was always about conquering fear and embracing courage. And now, here he was, living that promise.

Harper is going to the festival, no question! She was going to celebrate his success with him at his truck. Wasn't that what they'd always been for each other? Subtle reminders to leap, to chase what truly mattered.

More than just his food truck, she wanted to see him. If her own journey had taught her anything, it was that the boldest choices often set your heart racing. This could be her chance to reconnect meaningfully, moving beyond superficial texts and infrequent updates.

Aidan had been one of the first to encourage her to leave behind what didn't fulfill her and to take bold steps toward a life she could be proud of. And now, they were both living those choices, building lives they'd once only dreamed of. She felt she owed it to herself to see how much they had both achieved.

Her pulse quickened as she set her phone down. This wasn't just about celebrating his success. This was about unfinished stories, about second chances, about daring to ask, what if?

Twenty-Seven

The Myrtle Beach Food and Art Fest was in full swing when Harper arrived with Helen and Channing. The air hummed with the crowd's excitement, a festive energy that seemed to shimmer like heat waves under the early afternoon sun. Brightly colored flags fluttered above rows of vendor tents, their vibrant hues almost blurring together against the sandy path winding through the festival grounds. From somewhere close, she could hear the steady strum of a guitar mingling with the hum of voices, a lively soundtrack to the afternoon.

"Look, Auntie Harp! Over there!" Tugging at her hand, Channing pointed toward a face-painting booth where a kid was getting a tiger transformed onto his cheek.

"Do you want to be a tiger, buddy?" Harper asked with a grin.

He nodded eagerly, his eyes bright. "Or maybe a dragon!"

Harper chuckled, glancing over at her sister, who looked around with wide eyes and a contented smile. "This is a bit different from last year's fall craft fair, huh?" Helen murmured, taking in the bustling scene.

Harper nodded, drawing in a deep breath. The festival was a sensory feast: grilled meats, cinnamon, and salty air. She closed her eyes for a moment, letting herself sink into it, her heart beating in time with the rhythm of the crowd.

Helen nudged her with an elbow. "You're glowing. Someone's having fun."

Harper smiled, not bothering to deny it. It was true—she hadn't felt this alive in forever. It wasn't the glamorous NYC she dreamed of, but Myrtle Beach felt right with her family and all those artists and food trucks.

They meandered through rows of colorful artisan stalls, each a small world unto itself. There were pottery booths displaying glazed mugs and bowls in hues of teal and gold, hand-painted seashells strung into delicate wind chimes, and tables covered in handmade jewelry that sparkled under the sunlight. Channing stopped every few steps, his small hands reaching out to touch trinkets and treasures, eyes wide with wonder.

"Oh, Auntie Harper, look at this!" he gasped, picking up a tiny glass dolphin. He held it up to the light, admiring the way it glinted.

"That's beautiful, Chan," Harper said, bending beside him. She glanced up at the vendor—a kind-looking older woman with silver hair pulled into a braid—and handed her a couple of bills for the dolphin. She gave it to Channing, who held it like it was the most precious thing he'd ever seen.

Helen shook her head, smiling as she watched the exchange. "You spoil him, you know that?"

Harper just shrugged, giving her nephew a playful nudge. "Hey, that's the job of a cool aunt."

They wandered from booth to booth until the mouthwatering aroma of sizzling meat and roasting garlic caught Harper's attention. She turned toward the food trucks, where smoke curled lazily into the sky. Along the sandy path, vendors served everything from tangy barbecue to spiced tacos to exotic fruit smoothies.

Then she saw it: deep green and blue, Celtic knots around the serving hatch. Emerald Tide.

A tiny jolt, like a startled bird, fluttered in her chest.

It was really here. Aidan's food truck. Just as she'd seen in the social media posts, she'd practically memorized over the past month, but somehow more vibrant, more real, parked there against the ocean scenery with the festival crowd milling around it. Seeing it filled her with excitement and nerves, a potent mix that had her heart beating faster.

"Is that it?" Helen's voice broke through Harper's inner thoughts.

"Yup." Harper nodded, her throat tight. "That's Aidan's truck. Emerald Tide."

Channing, still clutching his glass dolphin, squinted in the direction she was looking. "Auntie Harper, is that the famous food truck you told me about?"

"Yep, that's the one," she replied, her voice soft.

Helen laughed, nudging Harper with a mischievous grin. "You're glowing. Is it the festival ... or the food truck guy?"

Harper shot her a warning look, but Helen just wiggled her eyebrows. "So ... what's the verdict? Did you wear your special underwear today? You know, just in case things heat up?"

"Helen!" Harper hissed, her eyes going wide as her cheeks burned crimson. She nervously looked around, but nobody noticed—not even Channing, who was busy checking out his incredible dolphin.

"What?" Helen asked, feigning innocence, her grin growing wider. "I'm just saying ... you never know what might happen. Gotta be prepared."

"Oh, my gawd, you're impossible," Harper muttered, shaking her head. "I didn't ..."

"Mommy, what's 'special underwear'?" Channing asked suddenly, his new trinket momentarily forgotten as he blinked up at them with wide, curious eyes.

Helen pressed her lips together, clearly trying not to laugh, while Harper froze, her blush deepening. "Uh ... it's just ... superhero underwear," Harper stammered, glaring at her sister. "You know, to help you feel brave and strong."

"Like superhero underwear?" Channing asked, his voice full of wonder. "Does Auntie Harper have superhero underwear?"

Helen snorted before doubling over with laughter, tears forming at the corners of her eyes. Harper groaned, rubbing her temples. "Yes, Channing," she said dryly. "But it's a secret. You can't tell anyone. Superheroes don't spill their secrets, okay?"

Channing gave a solemn nod, miming zipping his lips shut. "I won't tell nobody," he whispered.

Her hand trembling, Helen wiped her eyes, eventually regaining her composure. "Honestly, super-suit or not, that bra you've got on is doing fantastic work. Your boobs look like they could save the world."

"Helen!" Harper groaned, throwing her hands up. "Why do I even talk to you?"

"Because I'm your sister, and I keep life interesting," Helen quipped, patting Harper on the arm. "Now go on, get your food truck guy. Channing and I will be over there, keeping an eye out. You know, in case you faint or something."

With a shake of her head and a barely suppressed smile, Harper rolled her eyes and turned back toward the truck. Sometimes, her sister might be insufferable, but she wouldn't trade her for the world.

Reaching the window, a guy with a big smile and flour on his shirt was there to help. She recognized him from Aidan's posts as Sam, Aidan's right-hand man and former colleague from Murphy's.

"What can I get for you?" Sam asked, his voice bright over the hum of festival chatter.

Harper smiled. "I'll take an order of the Irish nachos, please." She leaned in, lowering her voice conspiratorially. "Could you let Aidan know an old 'sea buddy' is here to see him?"

"Wait, are you ... ?" Sam's thoughts wandered as he connected her to Aidan's tales. "Oh, he's gonna love this." Turning back into the truck, he called out, his voice carrying just enough amusement to pique Aidan's curiosity. "Hey, Aidan! There's someone here asking for you ... says she's an old 'sea buddy' or something."

Harper watched as Aidan stilled for a moment, his shoulders straightening before quickly wiping his hands on a towel and turning toward the window. When he saw her, he froze mid-step, his expression shifting from surprise to a broad, incredulous grin.

"Harper!" he said, the warmth in his voice carrying through the clamor of the festival. He stepped closer to the window, his face lighting up in a way that made her pulse quicken.

"Didn't think you'd recognize me, Murphy," she teased, resting her forearms on the counter. "Saw your post and figured I'd see what all the fuss was about."

Aidan laughed, running a hand through his hair in a gesture she recognized all too well. "You found me," he said, a hint of pride in his voice as he gestured to the bustling scene around him. "And here I am, drowning in sliders and whiskey wings."

She peeked past him into the busy, narrow kitchen, where dishes sizzled, and fresh ingredients were lined up in neat, organized rows. It was a beautiful kind of chaos, one fueled by passion rather than stress. She met his eyes, her smile soft. "I'd say you're thriving."

Aidan shot a quick look over his shoulder at the stacked orders, a sigh slipping out despite his smile. "Look, I'm swamped right now," he admitted, a hint of regret in his eyes, "but can you stick around? Maybe come back later? I'd love to really catch up."

"I'll be here, Aidan."

"Great," he said, his grin widening. They shared a lingering look before he returned to the grill, slipping seamlessly into his rhythm.

Harper stepped back from the window, watching him as he commanded the small kitchen. The buzz rippled through her, a quiet thrill at seeing Aidan bring his dream to life.

With her order in hand, Harper returned to the picnic table where Helen and Channing were waiting. "Finally!" Helen teased, scooting over to make room. "Thought you were gonna get lost staring into his dreamy chef eyes."

"Can you not?" Harper muttered, setting the tray of Irish nachos on the table. "Just eat something."

Helen smirked but didn't argue, grabbing a chip piled high with cheese and corned beef. "Mmm," she said through a mouthful. "I gotta say, your man knows his potatoes."

Channing leaned over, inspecting the food. "I wanna try!" He grabbed a cheesy slice and took a big bite, his eyes widening. "Mmm, these are really yummy!"

Harper smiled, shaking her head as Channing dove in for another bite. "See? I told you I came for the food."

Helen snorted, wiping her fingers on a napkin. "Right. The food. Definitely not the adorable guy making it."

"Do you ever let up?" Harper groaned, though her lips twitched into a reluctant smile.

"Never," Helen replied, her grin wicked. "But seriously, Harp. He looked happy to see you. That has to mean something."

Harper's attention drifted back toward the truck, where Aidan worked confidently. "Maybe," she said.

Helen stood, stretching. "Well, kiddo, time for your nap," she said, ruffling Channing's hair. "You sure you don't want a ride, Harper?"

Harper shook her head. "I'll stick around a bit longer."

Helen hugged her, her voice quieter now. "Go for it. He'd be an idiot to not fall for you."

As Helen and Channing walked off, Harper turned back toward Emerald Tide, glimpsing Aidan through the window. She took a deep breath and smiled.

As the festival crowd finally thinned, Harper settled herself at a nearby picnic table, enjoying the quiet shift in the atmosphere. The soft hum of live music drifted over the grounds, mingling with the salt-kissed breeze. Strings of lights flickered like fireflies as the sun dipped below the horizon, and from her seat, she had a perfect view of the Emerald Tide truck, now closed for the night. Painted in deep greens and blues, it looked like it belonged right there by the ocean—Aidan's dream brought to life.

Her phone buzzed on the table. Paige. Harper opened the message and laughed softly. It was a picture of a gleaming cruise ship under a pastel sunset, captioned:

Paige

> Let's go back! Grab your man and let's rejoin the ocean. I got a great deal for the four of us at Christmas.

Harper shook her head, grinning as she typed back.

Harper

> It's March. Isn't it a little early, even for you? Easy there, tiger. No second date yet.

Paige's reply came instantly.

Paige

> OMG! Harper!!! your first date was the cruise … last year!! Stop pretending it doesn't count. Call this one Date #2 and start packing. Christmas on the high seas, here we come.

Harper's smile lingered as she tucked her phone away—a year since the cruise. A year since their first and only date, and here she was, waiting for him again. Paige wasn't wrong—maybe it was time for something more.

The truck's back door swung open, and Aidan stepped out, hauling a trash bag over his shoulder. He stopped to talk to someone inside, probably Sam, before throwing the bag into a nearby dumpster. When he turned back, their eyes met, and his surprise melted into a warm, familiar smile that made her pulse skip.

Sam appeared at the door, giving Aidan a playful shove toward her. Aidan laughed, shaking his head before turning to Harper, his grin softening. As he closed the distance between them, her heart quickened.

This time, she wouldn't let another year pass.

As Aidan approached, Harper's lips curved into a smile, effortless and impossible to suppress. Like she always felt when seeing him, a familiar flutter of nerves stirred within her chest. It was strange, given how little time they'd spent together, yet it felt like they were picking up a conversation paused just yesterday.

When he reached her, she tilted her head, her tone playful. "Thought you might've forgotten about me."

Aidan shrugged, his grin easy and warm. "No rest for the road-weary chef, you know. Life's chaos in a food truck."

Her gaze dropped to his apron. It was a battlefield of sauce splatters and flour smudges. "Well, you look like a mess. A yummy mess, but a mess nonetheless," she teased. "What, did you do? Roll in the fryer?"

He laughed, glancing down at himself. "Close enough. Last week, a hand pie decided to blow up in there. Trust me, the fryer won."

She shook her head, her laughter light, carried by the soft festival breeze. "Why does every kitchen you work in sound like a disaster zone?"

"Hey," he said, his grin turning roguish. "Chaos makes for great food." He paused as his eyes swept over her. "But you ... you look amazing. Happy. I'd even say ... radiant."

Her breath caught, but she quickly masked it with a playful tilt of her head. "Thanks, Aidan. Living here, with the refreshing ocean air, it's difficult to not feel happy."

"Myrtle suits you," he said, nodding. "I knew you'd moved back after torching that New York agency, but I didn't think I'd actually see you here."

"Well," she replied, "when I saw Emerald Tide would be here, I had to see if the food lived up to the hype. Honestly, I wasn't sure it was really your account until I saw Sam in the background, looking perpetually exasperated."

Aidan chuckled. "Yeah, he's had a lot of 'what did I get myself into' moments. Busy, but good! We've been on the road for a little over a month now."

"You've really got this whole food truck thing going, huh? It's amazing," she said, her pride for him shining through.

He smiled, his voice quieting with sincerity. "It's been messy, exhausting ... but I think I've finally found it. That thing I've been chasing. Feels good actually ... to see it happen, you know?"

She nodded. "I get that. Really, I do." And she did—she recognized the same fulfillment in him she'd found on her own journey.

"So," he said, leaning casually against the counter, "how's Blue Horizon? Last I heard, you were picking up clients. Is it everything you hoped?"

She laughed softly, brushing her fingers against the table's edge. "Some days, it feels like I'm making it up as I go along. But it's good. I'm hooking up with some cool local spots: cafes, surf shops, and an artisan jewelry store. Helping them find their voice, telling their stories ... feels meaningful."

"I knew you'd crush it," Aidan said, the admiration in his voice unmistakable.

She smiled, tilting her head. "It's odd, but I enjoy doing things my way. No executive breathing down my neck, no endless revisions. Just ... people I care about. It's what I was missing."

He studied her, his voice low and thoughtful. "I can tell something's changed, and it's more than just your good mood. It's like you've found yourself again. Like you're home."

Her heart squeezed at his words. "I think so," she murmured. "New York was ... suffocating. Here, I get to set my own rules and take time to do things I love. Like, say, food festivals in the middle of the week."

"Speaking of food," he said, leaning in slightly, "what'd you think of those nachos? Too much cheese?"

She gasped dramatically. "Too much cheese? That's like asking if there's too much happiness in the world. Impossible."

He laughed, raising his hands in surrender. "Fair enough. So, they were good?"

"They were perfect," she said, her smile warm. "Honestly, Aidan, you've got something special here. I can see this really taking off."

He grinned, but rubbed the back of his neck sheepishly. "Full disclosure? I'm still figuring out the marketing stuff. For some reason, I thought I could just park somewhere, and customers would magically show up ... and, poof!"

"Poof?!" She let out a laugh. "That's your strategy?"

"Look, it seemed reasonable at the time!" he said. "Turns out you actually have to tell people where you are. Who knew?"

"Well," she teased, her tone light, "if you want help from someone who knows what she's doing, I could take Emerald Tide to the next level. No 'poof' required."

He didn't hesitate. "Harper, I don't need the pitch. I trust you. If you're in, I'm in."

Her voice cracked with surprise. "Just like that?"

"Just like that," he said, his grin widening. "Emerald Tide and Blue Horizon Creative—sounds like magic to me."

She smiled, feeling the energy between them shift. The festival's buzz seemed to fade, leaving just the two of them. He nervously cleared his throat, his voice lowering. "So, any chance you'd like to grab dinner sometime?"

Her pulse skipped. "Like ... a date?"

"Yeah," he said, a faint blush coloring his cheeks. "An actual date. You in?"

Her lips curved, and she paused, savoring the question. "Wow, we haven't had a date in almost a year. Not since the cruise."

His eyes flickered with realization. "You're right ... but I'd say we're overdue."

She didn't need to think about it. "Yes," she said softly. "I'd love that."

"Great," he replied, relief flashing in his smile. "The festival wraps up tomorrow. I'm free Monday."

"Monday it is." The words came quickly, her voice steady with certainty.

Without thinking, he opened his arms, and she stepped into them, her head resting against his shoulder. He exhaled, his arms tightening around her just enough to make her feel it—to make her know he didn't want to let go too soon. The world quieted, leaving only the secure rhythm of his heartbeat beneath her cheek.

When she finally pulled back, she didn't step away entirely, her hands still resting lightly against his arm. "Well, Murph, I'd better let you get back to work before Sam loses his mind."

His thumb grazed the inside of her wrist before he let her go completely, "It was really good to see you."

"You too," She turned, but after a few steps, she looked back. "Oh, and Aidan ... maybe wear a clean shirt Monday. First impressions and all."

His laugh rang out, warm and unguarded. "Noted!"

As Harper walked into the glow of the festival lights, his laughter wrapped around her like a soft breeze. Her heart felt light, her steps unhurried. She wasn't chasing anything anymore. She felt she was where she belonged; like a new chapter was beginning.

The festival lights twinkled above the quieting paths, their glow gentle, like stars brushing against the earth. Most of the booths had packed up, the hum of the day fading into a serene stillness. Harper delayed, savoring the peacefulness. It wasn't just the night winding down; it was a moment of clarity of the world, giving her space to breathe and hold on to this new feeling of possibility.

Aidan's voice and smile played in her mind, every word they'd exchanged replaying with crystal clarity. His dinner invitation, a simple question, carried the weight of something deeper: a promise. A door opening to a future she hadn't let herself dream of, especially not after all the near-misses, distance, and time. And yet, here she was, stepping forward.

At the edge of the festival, she instinctively pulled out her phone. Her unanswered "Hey, how's life?" still sat in her outbox. And then, as if the universe had been waiting for this moment, her phone buzzed.

Aidan.

She opened the message to find a single smiling emoji.

Simple.

Familiar.

Yet tonight, it wasn't just a message—it was a spark. A single emoji, small and insignificant to anyone else, but to her, it felt like an invitation. That tiny symbol wasn't just nostalgia—it was a bridge between brief encounters and something real, something waiting to unfold.

She slid her phone back into her bag, inhaling the crisp night air. They had both leapt—choosing courage over hesitation, passion over fear. This wasn't just a beginning—it was the sequel to a story she was finally writing on her own terms.

She was ready to see where this adventure would take her next.

About the Author

I'm J.D. Harbor, a romance novelist drawn to love stories set on the high seas. A former military photojournalist, I found my writing voice capturing real-life moments in the field. Now, I craft tales of connection, adventure, and self-discovery aboard cruise ships.

My RomantiSea Serenades series begins with Emerald Tide and Sapphire Seas, companion novels following two souls brought together by fate on a cruise. While their romance spans both books, each story delves into one character's personal journey. Inspired by my own experience of meeting my wife on a voyage, these novels embrace the magic of love unfolding when least expected.

Originally from Utah, I now live in Central Florida with my wife and two kids, always dreaming up our next adventure on the open water. I believe the best love stories begin with self-discovery—because only when we truly know ourselves can we fully open our hearts to love.

Also by J.D. Harbor

Embark on the journey of a lifetime with RomantiSea Serenades, a planned 15-book romance series set aboard the glistening Elysian Serenade cruise ship. This sweeping saga explores love, adventure, and personal growth against the stunning backdrop of the open sea.

Aboard RomantiSea Serenades, each Mingle at Sea cruise brings two solo travelers together, their love story spanning two companion novels. Each book offers a fresh perspective, following one protagonist's path through love, self-discovery, and transformation.

The series drops anchor with Emerald Tide and Sapphire Seas, companion novels that introduce readers to this vibrant world. As new couples set sail, they prove the best journeys aren't just about destinations—they're about the people who change us along the way. If you believe in love's power to surprise, this series is your escape.

A perfect match to Sapphire Seas, Emerald Tide takes readers on a voyage filled with passion, self-discovery, and a love that refuses to be left on the shore. Aidan, a talented chef, has spent years sailing in the safe waters of family expectations. Hoping for a little clarity, he books a singles cruise—only to find himself caught in an undertow of unexpected desire.

Harper, an ambitious advertising executive, wasn't planning on falling for someone at sea. But between stolen glances and late-night encounters under the stars, she and Aidan become tangled in something neither of them can ignore.

Sultry, seductive, and impossible to resist, Emerald Tide—paired with Sapphire Seas—delivers a romance that proves some connections are worth diving in headfirst for.